THE FAMOUS FIVE AND THE CAVALIER'S TREASURE

THE FAMOUS FIVE are Julian, Dick, George (Georgina by rights), Anne and Timmy the dog.

A summer holiday with their friends Tinker and Mischief the monkey gives the Famous Five a chance to explore an area a short distance from Kirrin Cottage. And it's not long before they discover buried treasure – which guarantees an exciting time for everyone!

Also available in Knight Books:

The Famous Five and the Cavalier's Treasure

A new adventure of the characters created by Enid Blyton, told by Claude Voilier, translated by Anthea Bell

Illustrated by Bob Harvey

KNIGHT BOOKS
Hodder and Stoughton

Copyright © Librairie Hachette 1976
First published in France as *La Fortune Sourit aux Cinq*
English language translation copyright
© Hodder & Stoughton Ltd, 1984
Illustrations copyright © Hodder &
Stoughton Ltd

First published in Great Britain by
Knight Books 1984
Third impression 1986

British Library C.I.P.

Voilier, Claude
   The Famous Five and the cavalier's treasure.
   I. Title   II. La fortune sourit aux cinq.
   English
   843'.914[J]   PZ7

ISBN 0-340-34592-6

Printed and bound in Great Britain for
Hodder and Stoughton Paperbacks, a
division of Hodder and Stoughton Ltd.,
Mill Road, Dunton Green, Sevenoaks,
Kent (Editorial Office: 47 Bedford
Square, London, WC1 3DP) by
Richard Clay Ltd, Bungay, Suffolk

CONTENTS

Chapter One

OFF TO ROSE COTTAGE

'Wake up, George! Are you asleep on your feet, or what?' asked Dick.

The four Kirrin cousins had just got off their bicycles, and were standing by the roadside, at the garden gate of a cottage. George had been staring straight ahead of her, absent-mindedly patting her dog Timmy. Now she turned to Dick.

'Of course I'm not asleep!' she said indignantly. 'I'm thinking, that's all!'

She and Dick were eleven years old. They both had dark, curly, short hair, and looked rather like each other. Dick couldn't help laughing.

'I say, you two, did you hear that?' he asked his brother and sister, Julian and Anne. 'George's mind is ticking over! George is actually thinking!

What marvellous idea will our brilliant cousin's superbrain come up with next?'

'Oh, don't be such an ass, Dick!' said Julian, smiling. 'If you two are going to *start* the summer holidays by squabbling, what *will* you be like by the end of them?'

Julian was thirteen, and he was the eldest of the children. He was very sensible for his age. He didn't look much like his brother Dick – he was tall, and had fair hair. So did their little sister Anne.

George's three cousins nearly always spent their holidays with her – and of course with Timmy her dog too. Timmy went everywhere with George, whose real name was Georgina. This summer the children had been going to stay at Kirrin Cottage as usual. George lived there with her parents, Uncle Quentin and Aunt Fanny – the house was by the seaside and near Kirrin village. But then, unfortunately, something unexpected had happened, and that meant a change of plan for the four cousins.

George was already opening her mouth to answer Dick back, but Anne got in first, in her soft little voice.

'What were you thinking about, George? Tell us, please do!'

'Oh,' said George, rather grumpily, 'I was only

thinking what a shame it is we can't stay at home in Kirrin Cottage after all!'

'Well, never mind,' said Julian. 'We'll only have to be away for two or three weeks, just so that Uncle Quentin and Professor Hayling can have time to finish their book in peace and quiet.'

'That's right,' agreed Dick. 'We're not being banished to Rose Cottage for so very long!'

'And just think of poor Uncle Quentin – he'd never get that important work of his done if he had us underfoot the whole time!' Anne reminded the others.

George suddenly smiled, and looked much better-tempered. 'Well, *you're* not the one who'd be most likely to disturb him!' she told Anne, truthfully. 'Nor Julian! But I suppose Dick and I do sometimes make rather a noise! And I know dear old Timmy can be *terribly* noisy when he feels like it. This is what comes of having a famous scientist for a father – you have to go about on tiptoe the whole time!'

'But it's just because Uncle Quentin and Aunt Fanny don't want to spoil our holidays by making us keep quiet that we're being sent to stay at Rose Cottage,' Julian pointed out. 'It's all turned out very well, really, seeing the Haylings' housekeeper, Jenny, owns the cottage, and she said she'd look after us if we went.'

'It doesn't look all that bad, either,' added Anne, glancing at the cottage beyond the garden gate.

The bicycle ride from Kirrin to Rose Cottage was only a couple of kilometres. Jenny's little house was a pretty white cottage, with green shutters at the windows, and the garden round it was full of trees, flowers and shrubs. They all grew in rather a wild, tangled way, but the garden still looked nice. No, it really wasn't a bad place at all!

'You're right, Anne!' George admitted. 'It *is* quite pretty.'

'And I bet we have some grand meals!' said Dick enthusiastically. 'You know what a wonderful cook Jenny is! She's bound to make us lovely cakes and buns and puddings – and we'll have Tinker to play with, too. Hallo, there *is* Tinker!'

A boy about the same age as Dick and George came dashing out of the house like a bullet shooting from a gun, and ran to meet his friends.

'Good – here you are! Welcome to Rose Cottage!'

Professor Hayling's son was always known as Tinker, because he loved tinkering about with cars. The Professor himself was a famous scientist, like Uncle Quentin, and the two men were great friends. They often worked together, and this summer they had something very important to do

— so to give them a bit of peace, Aunt Fanny had decided to send the children to stay with kind Jenny, the Haylings' housekeeper, who had looked after Tinker ever since his mother died.

Tinker opened the garden gate to let his friends in. 'I'm awfully glad my father's shut up our house at Big Hollow to go and stay at Kirrin Cottage,' he said. 'And he's let me come here to stay with *you*! This garden of Jenny's is a wonderful place for games. I've always loved playing Indians here!'

Jenny herself appeared on the white doorstep of the cottage. She was a plump little middle-aged woman, with a cheerful smile.

'Hallo, children!' she said. 'Come along in! I've got a nice tea waiting for you — it will do you good after such a long bicycle ride!' She was joking of course!

George and her cousins laughed at that. But before they could say hallo to Jenny, they heard a tremendous noise behind them.

'Woof! Woof!'

'Eeeak . . . chatter-chatter-chatter — *eeeak* . . . EEEAAK!'

George and Tinker burst out laughing.

'Listen to Timmy and Mischief saying hallo!'

'Just like the old friends they are!'

Timmy was standing braced with all four paws planted firmly on the ground, while a little monkey

11

gambolled affectionately round him. Mischief, Tinker's pet monkey, jumped up on the dog's back and then back down to the ground again, kissed Timmy's nose, and then repeated the whole performance, chattering away the whole time. Whenever the little monkey came within reach of Timmy's tongue, the dog gave him a friendly lick.

The two animals were really pleased to see each other, and went on playing until the children went indoors to sit down to a table covered with good things. There were egg sandwiches, Jenny's special home-made scones with cream and strawberry jam, and a big fruit cake. Soon Timmy came bouncing in to join the children, hoping for a sugar lump, and Mischief jumped up on Tinker's shoulder and begged for a biscuit.

As Jenny poured the tea, or milk for those who preferred it, she told the children, 'I don't know if Professor Hayling mentioned it, but I inherited this little cottage from my parents, and I thought I'd ask you to stay here because it's easier to look after than that big house of the Professor's at Big Hollow. But it will still take us all quite comfortably. Tinker's going to sleep in the big bedroom upstairs, with Julian and Dick, and there's another bedroom next to it for George and Anne to share.'

'We don't want to make a lot of extra work for

you, Jenny, so we'll help in the house!' Anne promised. 'We'll make our own beds, and I'll dust the furniture.'

'Yes, and I'll lend a hand with the heavy jobs,' added good-natured Julian. 'I'm sure George and Dick will be delighted to volunteer for the washing up!'

George and Dick didn't *look* particularly delighted – but they both really had kind hearts, and they knew it was only right for them to help Jenny in the house when she had so many extra people to look after, so they agreed, in chorus, 'All right, we don't mind washing up!'

After tea – and washing up! – Tinker and the Five went to their rooms to unpack. They had brought small suitcases on the carriers of their bicycles, and when they had put their things away, they spent the rest of the day exploring the garden. It was wonderfully wild, and there was pretty countryside all round the cottage too.

'And Kirrin isn't very far away,' said George, 'so if we want to go and play on my island, we can always go back to Kirrin Cottage for my rowing boat! It's still tied up in its usual place.'

George was a very lucky girl: she had an island of her very own! It wasn't very far from the mainland, but you could describe it as a 'desert island' because nobody lived there – except the

Five, now and then, when they went to camp on it. Uncle Quentin and Aunt Fanny had given George the island as a present. It still had the ruins of an old castle standing on it.

'You're right,' said Dick. 'You know, *I* think we'll really have more freedom here than if we'd stayed at Kirrin Cottage, George! I'm very fond of Uncle Quentin, but he does get a bit strict sometimes.'

'Yes, I must say Jenny's rather better-tempered than my father!' admitted George, smiling.

The last thing the friends did that evening was to draw up a list of all the expeditions they were planning to make during the next few days, and then they went upstairs to bed.

They had soon settled in at Rose Cottage. Except when they were helping Jenny in the house, the children were free to do whatever they liked. It was lovely weather, and the fine spell looked like lasting. They bathed in the sea, went for cross-country hikes, played in the garden, and did all sorts of interesting things.

And then, one fine day – or rather, one *not* very fine day – the weather broke and it began to rain. The rain came down in a thin drizzle, cold and very wet, and it went on and on as if it was never going to stop. Fancy having weather like that in the summer holidays!

After the children had tried going out several times, only to come home drenched, and with Mischief's and Timmy's coats sticking to them, they gave it up and decided they'd just have to play indoor games to pass the time. But it did get boring, having to stay indoors, and Jenny had her work cut out keeping her guests happy. She was a kind soul, and didn't like it when the children were cross and snapped at each other, but where many grown-ups would have scolded or threatened to punish them if they didn't behave, Jenny knew a better way to stop them squabbling. She told them stories – she knew lots and lots of stories, all of them different and all very amusing. The children thoroughly enjoyed listening to her, because she had a real gift for story-telling. What tales she had to tell! Stories about the naughty things she used to do when she was a little girl, stories about her brothers and sisters, old tales about the local countryside – they were all fascinating!

But the rain went on and on.

'Oh dear,' sighed George, 'if only we could have an adventure! Or a nice little mystery to solve – at least then we'd have something to think about. If it goes on raining like this, our talents for adventure will rust up!'

'Leaving the Famous Five out of a job!' smiled Dick. 'Well, that'll be something new!'

Jenny had a real gift for story-telling.

Jenny, who was sitting quietly knitting, glanced out of the window.

'As to adventures and mysteries, I really couldn't say,' she remarked, 'but you *could* go for a nice outing! Look – the clouds are blowing away, and it's stopped raining at last. You don't want to stay shut indoors, pacing up and down. I know a good place where you could go for an expedition too!'

Chapter Two

THE RUINED MANOR

George leaped to her feet.

'My goodness, Jenny, you're right! I never noticed the rain had stopped. I can't wait to get out of doors – let's take our bikes!'

'It would be better to go to the place I'm thinking of on foot,' Jenny told them. 'I thought you might like to have a look at the ruins of Mandeville Manor – it's a picturesque, round walk, and not a very long one. You could take your camera, Dick. I know you like taking photographs.'

'What way do we go for the round walk?' asked Julian.

'When you leave here, turn along the road to the

left,' said Jenny. 'Walk on until you get to the ruins up on the hill –'

'Oh, are those the ruins of the old manor house?' cried Anne. 'We noticed them on our way here.'

'Yes, it was once the ancestral home of the Mandeville family. They lived there for centuries, but then, at the time of the Civil War, Sir Rupert Mandeville was killed fighting for King Charles, and his wife had to flee the country with her son Hugh. That was when the house fell into disrepair.'

'Are there any of the family alive today?' asked Tinker.

'Oh yes! There's Mr Miles Mandeville, who's descended from Hugh, but not directly, so that's why he isn't 'Sir Miles'. He and his wife Sylvia are charming people. They have no children of their own, only a nephew called Benjamin, who will inherit the estate one day. I don't know him – he doesn't come here very often. The Mandevilles spend most of their time in London, but they travel a lot too. Mr Mandeville is an architect.'

'Do they live in the old ruins when they do come here?' asked Anne.

Dick roared with laughter, 'Don't be so silly, Anne! There isn't enough roof left on those ruins to keep a dormouse dry!'

Everyone else laughed too, including Anne, and

Jenny shook her head.

'No – the family did go on living in the house for some time after the restoration of King Charles II, but there was never enough money to repair it properly – and just think what such a place would cost to keep up, too! When there was a big fire in the house about a hundred years ago, the family gave up living in it and let it fall into ruins. After Mr Miles Mandeville inherited the estate he had a nice, modern house of his own design built a little way off, in a picturesque part of the old park. It's called Wistaria Lodge.'

'Oh, I think we've seen that house too!' cried Anne. 'I'm sure we cycled past it.'

'The Mandeville estate itself is very large,' Jenny went on. 'Wistaria Lodge and its garden occupy only a very small part of it. The Mandevilles own all the countryside round the ruins too, and a lot of the land beside the main road, as well as Coney Wood and part of the land on which this very cottage is built!'

'What?' said Julian, surprised. 'You mean Rose Cottage itself is on the Mandeville estate?'

'Part of it! I believe that at the time of the Civil War, there was a hunting lodge where the cottage now stands – and even today, though Rose Cottage and the front garden are mine, the *back* garden really belongs to the Mandevilles! But they let me grow anything I like there. As I told you, Mr and Mrs Miles Mandeville are very nice people.'

'What else is there to see?' asked George. 'Besides the ruins, I mean.'

'Well, if you go up the hill there's a fine view of the sea. And there's an old prehistoric burial mound not far off – what they call a tumulus. You don't have to come back the way you went. You can cut through Coney Wood, where there's a pretty little stream, with all sorts of wild flowers growing beside it.'

But just as the children were about to set off, something happened to delay them! Mischief decided that he'd like to borrow Timmy's collar. He took it off the dog's neck, and put it round his own! Good-tempered old Timmy didn't object. But as soon as Mischief was wearing the collar, the little monkey began to show off. He jumped around on the furniture, letting out his shrill chatter. Finally he leaped up on top of a tall cupboard and looked as if he was going to settle down there.

Tinker didn't think that was a good idea. He decided to get the little monkey down, so he put a chair on the table, and a stool on top of the chair, and then clambered up on them all, put out his hand – and tumbled down with a tremendous noise!

Luckily, he hadn't hurt himself, but Mischief was frightened. He jumped off his perch and caught hold of one arm of the light fitting hanging from the ceiling. It had several branches holding light bulbs. He swung there, looking ready to defy anyone. The children laughed and laughed, all except for poor Tinker, and Timmy barked.

Tinker, however, was very angry with Mischief, and went to fetch a broom to make the naughty monkey come down. He wasn't going to hit Mischief very hard with the broomstick, but the little monkey swerved to avoid it, lost his grip on the light fitting, slipped – and the dog collar, which was much too big for him, got caught on the branch he had been holding.

'Oh dear!' cried Anne in alarm. 'He'll strangle himself!'

Tinker was dashing about in a panic. George and her cousins ran to Jenny's boxroom. They knew she kept a pair of steps in there, so they fetched the steps, put them up under the light fitting, and Julian climbed up to unhook poor Mischief. Finally, George put Timmy's collar back on its rightful owner!

When all the excitement was over, the children looked out of the window and saw, to their dismay, that more dark clouds were coming up on the horizon.

They walked all around the crumbling walls.

'Oh well, never mind!' said George. 'Let's go out for a breath of fresh air anyway – if we just go as far as the ruins, then if it *does* rain again it won't be very far for us to run home!'

Jenny went to find their raincoats, and the children set off. Timmy was with them, of course, and so was Mischief, who had quickly recovered from his fright. He was clinging to Tinker's shoulder, snuggling close to his master.

The children walked at a brisk pace, and they were soon within sight of the ruined manor house. It so happened that although the place wasn't really very far from Kirrin, they had never visited it before, and it did look interesting. They walked slowly all around the crumbling walls. Blackened stones showed where there had once been a fire – that would have been the one Jenny mentioned, about a hundred years ago. No doubt the house had fallen into decay even faster since then.

'I say, what a gloomy spot!' muttered Tinker. 'It's a pity Jenny told us the old cellars are all blocked up and we can't explore them – I love exploring cellars!'

The ruins were attractive but there wasn't a lot else to see. Weeds and climbing plants had taken over all that was left of the manor house, and George, her cousins, and Tinker had soon satisfied their curiosity.

'There isn't anything very exciting here after all!' said Dick, at last.

Julian glanced up at the sky. 'No — but I think we're in for some excitement in the way of a downpour if we stay much longer!' he said. 'We'd better hurry home.'

'Yes,' said George. 'We can do the round walk Jenny suggested some other time.'

'Oh dear, here comes the rain!' cried Anne. 'Let's run!'

And run they did! The children and Timmy made a dash for the road, but the rain beat them to it. It was really pouring down by the time they reached Rose Cottage and, having dried themselves — and Timmy — thoroughly, they spent the rest of the day playing board games indoors.

But next day it looked fine again, although it was more like April weather than summer-time. The bright sunshine gave way to several sudden showers, and the children wished it would hurry and clear up properly!

That afternoon, as the sun suddenly shone out among the clouds again, Jenny told her young guests, 'Here's another sunny period, so you'd better make the most of it. Why not play in the orchard behind the house? You may be able to go for a real outing later on — showery weather like this often calms down towards the evening!'

'Orchard' was rather a grand name for the patch of grass in the back garden where a few apple trees grew, as well as a huge old oak, but it was a fine place for running about. The children organised a game of hide-and-seek, and Timmy and Mischief joined in with enthusiasm. The two animals were infected by the children's excitement. Timmy chased about, yapping and barking, and Mischief scurried all over the place, squealing and chattering like mad. They made no end of noise between them, but luckily Jenny hadn't got any neighbours living close to hear it!

Mischief decided the grass was too wet for his liking, and suddenly he jumped up to the lowest branch of the big oak tree and began to climb. Once he was well up the tree, of course he didn't want to come down again.

'Mischief! Come down! Come on down!' shouted Tinker, but it was no good. He was afraid they were going to have a repeat performance of that comical scene the day before! 'Come down, or I'll have to come and get you, and then you'll be sorry!'

'Eeeak . . . eeeeak!' squealed the monkey in reply.

'Woof!' barked Timmy, in his deep voice, telling Mischief to come down too.

But nothing his master Tinker or his friend the

dog said could persuade Mischief to leave his perch. Time was passing, and Jenny had already come out twice to call the children into tea.

'Come *on*, Mischief!' Tinker repeated angrily.

'Why don't the rest of us go in?' suggested George. 'I'm sure he'll follow us then.'

'That's what *you* think! You don't know how pigheaded he can be!'

'Ever see a monkey with a pig's head before?' asked Dick, laughing like mad at his own joke. 'Well, if we're ever going to dislodge your pigheaded monkey from his tree, *I* think –'

But the others never found out what Dick thought, because before he could finish his sentence, there was a tremendous clap of thunder, and heavy rain began beating down on the orchard.

'Here comes another storm!' cried Julian. 'Back to the house, everyone – quick! There's lightning about, and it's dangerous to stay here under the trees.'

Startled by the noise, Mischief the monkey was already scampering down the tree as fast as he could go. Tinker held out his arms to catch him as he jumped, but the little monkey landed in the grass instead. In his fright, Mischief was thinking of nothing but reaching the nearest shelter, so instead of setting off for the cottage, he made straight for the far end of the orchard.

'Help me catch him!' Tinker called to his friends. 'You wicked monkey – I'm drenched already!'

They all began chasing Mischief through the driving rain. Timmy obviously thought this was a lovely new game, and came bounding up to join in. He was the first to reach Mischief – and then the children saw a surprising sight. Mischief jumped nimbly up on his friend's back, and Timmy ran on to the end of the orchard, just as if he were obeying his 'rider's' commands. They disappeared among some tall weeds.

'Oh, bother!' said George crossly.

She was just going to call Timmy, when Anne pointed. 'Look – I think their idea is to take refuge in the shed!'

She meant an old toolshed at the far end of the orchard. It wasn't often used now, but the children had found it and played houses in it a few times, and Jenny had let them take picnic meals there.

'Anne's right,' said Julian. 'Timmy and Mischief knew by instinct that the shed was closer than the house. Good idea – let's join them!'

By the time the children had reached the shed they were wet through. Rain was falling on the roof with a noise like hailstones now. Timmy and the monkey were obviously rather frightened – and very pleased to see George and Tinker. Mischief jumped into his master's arms, and Timmy pressed close to his mistress. A flash of lightning shot across the sky, followed by a tremendous clap of thunder, and then another and another.

'I say!' exclaimed Dick. 'What a storm!'

'That lightning was awfully close,' said Anne, sounding rather scared

'And the storm seems to be coming closer still!' said George, listening. The time between the flashes of lightning and the rolls of thunder was getting shorter and shorter. 'I wonder –'

But she didn't finish her sentence, because just then a tremendous flash lit up the shed, dazzling the children as they huddled together a little way inside the door. Almost at once, there was a deafening clap of thunder, and the ground seemed to shake beneath their feet. Timmy barked, and Mischief squealed in terror. George and the boys let out startled exclamations, and Anne screamed with fright.

'The cottage! It's been struck by lightning – oh, poor Jenny!' she gasped.

'Hush, Anne – calm down,' said Julian, soothingly. 'It's all right! Look – the lightning didn't touch the house, but it *did* strike the big oak in the middle of the orchard. See that?'

And sure enough, peering through the driving

rain, the children saw that the magnificent old oak tree had gone – all that was left was a blackened column that had been its trunk, charred and smoking.

'My word!' said Tinker, turning pale. 'Just think – only a few minutes ago, Mischief was sitting on a branch of that tree!'

'And we were all standing underneath it, too,' added George.

Chapter Three

TREASURE!

The sound of the thunder was already dying away, and there were not so many flashes of lightning now. The storm was coming to an end.

The children heard Jenny's frightened voice, calling them. 'Tinker! Anne! George!'

'You stay here,' Julian told the others. 'I'll make a dash for the cottage, to let Jenny know we're okay, and then I'll be back with raincoats for all of us.'

He was back less than ten minutes later, running through the rain, and as well as the raincoats he had promised to bring he was carrying dry sweaters, and a big basket containing sandwiches, a huge chocolate cake, and thermos flask of hot cocoa.

'Jenny remembered the picnic cups and plates, too, so we can camp out here very comfortably until the storm's really over!' said Julian.

So they had an unexpected and very cheerful picnic. Timmy and Mischief were feeling hungry too, so the delicious picnic tea Jenny had packed in the basket was soon gone. Not a crumb was left.

'Gosh – I feel better now!' said Dick. 'It was pretty exciting, though, wasn't it? I say, I think the rain's stopped. Let's go and take a closer look at the damage that thunderbolt did!'

When they emerged from the shed, the children saw that the sun had come out again, and the wind was chasing the clouds away. They were certainly having changeable weather!

'My word, there's not much of that huge oak left now,' said George, rather sadly. 'What a shame – it was such a fine tree!'

'Yes, and while she was packing up our picnic just now, Jenny told me it's one of the few trees on the Mandeville estate supposed to date back to the time when Sir Rupert and Lady Mandeville lived at the Manor before the Civil War,' said Julian.

The children looked at the place where the tree used to stand with even more interest than before. They saw that when the thunderbolt struck, it had dug a sort of circular crater all round the charred stump of the tree.

'Look how deep it is,' said Tinker. 'It would take ages for anyone to dig a hole like that themselves – and they'd have got blisters on their hands, too.'

Mischief, feeling playful again, jumped down into the hole. He seemed to have spotted something interesting, because he started digging away in the earth with his tiny hands. Timmy jumped in too, to help him, and began scraping soil aside with his paws.

'Do look at them – they're playing Hunt the Thimble, or something!' said Tinker, laughing.

But George had a thoughtful frown on her face. She bent down to get a better look inside the hole. She had heard the dog's claws scrape against something hard, buried in the ground – and then she heard the same sound again. What could it be? George felt intrigued.

'Seek, Timmy! Good dog – go on, seek!' she told her dog.

Hearing the encouraging note in her voice, Timmy dug harder than ever. Suddenly, all the children let out exclamations. The dog's busy paws had just uncovered something – something dull-coloured and rusty, but easy to recognise. It was the lid of a metal casket.

'Hallo!' said Dick. 'I wonder what that is?'

'Perhaps it's buried treasure!' said Anne, just for a joke.

Julian and Dick soon managed to dig the box up.

'An old dustbin lid, more likely!' said Tinker.

Dick and George were already down in the hole with Timmy, trying to tug the metal box out of the earth. But it was well embedded, and they couldn't get a good grip on it anywhere.

'Wait a sec!' said Julian. 'I'll go and fetch some tools!'

He ran back to the toolshed, and came back with a spade and a pickaxe. He and Dick soon managed to dig the box up and hoist it out of the hole. George lifted the lid – that was easy enough, because rust had eaten away the lock and the hinges.

And then they all exclaimed again, in sheer amazement!

'I don't believe it! It really *is* buried treasure!'

'Gold! Gold and jewels!'

'Golly – there must be a fortune in there!'

'Just pinch me, will you, Dick? So I know I'm not dreaming!' George asked her cousin.

Dick was quite ready to oblige – and she *wasn't* dreaming. She was gazing at a wonderful treasure, the kind of thing you'd expect to find only in a story-book.

The Five had already found valuable lost or stolen property on a number of occasions – but only after they had worked hard searching and making inquiries. This was the first time they had ever stumbled across such riches quite by chance, without having to go to any trouble at all! They were dazzled!

'I tell you what – it somehow doesn't seem *right*!' said George to the others. 'Fancy finding a treasure like this, just by accident!'

'A bolt from the blue!' said Dick, laughing.

Julian quickly pulled himself together.

'Come on, let's take this box into Rose Cottage and show it to Jenny,' he said. 'I wonder who can have buried it in the orchard? Perhaps she'll know.'

Jenny looked relieved when the children came in. 'So there you are at last!' she said. 'I was just beginning to worry about you. Are you terribly wet?'

'Never mind about that!' Tinker interrupted, impatient to show off their find. 'See what we've got here!'

Julian and Dick put the box on the kitchen table and opened it – and Jenny's mouth dropped open as she stared at the contents. It was at least half a minute before she could utter a word.

'My goodness, children!' she said at last. 'It can't be possible – why, I can hardly believe my eyes! So it really *did* exist! Oh, goodness gracious me! Won't Mr Mandeville be pleased! And what a shame poor Hugh Mandeville couldn't benefit from it, all those years ago.'

It was the children's turn to be baffled. 'What are you talking about, Jenny?' asked George.

'Why, the Mandeville treasure, of course! The lost treasure! Didn't I tell you that part of the story? It all happened so long ago, you see.'

'Tell us *now*, Jenny – quick, tell us!' cried Tinker.

'Well, do you remember how I was telling you, the other day, about Lady Mandeville and her son Hugh, who was only a little boy at the time of the Civil War? My own family has lived round here for hundreds of years too, you see, and one of my distant ancestors, called Andrew Foster, was a servant of Lady Mandeville's in those days. That's how I come to know the Mandevilles' family history so well. Lady Mandeville was quite a young woman when she was widowed, and beautiful too. It was very sad for her when Sir Rupert was killed fighting for the King – and when the Roundheads became very powerful in this part of the country, she didn't feel safe any more.'

'Not even in her own home?' asked Dick.

'No, because, you see, her husband had always supported King Charles, and she knew that all the people hereabouts who supported Cromwell would bear her a grudge too.'

Anne couldn't help shivering. 'Oh, poor Lady Mandeville!' she said.

37

'And more and more people were going over to Cromwell all the time, now that he was winning the war,' Jenny went on. 'Soon the whole of this part of the country was in turmoil. Andrew Foster was still able to go between the manor house and the village, and he told Lady Mandeville she was in danger. He was devoted to the Mandeville family himself, and he advised her to escape at once, taking her little boy with her. Lady Mandeville knew he was right. She decided to go to France, like a great many other aristocratic people about that time, including the King's son himself. At least she and Hugh would be safe in France, though she hoped they wouldn't have to stay there long.'

'Where does this treasure come into the story, though, Jenny?' Tinker prompted her.

'Well, before she left the Mandevilles' ancestral home, Lady Mandeville hid her gold and jewels, with Andrew Foster's help' Jenny said. 'She dared not take them with her, for fear they'd be stolen, and if she left them behind it was more than likely the house itself might be ransacked. So she took only what she knew she would need, put the rest in a casket, and Andrew found a good place to hide it. Lady Mandeville and young Giles watched him bury the treasure, and then they all went away to France. Faithful old Andrew wasn't going to be left behind! But poor Lady Mandeville died abroad, and so did Andrew Foster – Hugh was brought up by friends in France, and many years later he came back to England on his own. He found the manor house empty and derelict, and he couldn't tell where the treasure was buried. Hard as he searched, he never did find it!'

'Why not?' asked George. 'You mean he just couldn't remember where to look?'

'No – Hugh had been very small when Andrew Foster buried the treasure, and all he could remember was watching the old man dig a hole somewhere in the grounds while he and his mother looked on.'

'But didn't Lady Mandeville or old Andrew tell him where to look, before they died?' asked Dick.

'Lady Mandeville died very suddenly, you see – it was said she left her son some family papers, and I expect they gave a clue to the whereabouts of the treasure but they were lost. People in France wouldn't have thought much of papers written in English – and this was a time when most people couldn't read or write at all, remember! Oh, dear me, children – just to think that the Mandeville treasure has been lying under the big oak tree all this time! And but for you, and the thunderstorm, it would still be there!'

'But how can we be sure it really *is* the

Mandeville fortune?' asked George.

Jenny looked at the open casket and picked something up. 'There's no doubt about that!' she said. 'Look – here's a miniature painted on ivory, showing a little boy, with his name written underneath. Hugh Mandeville! To tell you the truth, my dears, I didn't entirely believe in the existence of the treasure myself. People have talked about it for so long, you see, and yet nobody has ever found it. And now you children just stumble across it! George, we ought to let your father know, and then I'm sure he'll see to it that Mr Miles Mandeville gets his ancestors' fortune back. Why, I believe Mr and Mrs Mandeville are returning home today – how lucky!'

George said nothing. She didn't want to leave it to her father! She wanted to get in touch with the owners of Wistaria Lodge herself, and see their faces when she gave them the precious treasure Timmy had dug up on their land.

'Let's make a list of all the things in the box,' suggested Tinker. 'You know – what they call an inventory! That would be fun.'

It *was* fun, and very exciting, too. The children counted over six hundred gold coins with the head of King Charles I on them, and there was a whole set of emerald jewellery, a diamond and sapphire bracelet, a huge, unset ruby, a tiara, a diamond pendant, and a great many rings and earrings set with precious stones. Then there was an enormous pear-shaped pearl, three engraved gold bracelets, three gold chains, two gold watches and chains, four medallions, several miniatures painted on ivory – among them that picture of little Hugh, and another of his mother – and a signet ring with the arms of the Mandeville family on the seal. That certainly proved whose the treasure was.

'Are you sure Mr Mandeville and his wife are at Wistaria Lodge now?' Dick asked the housekeeper.

'Well, that's what they were saying in the grocer's earlier today – the Mandevilles were expected to arrive about ten o'clock this morning.'

George glanced out of the window. 'The storm's quite finished now – why don't we go and tell them the news?' she suggested.

'Yes, that's a good idea!' Julian agreed. 'We must leave the casket here in Jenny's care, of course. It wouldn't be safe to go carrying all those precious things round on our bicycles! But if the Mandevilles don't want to come straight over and fetch the treasure themselves, I'm sure Uncle Quentin or Professor Hayling will take it over to them by car if we ask them to.'

'Yes, and don't you remember? Aunt Fanny is coming to see us tomorrow!' Anne said. 'Maybe she'd like to take it back to them. Oh yes, George,

41

do let's cycle over to Wistaria Lodge and tell the Mandevilles what we've found!'

With such good news to tell, the children cycled fast and energetically. Vapour was steaming up from the wet ground in the hot sunshine, and the clouds were all blowing away at last. George and Dick led the little procession, with Timmy running along beside them. Julian, Tinker and Anne followed, more sedately, but they were all keen to get to Wistaria Lodge and see Miles and Sylvia Mandeville. What a lovely surprise to the architect and his wife! The children could just imagine their amazement and delight.

But sad to say, things didn't turn out exactly as they expected . . .

Chapter Four

THE DISAGREEABLE CARETAKER

The children cycled past the ruined manor house, and soon saw the white paint of Wistaria Lodge ahead of them. It was a square, pleasant house, with pretty purple wistaria and other climbing plants growing over it. There were neat flower beds and well mown lawns in the gardens. The children looked through the railings and saw a man walking along the garden path. When Julian pulled a chain hanging by the garden gateway, a bell rang in the distance.

The man in the garden stopped, turned round, and then came towards the gate. They heard the gravel of the path crunching under his feet.

'Good – here comes somebody!' said Dick. Like

George, he was so excited he could hardly keep still.

When the man reached the gate, they could see that he was middle-aged, with thin, greying hair. His face was rather forbidding, and he had a thin-lipped mouth. He didn't smile at the children. George noticed that he was wearing corduroy trousers and a blue overall.

The man looked at the children. He didn't seem to be in any hurry to open the gate.

'What do you want?' he asked.

'We'd like to see Mr Mandeville!' said George eagerly. 'Is he at home?'

The man did not reply at once. He was looking hard at the children, and finally he seemed to make his mind up. 'My employer doesn't talk to strange kids!' he said. 'He's got better things to do!'

George opened her mouth to protest, but he went on, 'I'm the caretaker here, and it's my job to keep unwanted visitors out!' He spoke in a most unpleasant tone of voice.

George went crimson with rage! Patience was not her strong point anyway, and the way the caretaker was behaving was really infuriating. 'I'd have thought it was up to Mr Mandeville to say if he wants to see us or not,' she said, doing her best not to lose her temper. 'So would you go and tell him we'd like to talk to him? We have something

The caretaker was being most infuriating.

extremely important to say to him!'

The caretaker began to laugh. 'Well, well, well!' he said sarcastically. 'Just hark at the lad! Sharp-tongued, aren't you? And impertinent too! Well, well – and just who do you think you are, my boy?'

George felt her temper rise to boiling point. Of course, it wasn't at all unusual for people to think she really *was* a boy, and she did look like one. Most of the time she didn't mind a bit – in fact, she rather liked it. But she didn't care for being treated as a cheeky brat by this horrible man! She was about to answer when Julian, realising that she was about to explode, hastily stepped in.

'You're making a mistake,' he told the caretaker coldly. 'My cousin here, Miss Georgina Kirrin, really has got some very important news for Mr Mandeville, so would you kindly let him know we're here?'

The caretaker looked suspiciously at the children again, and they could tell he wasn't quite sure what to do now. However, it didn't look as if he was going to oblige Julian, so Dick thought he'd put a word in too. 'That's right!' he said. 'And it's very, very *good* news we've got for Mr Mandeville, too!'

Anne spoke up as well. 'Oh yes!' she said, with her nicest smile. 'Please do believe my brothers! It really is *very* good news – about the lost treasure!

We've found –'

George quickly interrupted, glaring at her cousin. 'Be quiet, Anne, you little chatterbox!' she snapped.

Realising how thoughtlessly she had been chattering away, the little girl blushed and bit her lip.

But George's warning came too late. The caretaker had caught what Anne said, and he was certainly interested now! His manners improved as if by magic, and his voice became gentler.

'Treasure? What treasure?' he asked. 'You don't mean the Mandeville treasure said to have been buried by old Andrew Foster during the Civil War, do you?'

None of the children felt like telling him any more. Anne hung her head. She would have given a lot to take back the words she'd so stupidly let slip! Seeing that they were all silent, the man went on, 'I think you *do* mean Lady Mandeville's treasure! Am I right?'

George looked him up and down. 'We don't want to talk to you – only to Mr Mandeville!' she said firmly. 'Now, are you or aren't you going to let us see him? Make up your mind!'

A gleam came into the caretaker's eyes. 'It's like this, children,' he said in a much gentler tone than before. 'Mr and Mrs Mandeville aren't at home at the moment – they won't be back until tonight, or maybe tomorrow, or they might even be staying for a day or so longer. I think it would be best if you told me your story, since they're not here. Well – what's it all about?'

He wasn't so cross now, but Julian didn't like his manner any better than before. Timmy was sniffing the man's shoes through the railings, and growling quietly. *He* didn't take to the caretaker any more than George did.

'Sorry, but that's our business – and Mr Mandeville's,' said Julian firmly. 'Well, we'll just have to come back tomorrow, and the day after too if necessary.'

'Oh, it really isn't worth your while to put yourselves to all that trouble,' protested the caretaker. 'You might have a wasted journey, too. Why not give me your address? Then I can let you know as soon as Mr and Mrs Mandeville get back!'

It was Tinker who put his foot in it this time! He was slow to realise that his friends didn't want to tell the caretaker any more than he already knew, and without meaning any harm, he let out the information the man was after.

'My name's Tinker Hayling,' he said, 'and I'm staying at Rose Cottage with my friends here – perhaps you know where it is?'

'Why yes, I certainly do! I often pass the cottage

48

on my way down to the village, so just leave it to me! I'll drop a note into your letter-box as soon as Mr Mandeville comes home.'

The caretaker was smiling now. George thought she rather preferred his rudeness to that sugary smile!

On the way back from Wistaria Lodge, she told her cousins and Tinker, 'That man was really horrible! I didn't like him a little bit.'

'We shouldn't judge by appearances, you know,' said Julian, who had a strong sense of fair play. 'He may be kind at heart, even if he has a surly sort of way with him.'

But George wasn't convinced. 'Well, Timmy agrees with me,' she said. 'I could tell that *he* couldn't stand the man either. And believe me, Ju, old Timmy isn't often wrong about that sort of thing. You can rely on his instinct!'

Dick agreed with his cousin. 'He was working in the garden – how do we know he's really a caretaker at the house at all, and not just a gardener who was trying to make out he was Mr Mandeville's right-hand man so as to gain our confidence? I didn't take to him at all!'

'Nor did I! He didn't begin to sound polite until the moment Anne mentioned the treasure,' said Tinker. 'Honestly, Anne, how *could* you be so silly?'

'No sillier than you, old chap!' Julian pointed

out gently. 'Why on earth did you have to go and give that man our address?'

Tinker looked at Julian, puzzled. 'What's that got to do with it?'

Dick explained. 'Tinker, we didn't want the man to know where he could find us – and the treasure!'

'Oh dear, – yes, I see now,' said Tinker ruefully.

'Well, there's no point in arguing!' interrupted George. 'It's no use crying over spilt milk, either! The important thing now is to keep a close watch on that precious casket until my mother arrives tomorrow and we can get her help.'

'Yes, George is right,' said Anne. 'I expect Aunt Fanny will tell Uncle Quentin, and he'll come to fetch the treasure, and then it will be safe.'

When they got back to Rose Cottage, the children told Jenny about the disappointing result of their expedition.

'Oh, I know the man you mean,' the housekeeper told them. 'Yes, he's caretaker and gardener at Wistaria Lodge all right – his name is Johnson, and he's fairly new to these parts – nobody seems to like him much round here! He's rather sly, and mean too. In fact, I don't know why the Mandevilles employ him, but as they aren't here so very often, perhaps they don't know what he's like – and they're very kind-hearted, too. Too kind-hearted for their own good, if you ask me.'

Next morning the children had another disappointment. Aunt Fanny telephoned to say she had a slight cold, and so she didn't think it would be a good idea for her to come and see the children that day after all. 'I'd better stay indoors, George,' she told her daughter, 'and then I'll soon be well again.'

'Can *we* come and see *you*?' asked George.

'That wouldn't be very sensible either — since you're out of reach of my germs at Rose Cottage, I don't want to pass them to you! I'll see you in a few days' time, dear!' And Aunt Fanny hung up, sneezing, before George could say any more.

'You didn't mention the treasure,' said Julian, who had been standing beside her.

'No, I didn't get time! But I've been thinking why *don't* we take it to the Mandevilles ourselves, after all? We can walk instead of bicycling to Wistaria Lodge, and we'll take jolly good care not to hand it over until we actually see Mr or Mrs Mandeville in person.'

Julian didn't look as if he thought this was a very good idea — but before he or the others could say anything about it, Mischief had darted off to the garden gate. He had seen a piece of white paper lying in the letter-box fastened to the gate itself, and he was soon back, triumphantly clutching an

51

envelope in his little paw. He held it out to Tinker. The note was addressed to Miss Kirrin and Mr Hayling. The envelope turned out to contain a card with Mr Mandeville's name at the top, and the message on the card was very brief.

'Mr Mandeville regrets that he is too busy to come to see you himself or to ask you to visit him. However, his nephew, Benjamin Latchford, will call on you today before noon, to thank you on Mr Mandeville's behalf. Would you be good enough to give Mr Latchford what you have found?'

The note was signed 'Miles Mandeville'.

'Well!' said George, disgusted. 'How *rude*! Short and not very sweet – not only can Mr Mandeville not be bothered to see us himself, he's hardly even saying thank you!'

Dick shook his head. 'If you ask me, he doesn't believe in the treasure!' he said. 'Goodness knows what that caretaker man, Johnson, has told him about us! He probably said we're just kids playing a practical joke, or something like that! So Mr Mandeville doesn't trust us, or believe we've got anything worth his while.'

'I think Dick is right,' Julian agreed. 'Mr Mandeville wouldn't want to run the risk of looking silly by dashing off after a treasure that doesn't really exist!'

'But it jolly well *does* exist!' said Anne, glancing

at a shabby little suitcase on the floor. Jenny had thought it might be a good idea to hide the casket inside this suitcase for camouflage.

George sighed. 'Oh well, we'll just have to wait here for Mr Mandeville's nephew. Still, fancy just sending someone else to collect such a treasure! I really do think he's being offhand about it, don't you?'

So the Five, Tinker and Mischief spent the morning in the garden, keeping an eye on the gate. They were eagerly waiting for Benjamin Latchford to appear. They rather looked forward to the moment when they'd show him all the precious things, and see his face when he realised that the treasure *was* real, whatever his uncle thought – and fabulously valuable!

It was still well before noon when they heard the noise of a motor-bike coming along the road. That must be Benjamin, they all felt sure!

Chapter Five

BENJAMIN – OR IS IT?

Sure enough, the motor-bike stopped outside Rose Cottage, and a tall, thin, dark-haired young man of about eighteen got off it. He rang the bell.

The children all went to open the gate. 'You the kids, are you?' asked the newcomer. 'I'm Benjamin Latchford.'

George frowned. She didn't much like the young man's high-and-mighty tone, nor the way he called them 'kids' – it was as if he didn't think they were worth his attention! But Tinker went up to the motor-cyclist.

'Yes,' he said. 'We're the people who discovered your family's ancestral treasure!'

'Well, that's wonderful! My uncle will be delighted. Let's have a look at the loot, then!'

It was Julian's turn to frown. He didn't take to this Benjamin at all. He thought his manner was very offhand and unattractive. All the same, he politely introduced the others – not forgetting Timmy, who had been the first to sniff out that casket full of gold and jewels.

Benjamin Latchford listened with obvious impatience, and he seemed very tense, although the children couldn't think why. But a gleam came into his eyes when Julian mentioned the gold and jewels. He still didn't smile, though, and Anne noticed that he was involuntarily clenching and unclenching his fists as he said curtly, 'Okay, now show me the goods, will you? I haven't got much time, and my uncle's waiting.'

The children led Benjamin to the cottage door, and Jenny welcomed him in her usual friendly way. However, Timmy was growling softly and sniffing at the visitor's ankles.

'Oho!' George thought with amusement, 'it looks as if Timmy doesn't like Benjamin any more than we do!'

Jenny produced the suitcase and put it on the living room table, Julian opened it, Dick lifted out the rusty old casket, and George unpacked all the wonderful things inside it. They certainly *did* impress Benjamin, just as the children had expected. He let out a low whistle of amazement.

'Crikey!' he exclaimed. 'How about that for a real little gold-mine!'

Julian thought Benjamin's way of putting it was really rather vulgar – it was obvious that *he* wasn't out of the top drawer, even if his uncle was such a perfect gentleman as Jenny said! Benjamin got over his surprise, briskly swept the gold coins and jewellery into a heap and put them into the casket again, and returned the casket itself to Jenny's old suitcase.

'Well, I'll be off now, and take this straight to my uncle,' he said. And he was about to pick up the suitcase and walk out with it.

Jenny hesitated. She had an uneasy feeling that something wasn't quite right, and she did wish Aunt Fanny was there. Julian, Dick and Anne glanced at each other, not sure what to do. Anne wondered why they were so quiet all of a sudden.

Then George stepped forward, placing herself between Benjamin and the door. 'Wait a minute!' she said. 'Mr Mandeville certainly told us his nephew Benjamin Latchford would be calling, and he did ask us to hand over the treasure to Benjamin. But I hope you won't mind if we ask you to prove your identity! After all, we don't know you, do we?'

'My cousin's quite right,' said Julian. 'Have you got any documents on you to prove who you are – a driving licence or anything like that?'

The boy went pale, and shot a furious glance at the two cousins. 'How dare you speak to me like that? I *am* Miles Mandeville's nephew!' he shouted.

'Okay, then prove it!' said Dick, walking over to stand with his own back to the door. 'And if you don't happen to have any proof with you, I expect you can go and find some papers to back up your claim, and *then* we'll hand over the treasure!'

'Oh, very well! I'll go straight away!'

'But put that suitcase down first,' Tinker told him.

However, instead of obeying, the young man made for the door. Julian, Dick, and George barred his way. With a shout of fury, he swung round, pushing Jenny aside, and fending off Anne and Tinker as they tried to grab hold of him. He was making for the window!

But he had reckoned without Timmy. The good dog, who had been sniffing round the stranger, growling, all this time, sprang at him, caught him by his leather jacket, braced himself on all four paws, and clung on with all his might.

The fake Benjamin – for by now it was clear to all of them that this young man was an impostor – turned, dropped the suitcase, and tried to pull the dog off him. It was no good! Timmy let go of the

The young man was making for the window.

jacket for a moment, but only to take a firm hold of the seat of his jeans. With a growl of triumph, he tore away a big piece of denim – and maybe a little bit of skin too, because the young man let out a howl!

As 'Benjamin' made for the door, abandoning the suitcase, George held it open for him with a mock-polite gesture. He rushed out, clutching his behind with both hands. The children were in fits of laughter! Then Mischief decided that *he* would take a hand too. Jumping up on the fugitive's shoulder, the little monkey climbed on to his head and began pulling his hair very hard. The young man howled louder than ever, and ran for it, disappearing from the children's sight. But a moment later, they and Jenny heard the sound of his motorbike starting up, and Mischief soon reappeared, looking very pleased with himself. He started chattering away to Timmy in shrill tones, no doubt telling his friend all about his brave deeds!

When the children's laughter had died down a bit, Dick said, 'Well, that was a close shave! The Mandeville treasure would have fallen into quite the wrong hands but for you, George.'

'But for Timmy, you mean,' said George, patting her dog.

Julian had stopped laughing now, and was frowning instead as he thought it all over. 'How did that young man who was pretending to be Benjamin Latchford know that Mr Mandeville's nephew was going to call here this morning?' he said. 'He was running quite a risk, wasn't he, counting on getting here first!'

George shook her head. 'If you ask me, the real Benjamin won't turn up at all,' she said. 'The whole message telling us to expect him was probably faked!'

'What do you mean?' asked Anne and Tinker.

'I mean it almost certainly wasn't Mr Mandeville who sent us that curt, rude note! Jenny says he's such a gentleman! We ought to have suspected something from the start.'

'Then who did write it?' asked Tinker.

'I can only think of one likely person,' said George, 'and that's Johnson, the caretaker at Wistaria Lodge. After all, *he's* the only one who knows we've found Lady Mandeville's treasure.'

'But he didn't come for it himself,' Tinker protested.

'No – he knew we wouldn't hand it over to him, so he sent an accomplice instead! I don't think we need expect to see the real Benjamin today.'

They did wait until twelve noon, however. But sure enough, nobody else turned up. All the evidence showed that George had guessed right.

'Oh dear, that Johnson is a real bad lot!' sighed

Jenny. 'I do wish he didn't know you've got the treasure, children.'

'Well, we must do something!' said George briskly. 'Perhaps Johnson was lying to us, and Mr Mandeville is at home after all. If so, we'll try to see him again – that will be one in the eye for Johnson!'

So directly after lunch, the children got on their bicycles and went off to Wistaria Lodge, followed by Timmy, as usual. When they reached the garden gate they dismounted. Much to their disappointment, all the windows of the house were closed, and the place looked shut up. Julian rang the bell by the gate, but nobody appeared, not even Johnson.

Feeling rather flat, the five friends looked at each other. They decided to wait a little longer, in case somebody came home, but it didn't look as if Mr Mandeville was back yet after all. It was really very frustrating! Then a girl came along the road with a basket of eggs.

'Looking for somebody?' she asked the children. 'If it's the Mandevilles you want to see, you'll have to wait another twenty-four hours. They're still in London, but they expect to be back tomorrow. Our farm is just along the road, and they've written to my father to order milk every morning from then on.'

That sounded like better news! George and the

61

others thanked the girl, and when she had disappeared round the next corner, Dick cried, 'So you *were* right, George! If Mr Mandeville isn't here, he couldn't have written us that note, and it must have been Johnson who did!'

The children stood by the garden gate for a few minutes longer, working things out. 'I wonder who the fake Benjamin really is?' Tinker wondered. 'I just hope that once Mr Mandeville hears about all this, he'll be asking his caretaker a few questions. And getting answers to them, too!'

'What are we going to do until he gets back?' said Anne, worried.

'Nothing,' said George. 'We must just wait! We'll come back here tomorrow, and *then* we should be able to talk to the owner of Wistaria Lodge.'

'But meanwhile we ought to make sure the treasure's safe. Maybe we ought to hand it over to the police,' suggested Julian, who was the most thoughtful and sensible of all the children.

'Oh no, please, Ju!' begged George. She really *did* want to give it to the Mandevilles in person! 'I mean, it would be silly, just for such a short time – and think how pleased Mr Mandeville will be to have his inheritance back without any formal fuss and bother!'

'But that means we have to keep it for another

twenty-four hours – and we'll be responsible if anything happens to it,' Julian pointed out, sounding very worried.

'Twenty-four hours isn't long!' said Dick, who always tended to back George up. 'Who do you think would go off with it?'

'Have you forgotten that Johnson and that young man pretending to be Benjamin have already tried going off with it?' asked Julian.

'No, of course not, but they'll never have the nerve to try again! Why don't we hide the treasure somewhere safe until it's time to hand it back to the rightful owner?'

'Good idea!' agreed Tinker, getting on his bicycle. 'Let's go home, quick, and find it a safe hiding place!'

Chapter Six

A SAFE HIDING PLACE

The children cycled back fast, in a great hurry to put the precious treasure somewhere safe. They only hoped nothing had happened to it while they were out!

However, when they reached Rose Cottage everything was all right. But Jenny told them she was very worried. 'I just don't feel easy in my mind, children, with all those golden coins and precious stones about! Such a fortune to have in the house!'

'It'll be off our hands tomorrow, Jenny!' said Tinker. 'And meanwhile, we're going to hide it so well that the cleverest of thieves couldn't find it!'

First of all, George, Julian, Dick, Anne and Tinker took the case containing the precious casket up to the attic. Dick had suggested slipping it under one of the beams there, but they found the case would stick out quite a long way, so that anyone could see it, and they dropped that idea.

Then Anne asked why they didn't put it inside a trunk – but Tinker pointed out that that would be one of the very first places where a burglar would look for it. Julian and George suggested that they should try the cellar, so they all went downstairs again.

'I know – let's hide the treasure in the boiler!' said Julian. 'It's not on at the moment, because it's summer-time, and it would make a grand safe!'

But although the suitcase wasn't very big, it was still too large to go through the opening of the boiler, and they soon gave up the attempt to get it in. George suggested simply stuffing it under the old sacks piled against the end wall of the cellar, and putting an old bedstead in front of it. Everyone agreed to this idea, and George began directing operations.

'Julian and Dick, you take one end of the bedstead each,' she said. 'Pick it up carefully and put it down over here, and whatever you do, mind you don't drag it over the floor.'

Tinker was looking puzzled. 'Why all these precautions?' he asked.

'Because if we go dragging the bedstead over the

dusty floor it'll leave marks,' George explained. 'Then anyone will be able to see straight away that it's been moved, and it'll be an obvious place to look for something hidden!'

'You think of everything, George!' said Anne admiringly.

Tinker helped the other boys move the bedstead. Still taking care not to leave any tracks, George picked up the dusty sacks and hid the suitcase behind them.

'There!' she said, straightening up. 'Now the treasure's safely hidden, and all we have to do is put the bedstead in position in front of it!'

No sooner said than done! Then, with their minds at rest, the children went off to the kitchen, where Jenny had made them a delicious tea, with a big plate of chocolate biscuits as a special treat. That put them in a good mood again, and the rest of the day passed pleasantly if uneventfully.

At breakfast next morning, the children discussed the best way of getting in touch with the Mandevilles at Wistaria Lodge.

'If I were you I'd telephone instead of just turning up on the doorstep,' said Jenny. 'If you arrive too early, maybe nobody will answer the door – or you might meet that Johnson again, and find he won't let you in!'

'Yes, why don't we telephone?' cried Tinker.

George hid the suitcase behind some dusty sacks.

'That's a good idea – we ought to have thought of it before!'

'What's the Mandevilles' number?' asked George.

'I don't know, but you're sure to find it in the telephone book,' said Jenny. 'I should call at about ten o'clock, I think.'

The children took Jenny's advice, and at ten o'clock, George picked up the telephone and dialled the number of Wistaria Lodge.

A man's deep, pleasant voice replied.

'This is Georgina Kirrin speaking,' said George, very distinctly. 'I'd like to talk to Mr Miles Mandeville, please. It's personal!'

'Miles Mandeville here,' said the voice, sounding a little amused. 'Go ahead – I'm listening!'

So in a few sentences, George told the tale of their amazing adventure, and the fabulous treasure they had discovered.

For a moment or so, Mr Mandeville said nothing at all. Then he began, 'If this is some kind of joke –'

'No honestly it isn't!' George protested. 'It's nothing but the truth! If you'll let us come and see you, we'll explain all about it, and then you can come back to Rose Cottage with us and we'll hand over your property.'

There was another moment's silence at the other end of the line, and then Mr Mandeville said, 'Very well! I'll expect you at Wistaria Lodge at about three this afternoon – but I must say, your story sounds very strange to me!'

With a sigh of relief, George put the receiver down again. 'Phew! Done it!' she told the others. 'Mr Mandeville will see us this afternoon!'

The children were very excited. They stayed in the garden of Rose Cottage all morning, looking forward to their meeting with the Mandevilles that afternoon. Anne, who loved pretty things, kept imagining Sylvia Mandeville's delight when she saw the jewels.

'She'll be so pleased and happy! I can just see her putting on that diamond tiara, like a queen wearing a crown –'

'And then going out to do her shopping in it, I suppose!' finished Tinker, laughing.

The children were still in the garden when the bell rang at about eleven. A tall, distinguished-looking man stood at the garden gate.

'I'd like to see Miss Georgina Kirrin, please,' he said politely. 'I believe she's staying here, isn't she?'

George stepped forward. 'I'm Georgina Kirrin – oh, I bet you're Mr Mandeville!'

The visitor smiled. 'Yes, that's right! Forgive me

for coming over on impulse like this, but when I thought about it, I hadn't got the patience to wait until this afternoon to meet you and your friends!'

George smiled, with a mischievous gleam in her eye. She guessed that Mr Mandeville, doubting the truth of her story and afraid that someone was trying to play a trick on him, had come to make sure for himself that the children really *did* live at Rose Cottage, as she had said, and weren't just anonymous practical jokers. But she was too well brought up to say exactly what she was thinking out loud!

First of all she introduced her cousins and Tinker, not forgetting Mischief and Timmy too.

'It's thanks to my dog Timmy we found your family treasure at all, Mr Mandeville,' she said. 'But for him, we'd never have guessed there was anything there!'

The children could tell that Mr Mandeville still wasn't quite sure whether or not to believe them, so they invited him to follow them into the cottage, where Professor Hayling's housekeeper confirmed their amazing story.

'Yes, sir, Miss Georgina has told you the exact truth,' said dear old Jenny. 'When the children brought in that rusty old casket after the storm, I could hardly believe my eyes. All those gold coins! And the jewels – precious stones all sparkling with different colours! It was like something in a fairy-tale!'

Mr Mandeville seemed quite staggered by what Jenny told him. 'This is astonishing!' he said. 'To think of my ancestral inheritance being found quite by accident, after such a long time! Forgive me if I seem a little upset, but I can scarcely get over it!'

Julian nodded sympathetically. 'We under-stand, sir! It certainly must make you feel odd!'

'But you just wait till you see the treasure for yourself!' added Dick, cheerfully.

'We hid it down in the cellar, for fear of jewel thieves,' explained Tinker.

'Jewel thieves?' said Mr Mandeville, smiling. 'I don't imagine there are many jewel thieves about in this quiet part of the country! And I suppose you didn't tell anyone else you were looking after such a fabulous treasure!'

Anne looked guilty, and glanced at George. George frowned. She had told Mr Mandeville about the casket itself, and how they found it at the foot of the oak when the tree was struck by lightning, but so far she hadn't mentioned Johnson, or the young man pretending to be Benjamin Latchford. She quickly put things straight now – and Mr Mandeville himself seemed thunderstruck, like the oak tree!

'I'd never have believed it of Johnson!' he exclaimed. 'And to think how we trusted him! As for my nephew Benjamin – the real Benjamin – he's fair, not dark, and doesn't sound in the least like the young man you met. What's more, he's on holiday abroad at the moment!'

'Quick, let's go down to the cellar!' cried Dick. 'Coming, George?'

'We'll all go,' said Julian.

'So will I, if I may!' said Mr Mandeville.

Jenny went back to the kitchen, and a little procession set off down the cellar steps. George was leading the way – and the moment she entered the cellar she let out a cry. The old bedstead had been pushed aside, the sacks were scattered round the floor – and there was nothing else on the floor at all!

Julian, Dick, Anne and Tinker all exclaimed in horror too.

'The treasure's gone!'

'Woof!' agreed Timmy, running over to the sacks and sniffing them as he growled. Then he barked again. 'Woof, *woof*, WOOF!'

Mr Mandeville had turned very pale. 'Are you *quite* sure that's where you hid it?' he asked.

'Absolutely certain!' Julian told him. 'George took a lot of trouble to hide any traces that we'd been here, too!'

'And now,' said Dick, gloomily, 'anyone can see someone's been dragging the bedstead over the floor and scattering the sacks about without taking any precautions at all!'

George was standing perfectly still, thinking.

'I wonder how the thieves managed to get in here?' she murmured. 'This stone cellar is very old – Jenny told me it was part of the old hunting lodge that once stood here, and Rose Cottage was built on top of it. The door to the cellar steps is always locked, and Jenny keeps the key in a safe place. She had to go and fetch it for me when we hid the treasure here. And there's only one little window, high up in the wall, to let light into the cellar . . .'

Julian walked over to look at the window. 'That's closed, too, and looks as if it can't have been opened for centuries!' he said.

'The Mystery of the Locked Room!' said Anne, who had once read a very exciting detective story with that title. 'Well – if nobody could come in or go out, how can the treasure have been stolen?'

Mr Mandeville too was checking the window and the door.

'*I* can't see any signs of a break-in,' he said, rather sternly. 'Are you really sure this is not a practical joke you've been playing on me?'

At that moment, Mischief dived into the dusty jumble of sacks. He picked up something shiny with his soft little paw, and held it out to Tinker.

'Oh, Mr Mandeville!' cried Tinker. 'Here's proof that we're not lying! Look! This jewel must have rolled out of the treasure casket. We've seen it before – a big, unset ruby! It's yours, sir – here you are!'

Mr Mandeville took the stone, put it in the hollow of his hand, and looked at it. It was translucent and deep red, with a wonderful pure glow.

'A ruby!' he murmured in amazement. 'One of the finest rubies I have ever seen! My dear young people – I am so sorry I ever doubted you! This certainly looks as if it proves the existence of the treasure. The thieves must have been quite dazzled by the contents of the casket if they let a wonderful jewel like this roll away, and never noticed!'

Meanwhile George had joined Timmy, who was still sniffing round the sacks, growling. She noticed several things, but she decided it would be better to keep quiet about them for the time being.

Mr Mandeville was already climbing up the steps out of the cellar. He went to find Jenny and tell her what had happened. Poor Jenny let out a cry of horror.

'Oh dear – oh, Mr Mandeville, whatever shall we do?'

'We must tell the police at once,' said Mr

Mandeville. 'You come with me, children! We'll make a statement. You must tell the police the whole story, not forgetting that note signed with my name, and the visit from the young man pretending to be my nephew. Johnson is going to have some trouble proving his innocence!'

Chapter Seven

DOWN IN THE CELLAR AGAIN

Sure enough, as Mr Mandeville and the children had expected, the police immediately suspected Johnson. He was called to the police station – but he swore that he was innocent, he hadn't sent the note, he didn't know the fake 'Benjamin', and – so he said – he certainly knew nothing whatever about any burglary at Rose Cottage.

When the children and Mr Mandeville confronted him, he just stuck to his story, and said firmly, '*I* don't know this dark haired lad with the motor-bike, however much you want to make out I'm in league with him. Never set eyes on him in my life! As for knowing about the discovery of the old treasure, why, that little girl –' and he pointed in a scornful way at poor Anne – 'that little girl was chattering away about it for anyone to hear! Anyone could have overheard her talking and tried to get hold of the treasure. I didn't believe a word of it, myself!'

So it was impossible to prove that Johnson had written the note – especially as the children hadn't got it any more! That naughty little monkey Mischief had torn it up. The police had no solid evidence at all to back up their suspicions, so they had to let Johnson go home.

George, her cousins and Tinker were very disappointed. They were sure the man was guilty! Lunch at Rose Cottage that day was a dismal meal, and as soon as they had finished eating, the five friends held a council of war.

'I tell you what – we'd better make our own inquiries, in case the police don't get anywhere with theirs!' said George firmly. 'For a start, there are one or two things I'd like to show the rest of you. Let's go down to the cellar.'

The others followed her, wondering what she could mean. A little earlier, the police had been round for a brief look at the scene of the crime, and they had glanced at the cellar themselves, but they didn't seem to have been able to deduce much from anything there.

When they were all down the steps, George waved her hand round at the cellar. 'Right!' she said. 'Here's a good test of our powers of observation! Does anything in particular strike you about this burglary?'

'Yes, it does!' said Julian at once. 'None of the other rooms in the cottage were disturbed at all. The thieves went straight to the cellar and took the treasure, just as if they already knew where to find it!'

'Well done, Julian! Good thinking!'

Anyone less good-natured than Julian might have been annoyed with his younger cousin for sounding a bit patronising, but he merely grinned and pretended to aim a blow at her!

'But apart from us and Jenny, nobody knew where the hiding place was!' Dick objected.

'Correct!' agreed George. 'So what do you deduce from *that*?'

'Well – the burglars must have begun their search of the house down in the cellar, and they struck lucky. They found the treasure straight away!'

'That's what I'd have thought, too, if I hadn't taken a very close look,' said George, shaking her head. 'See those marks on the floor. Now, tell me what you make of them!'

Julian, Dick, Tinker and Anne looked at the marks left on the dusty floor by the bedstead and the sacks when they had been moved.

Rather surprisingly, Anne was the first to speak up – not that the little girl was at all stupid, but she did tend to be rather shy.

'That bedstead wasn't just dragged aside,' she remarked. 'It's been turned over first. And the sacks are scattered in a funny sort of way – as if they'd been pulled away from the wall into a kind of semi-circle.'

'Not pulled away, exactly,' George told her cousin. '*Pushed* away!'

'Pushed away?' Dick looked at George blankly. 'What do you mean?'

'I mean the burglars weren't *facing* that end wall when they came into the cellar – they had it *behind* them!'

'But that's impossible!' cried Tinker. 'The only way in would have been that little window, and it's tiny, and tightly closed. They could never have got through it.'

'No, they didn't come through the window,' agreed George. '*Or* through the door, either!'

Julian looked at his cousin with interest. 'What are you getting at, George? Come on, spill the beans!'

'Well, those sacks lying in a semi-circle, and the way the bedstead was upside down, as if something had knocked it over, all make me think the thieves came through a secret doorway in the end wall!

It was the entrance to a secret passage!

And when they pushed the door open, they pushed away everything we'd piled in front of it. So then, there they were, face to face with the treasure which we'd so kindly put there for them. All they had to do was pick it up!'

'What an amazing coincidence that would be!' said Julian.

'Julian, my revered and respected cousin, life is *full* of amazing coincidences!' pronounced George, in a comically solemn tone. 'Anyway, we can check my theory!'

The five children scrambled over the bedstead, and began feeling the stones of the cellar wall. It was an unusually thick wall, the kind you sometimes see in very old buildings. Yes, it could easily be hiding a secret passage.

'And don't forget, this cellar is part of the old hunting lodge,' said George. 'Oh, I say – this stone seemed to move! If we all push together –'

Tinker was pushing so hard that when the stone pivoted on its own axis and swung aside, to reveal a dark, gaping hole, he almost fell into the hole head first.

'So I was right!' cried George, delighted. 'I know the country round here pretty well, you see – and almost all the old manor houses in these parts have underground passages like this one! I bet the other end comes out in the ruins of what used to be the

Mandevilles' ancestral home. And it must pass close to Wistaria Lodge, too. I feel sure Johnson knows about it! Now, let's think. Nobody but Johnson knew the treasure was at Rose Cottage, so he must have come along the secret passage to get in and look for it – and he was lucky enough to find it straight away! Oh dear, I could *kick* myself for thinking it would be such a good idea to hide the suitcase containing the casket down here in the cellar!'

'You weren't to know what would happen,' said Julian, gloomily. 'But I rather think you're right, George. Working for the Mandevilles, Johnson has probably come to know the estate like the back of his hand. And we've already worked out that he's the only one who can have committed the crime, knowing what he did know.'

'Gosh!' cried Dick excitedly. 'Listen, why don't we go and get the treasure back? We can go the same way as Johnson, only in the opposite direction. Come on!'

'Not so fast, Dick! Calm down!' said Julian. 'Never mind the treasure now – we don't know where he may have put it. But we *can* make a little reconnaissance trip along this passage, for a start!'

Saying nothing to Jenny for fear of alarming her, the children went to get their electric torches. Then they climbed back down the cellar steps and into the secret passage. Beyond the doorway made by the pivoting stone, they found a staircase climbing down underground. It led to a narrow passage of solid masonry – luckily, though it must have gone down quite deep, it was quite dry.

George was leading the way – and suddenly she switched off her torch. The others followed suit instinctively. 'Ssh!' she hissed. 'I thought I heard something!'

They waited a few minutes, but nothing happened. It had been a false alarm. But as they stood there in the dark, the children realised they could see light ahead of them.

'Daylight!' whispered Anne. 'It must be the far end of the passage.'

They moved on again, taking even more precautions now. The floor of the passage was sloping upwards all the time at this point. Soon they reached the top of the slope – and saw the sun shining brightly through thickly intertwined branches just above their heads.

Cautiously, George peered out of the opening of the tunnel. When her eyes were at ground level, she let out a soft little cry of triumph.

'We're in the garden of Wistaria Lodge!' she whispered to her companions, who were standing perfectly still behind her. 'I can see the back of the house from here.'

So her theory had been correct. The secret passage *did* come out in the Mandevilles' garden, which had once been part of the grounds surrounding the old manor. But what should their next move be?

'What do we do now?' muttered Dick, echoing George's own thoughts. 'Shall we go and tell the Mandevilles what we've found – or what?'

'Wait a minute!' said George suddenly. 'Hm . . . that's funny! All the windows of Wistaria Lodge are closed – on this side of the house, at least!'

'Let's get a move on, anyway,' said Tinker. 'I'm stifling down in this hole!'

'We must go carefully, though,' George warned. 'We'll be in real trouble if we meet Johnson now!'

But the place seemed to be deserted. The children clambered up out of the underground passage. It ended in the middle of a thick hedge, and you'd never have seen it if you weren't looking for it. George guessed Johnson must have discovered it quite by chance while he was cutting the hedge, or something like that. Obviously even Mr Mandeville himself didn't know about it!

Very cautiously, the Five and Tinker went all round the house. But Wistaria Lodge was silent and shut up.

'The Mandevilles must have gone away again,' murmured Anne.

'Let's leave,' said Julian. 'We're trespassing, you know – I shan't feel happy until we're well away from here.'

All the five friends had to do was push open a little gate, which wasn't locked, and then they were out in the road. The cottage where, so Tinker had told them, Johnson lived was not far away.

'Why don't we try to find out if he's there?' suggested George. 'After all, if he's stolen the treasure, where can he be hiding it except in his own home?'

'This could be dangerous,' Julian warned the others.

'Nothing venture, nothing win!' said George.

'And fortune favours the bold!' added Dick, showing he could cap George's proverb and backing her up as usual.

The Five and Tinker went into the little garden behind Johnson's cottage, taking great care not to make any noise – and as they got closer they realised they could hear two men talking inside the little house.

'Johnson's at home!' whispered Tinker. 'And he's not alone, either!'

'Let's see if we can get a glimpse of him!' said Dick, going down on all fours and crawling over to the ground floor window from which the voices were coming. Then, slowly and cautiously, he raised his head to look in. 'I say!' he breathed. 'Look at that!'

The others followed him over to the window. It had taken them quite a long time to explore the cellar and go along the underground passage. The sun wasn't so hot now, and there were big clouds coming up to cover the sky. Looking into the room from outside, they had to peer hard to see anything, and as they didn't want to be seen themselves they had to be very, very careful too. But they could all make out the figures of two people. One was Johnson, and the other was the dark-haired young man who had pretended to be Benjamin Latchford. They were sitting at the table with two bottles of beer in front of them, talking quietly, with no idea that five pairs of ears were listening most attentively to their conversation!

Chapter Eight

AN INTERESTING CONVERSATION

'I'm surprised you didn't meet any of the police on your way here,' the caretaker of Wistaria Lodge was saying. 'They came to search the house not so long ago – but they left empty-handed, that's what matters! A real laugh, that was!'

'Acted all innocent and indignant, did you, Uncle Jim?' said the young man, laughing. 'I bet you had 'em puzzled! How were they to know you'd already got the goods safe away?'

'We've hit a winning streak all right, Gary!' said Johnson.

'Specially finding the treasure straight off like that, first go! Just think of those stupid kids hiding it down in the cellar, right in front of the secret door! And *what* a treasure, too!'

'When I opened up that rusty old box, you could have knocked me down with a feather!' agreed Johnson.

'The only thing is, Uncle Jim – well, all that gold and those jewels, they're kind of conspicuous! How are we going to get rid of them?'

'That'll be okay. Potter knows a man in London – what they call a fence. He'll be getting in touch with his friend. But there's no tearing hurry. Don't want to draw attention to ourselves, do we? We'll wait for the sensation to die down a bit. Meanwhile the loot's safe enough where it is. Well, here's to our success, Gary!'

The two men drank their beer, and then the younger one, Gary, left. The children could hear him starting his motor-bike and riding off down the road.

They looked at each other. Well! They'd learnt a lot in a very short time! So the police had searched Johnson's house and found nothing. The young man who had pretended to be Benjamin was really the caretaker's nephew and was called Gary. He and his uncle were certainly guilty of stealing the treasure, and they had an accomplice called Potter. Moreover, George's theory about the way they used the underground passage had been right. And last but not least, Johnson planned to hand the gold and jewels over to a 'fence', who would get rid of them for him – but not just yet! That meant the Five and Tinker still had time to do something about it.

However, talkative as Johnson and his nephew had been, they hadn't been kind enough to mention the most important point: just *where* they had hidden the treasure!

When the sound of Gary's motor-bike had died away, the children went back to Rose Cottage, wondering what to do next.

'I wish the Mandevilles hadn't gone away,' said Julian. 'But it does look as if they have, so let's hope they're back tomorrow. Then we must tell them what we've discovered!'

'Meanwhile, don't you think we ought to go to the police with our story?' asked Anne.

'What would be the use?' said George gloomily. 'All the police can do is question Johnson again, and he'll deny everything! What's more, it might make him decide to dispose of the treasure sooner then he planned at first, and get it away from here! No, that won't do at all. We must try to recover it ourselves. Why, for all we know it may actually be inside Wistaria Lodge itself! At any rate, Johnson can't have hidden it very far away. And I bet you he goes to look at it from time to time, to gloat over it and make sure it's still there in its hiding place. All we have to do is keep a close watch on him, and

I think he'll lead us to it!'

Dick agreed with his cousin, and Julian decided, 'All right, then, that's what we'll do. We'll take turns keeping watch on Johnson, starting tomorrow!'

Next morning Jenny went out shopping very early, and came back with some news that interested the children a great deal. The postmistress had told her that Mr Mandeville had been unexpectedly called back to London on urgent business the day before, and as his wife didn't like being left alone in the house she had gone with him, but they both expected to be back soon.

George, her cousins and Tinker exchanged meaning glances as Jenny told them this. If Johnson's employers were away, he'd be free to visit his treasure in Wistaria Lodge – that is, if he really had hidden it there! In any case he'd be more likely to move about without taking so many precautions, and that might well make things easier for the children.

They immediately drew up a rota for following Johnson. They intended to take turns keeping an eye on him the whole time, except at night – from what he'd been saying to Gary, they didn't think he planned to move the treasure yet, so they needn't keep a watch on him all round the clock at this point. During the day, however, somebody would be near him, even at mealtimes.

Disappointingly, however, Johnson's daily life turned out to be very dull! He didn't go out much at all, except to work in the garden of Wistaria Lodge or to do a little shopping. And this went on for two days.

'You know, I'm beginning to think he's got the treasure hidden in his own cottage after all,' George said, several times. 'I know the police searched it and didn't find anything, but he may have a very good hiding place there.'

And in the end Julian, Dick, Anne and Tinker came round to George's point of view. It was true that Johnson hardly ever left his cottage – he was like a dog jealously guarding a bone!

'Well, we can't go on like this!' said George, on the third day. 'We must *do* something! Next time that horrible man goes out, let's go and search his cottage ourselves. After all, he can hardly complain of *us* breaking in – that's just what *he* did!'

Julian wasn't at all sure that this was a good idea, but the others all agreed with George, so in the end he had to give way.

And they got their chance that very afternoon! Johnson went off to Wistaria Lodge to mow the lawns. The children went straight to his cottage, thinking they would have plenty of time to look round.

As it turned out, getting into the house was quite easy, because one of the ground floor windows at the back had been left open. They quickly searched the cottage, but they didn't find anything.

Dick sighed. 'Just what we might have expected, I suppose!' he said. 'If the police didn't find anything, we couldn't really hope to have better luck!'

'No, and the police must have had a search warrant too, which is more than we've got!' said Julian. 'Come on, you've had your way, George, and now we'd better clear out!'

'Oh, Ju, I'm *sure* the treasure can't be far away!' George protested. 'There are a couple of little outbuildings – let's search those before we go, and see if –'

But Anne interrupted her. 'Ssh!' she hissed. She was looking very frightened. 'Oh dear – I can hear footsteps. It must be Johnson, coming back!'

Glancing quickly round to make sure no trace of their presence in the cottage was left behind, the children scrambled out of the window again. Timmy had run on ahead, and they retreated without a sound. Only just in time! Anne was right – Johnson was coming home.

On the way back to Rose Cottage they stopped in a meadow, under a shady oak tree, to get their breath back.

'We mustn't give up hope,' said George. 'We'll

go on searching tomorrow if we can. Don't forget, Johnson's cottage is on the Manor grounds too — and for all we know the whole place is riddled with underground passages. Maybe there's another one somewhere close, and Johnson has hidden his loot there!'

Luck was with the children again next day. Johnson went back to Wistaria Lodge to cut the hedges. The five friends didn't go into the cottage itself today, and that set Julian's mind more at rest! Instead, they searched the garden and the yard. There was a sort of toolshed without a front wall, so it was open to all weathers, and nothing much of value could be stored in there. But then George's attention was attracted by another little structure built in the yard — an old stone washing trough with a roof over it to shelter it and a little raised stone wall round it. It was the sort of thing that would have been used for a huge family wash in the old days, and the bottom of the trough itself was paved with several big flagstones. Followed by Timmy, George prowled round the structure, examining every stone. She soon found that one stone stuck out a little farther than the others, and she called to her companions.

'Hey, come over here, will you? I'd like to try moving this stone!'

Julian and Dick hurried over to lend her a hand

One of the big stones paving the trough began moving aside.

– and they found they could lift the stone right out of place. A kind of rusty handle came into view behind it. Julian pulled the handle, and one of the big stones paving the trough began moving aside! George had suspected another underground passage might exist – and it looked as if this could be the way into it!

'What did I tell you?' she cried, delighted, and she plunged straight into the dark hole under the stone. 'Come on! What a good thing we've got our torches with us!'

The other children followed her. Julian brought up the rear. He wanted to make sure that once he'd put the flagstone back in place, he could move it easily from underneath, and to his great satisfaction he found there was a lever inside the tunnel which was obviously meant to do the job. He was just using it to close the opening when he let out a soft exclamation. Heavy footsteps were approaching! Johnson must be back earlier than they'd have expected again – he certainly wasn't keen to leave his cottage for any length of time. He had just come into the garden, and was walking towards the big trough!

'Watch out!' whispered Julian, manoeuvring the flagstone back into place in a hurry. 'Johnson's back already. I don't think he's spotted us, but it was a close thing! Let's hope *he's* not going to come

95

down here too.'

They daren't hang about. There was nowhere the children *could* go but straight ahead, and if they were out of luck and Johnson followed them into the passage, they'd have to find a hiding place as fast as they could and hope he wouldn't discover them.

Anne's heart was beating fast as she followed her intrepid cousin George along the underground passage. Tinker and Dick were just behind her, and Julian came last. George had advised the others not to use their torches – they didn't want the least little bit of light to show if there were any openings along the way. She kept only her own, small torch switched on, and as they moved forward she shone its narrow, golden beam down on the ground ahead of her.

Chapter Nine

ADVENTURE UNDERGROUND

The floor of the underground tunnel was uneven, and the children kept stumbling. Suddenly the passage turned a corner, and they stopped to listen.

'It's all right. I can't hear anything,' whispered George.

But Timmy had pricked up his ears. He was whining very quietly, as if to tell her she was wrong. The children listened harder, and they thought they heard a sound behind them.

'I think it's Johnson moving the flagstone away!' whispered Tinker.

'Come on, quick!' Julian gave his brother a little shove. George had already started to hurry forward, and was helping Anne along. This was a risky situation! If Johnson found them down here he might not actually hurt them, though they couldn't be sure of that, but it would be a disaster all the same. He'd be very suspicious, and would probably move the treasure somewhere farther away at once. He might even decide to run for it earlier than he'd planned, taking his haul with him.

Timmy was going ahead now, sniffing the ground, his sensitive nose twitching. The children could hear Johnson's heavy footsteps coming closer behind them. The caretaker probably knew this place inside out, and he was going faster than they were. He'd catch up with them before very long!

Suddenly the children stopped short. They had come out in a little, round, underground cavern. Fallen rocks littered the floor. The passage obviously went on beyond this cavern, but there was a grating over its mouth to stop anyone getting into it. The children were caught in a trap!

Timmy whined again, and Anne bit back a cry of terror. Dick, Julian and Tinker looked frantically round. Then George, who was keeping quite cool, saw a heap of old sacks thrown carelessly into a corner.

'Quick!' she said. 'Let's hide under those!'

They hurried over to the sacks. George made

Timmy lie down and covered him up. Then she and the others slipped under the sacks too and waited there, motionless and huddling together, hardly daring to breathe. George had switched her torch off, of course, so it was pitch dark. Mischief snuggled close to Tinker, and kept as still as his master.

They could hear Johnson's footsteps quite clearly now – and they could make out the faint light of a lantern as they peered through the coarse sacking.

'Oh, I do hope he doesn't look this way!' thought Anne to herself.

She needn't have worried. Even if Johnson *had* looked in their direction he couldn't have told there was anyone there. The children were quite invisible in their hiding place in such dim light.

Johnson went up to the grating – and thinking he was alone, he began talking to himself out loud. He sounded very cheerful indeed.

'A nice fit, this little grating!' he said. 'The door to Jim Johnson's private safe, eh? Ha, ha, ha!'

Julian and his companions heard a slight click, and they realised that the caretaker of Wistaria Lodge must be opening up the grating. Then there was a very faint squealing sound, not at all loud. They guessed Johnson had been careful to give the hinges of the door of his 'safe' plenty of oil!

George ventured to lift one corner of a sack and look out of her hiding place. She could see Johnson's back. The grating was open now, and he was moving on along the tunnel, carrying his lantern.

'Now what?' whispered Dick, who was just behind her. 'Shall we go back down the passage and get out that way?'

'No,' said Julian at once. 'Johnson's still too close – he might easily hear us!'

'Listen,' said George softly. 'I've an idea he's gone to take a look at the treasure – so let's stay here till he leaves again, and then we can go on the same way he went and recover our property, or rather, Mr Mandeville's property. That's what we came for, isn't it?'

The children had to wait patiently for quite a long time, but at last Johnson came back. He seemed to be in a very good mood, and was chuckling away like an old hen cackling!

'Ho, ho – those lovely gold coins!' he muttered; closing the grating. 'Wonder what they'll fetch? Whatever it is, Jim Johnson's going to be a rich man – ha, ha, ha!'

His chuckling died away as he went back along the part of the underground passage that ended in the old washing trough in his cottage yard.

'Did you hear what he said?' asked George,

triumphantly. 'I was right! The treasure's somewhere here, quite close. All we have to do is go and get it!'

Quickly, the children threw off the sacks which had done such a good job of hiding them. Timmy jumped about to get the circulation in his paws going again. George hurried over to the grating. She took it in both hands and shook it, but it wouldn't budge.

'Oh, bother!' she said.

'Half a sec!' said Julian, 'There's no lock, so that means there must be a lever or a secret spring or something to work the mechanism, if we can just find it.'

In the end it was Anne's nimble fingers that found the little knob to open the grating. All you had to do was press it, hard, and the grating swung open with that slight squeal the children had heard before. They felt jubilant!

It turned out that the passage didn't go much farther beyond the grating. Instead, they came to a sudden opening. They were on the edge of a circular well! Or rather, as they realised in a minute or so, when they had got their bearings, they were about half-way down the well-shaft. It extended above and below them, and they saw the gleam of water a couple of feet down. There was no way to go on – only up or down!

'Well, this means that Johnson must have hidden the treasure somewhere along this last short stretch of the tunnel' said Dick happily. 'It shouldn't take us long to search the place thoroughly. Come on!'

However, the children were in for a disappointment. Hard as they searched every nook and cranny of the underground passage, there was no sign of the suitcase containing the casket, or the casket itself. The treasure didn't seem to be anywhere here.

'What a nuisance!' said Julian. 'I just can't make it out!'

And then, for the third time, the children heard a now familiar sound.

'Oh no!' cried Dick. 'That grating's swinging shut again! We ought to have wedged it open with something!'

They all ran back, but they were just too late to catch the grating and hold it open. It closed right in their faces, with a dry click.

'Just our luck!' exclaimed Tinker. 'We're prisoners here now!'

'Well, all we have to do is press the knob that works the grating,' Dick pointed out. But that was easier said than done. The knob was in the underground cavern on the other side of the grating – and it was out of reach! Julian was the biggest of the children, and had the longest arms, but though he tried putting his arm through the bars he still couldn't touch the knob.

Then Tinker thought of making Mischief slip out through the bars to get at the knob. Mischief could do that all right, and he tried to obey Tinker's signs that he was to press the knob, but unfortunately he wasn't strong enough to push it right in hard. He did his best, but the grating stayed closed. At their wits' end, the children tried to tear it down, all together, but that was no use either.

'Well, there's no point in exhausting ourselves struggling with this stupid grating!' said George. 'Why don't we go back to the well and see if we can find some other way out?'

George, Julian and Dick were all being very calm and brave, and but for that Anne and Tinker might have been even more frightened than they were. For they were in a very unpleasant situation, trapped underground! And as nobody knew where they had gone, they couldn't hope for any help to arrive.

However, George marched back to the well with determination. Leaning over, she shone her torch inside. She couldn't tell how deep the water at the bottom was, but obviously they couldn't get out that way. Next she shone her torch up, but she could see nothing at all. She switched the torch off, but went on looking up, and when her eyes got used to the dark she could make out a faint circle of light overhead. But not too far overhead!

'Good!' she said. 'It's not so very far up to the top of this well-shaft, and though I think there's a round lid over it, so long as the lid can be moved from inside we'll be all right if we can hoist ourselves up there! I bet we can get out that way!'

'But how can we ever climb that far?' asked Tinker. He sounded worried.

George switched her torch on again and shone it round the sides of the well. She gave a cry of triumph. 'Look — I thought there'd be something of this kind! Iron rungs set in the wall to make a sort of ladder. Quick, let's go up!'

'Oh no!' cried Anne. 'I can't! I'd be too scared!'

'You'll be much more scared if you stay down this well!' said George briskly.

'Wait a minute,' said Julian, stretching his arm out to take hold of a rung and put all the weight he could on it. 'We've got to make sure it's safe first!'

But it turned out that all the iron rungs were firmly fixed in the side of the well. George insisted on going first, and the others all watched anxiously as she climbed up. She soon reached the top of the well. With a heave of her shoulder, she tried raising the circular wooden lid, and to everyone's relief it came away easily. George stepped out into broad daylight.

A glance round her told her just where she was – at the bottom of the garden of Wistaria Lodge, not very far from the tangled hedge which hid the end of the other underground passage!

Leaning over the side of the well, she called down, quietly, 'Dick! Tinker! Anne! Come on up – hurry! Ju, do you mind waiting a bit? I must go and look for a rope, so we can haul Timmy up.'

While Anne and the two younger boys climbed out of the well, George ran to the tool shed in the garden of Wistaria Lodge, and was lucky enough to find a length of good strong cord, which would do for pulling Timmy up. She went back to the well and let one end of the cord down to Julian. He wrapped his jacket round the dog, then tied the cord round him, and a moment later George and Dick were hauling away. Up went Timmy, like a passenger in a balloon!

Then Julian too climbed out of the well, and they put the lid back on top. Now all they had to do was go back to Rose Cottage, though they put the cord they had borrowed back in the toolshed first.

However, they still hadn't found the treasure, and next day they decided to go in search of it again. As it certainly hadn't been in the part of the underground passage they had searched so thoroughly, they deduced that it might be actually inside the well itself, or at least somewhere very near it.

Julian was not quite happy about this expedition, and kept saying they must take great care, but George was determined to climb back down the well and see if there was anything at the bottom.

The children thought it would be good idea to wait until dusk until they set out to explore the well – they didn't want Johnson to find them at it, and he might well be working in the garden of Wistaria Lodge again during the day. Directly after supper, however, they got their bicycles out and told Jenny they were going for a ride.

They reached Wistaria Lodge, got into the garden through the little side gate, and made straight for the well. They had brought their torches, and a length of good stout rope. Julian insisted on George's tying it round her waist before she climbed down the iron rungs inside the well.

'And we'll tie the other end to this tree,' he said. 'Then if you do happen to slip, we can soon haul you up again!'

So George tied the rope round herself, and began climbing down. Once she had reached the level of the water down below, she got a stone out of her pocket. It had a hole in the middle, and she had tied it to a piece of thin string. She let the stone down into the water, and found that it very soon touched bottom. George fished it out again, and now she could tell how deep the water was by looking at the wet part of the string.

'Good!' she called up to her cousins, who were leaning over the edge. 'The water's not at all deep. Now, I wonder . . .'

As she spoke, she was shining her torch round the walls of the well that surrounded her. An idea had suddenly come into her head! Suppose Johnson had hidden the treasure *underwater*?

Suddenly a gleam came into her eyes. She had just spotted a cord tied to the bottom iron rung, and hanging down into the water. She pulled it with her free hand, and soon a package came in sight. A heavyweight plastic bag, wrapped round a rusty old casket – the casket containing the treasure! She recognised it at once through the transparent plastic.

George let out a shout of triumph! 'I've got the treasure!' she called. 'It's here! I'm coming up again!'

As she fastened the cord tied to the casket to the rope she was wearing, Julian, Dick, Anne and Tinker all called down their congratulations, but quietly, because they didn't want to be heard. However, their excitement infected Timmy too.

He bounded forward to the edge of the well, and as *he* didn't mind how much noise he made, he started barking at George, who was just coming up. The weight of the treasure slowed her down. Tinker raised his hand to give Timmy a tiny little tap, just to make him stop barking, but Timmy swerved to avoid it – and lost his balance!

The poor dog tumbled down the well just as his mistress was emerging into the open. George wasted no time in going to the rescue. Quickly, she untied the casket which she had brought up the well, dumped it in Dick's hands, and then climbed down again as fast as she could. Down below, poor Timmy had hit the water with a mighty splash, but he was up above the surface again by now, dog-paddling round and round with a lot of spluttering.

'Don't worry, Timmy! I'm coming!' she called.

She was soon within reach of Timmy. 'Gosh, we *are* having what you might call a ropy sort of evening!' she muttered, as she grabbed him by the collar. Undoing the rope Julian had made her wear, she tied it round Timmy, with some difficulty.

'Ready up there?' she shouted. 'Haul Timmy up, then!'

The rescue operation was carried out in complete silence. Then George came up again too – and almost fell back in, in her surprise at the sight

Johnson had a shotgun and Gary was looking for the treasure.

that met her eyes!

Timmy was safe and sound all right, busy shaking himself. But Julian, Dick, Anne and Tinker were standing perfectly still, looking rather pale and scared. Johnson the caretaker was facing them, aiming a shotgun at them, while his nephew Gary investigated the plastic bag to make sure the treasure was still there!

Chapter Ten

PRISONERS

So that was why everything had suddenly gone so quiet during Timmy's rescue! The children had fallen right into their enemies' hands.

George immediately realised that they were in a tight spot. Johnson and Gary had been unmasked – they couldn't pretend to be innocent any longer. The discovery of the treasure proved their guilt. And now they'd got it back again!

'They'll never let us go!' thought George, with a shiver. 'We'd be much too dangerous as witnesses.'

Julian exchanged a despairing glance with his cousin. *He* was thinking much the same thing too. 'What will they do with us now?' he wondered.

Far too late in the day, George was wishing she

hadn't been quite so daring. *She* was the one who'd led the others into this mess. Getting over his fright, Timmy suddenly began growling.

'Quiet, Timmy!' George ordered, terrified in case Johnson shot her beloved dog to keep him quiet.

The good dog obeyed her, and the five children pressed close together as they faced their enemies.

'It's okay!' said Gary, straightening up. 'They didn't get time to open the bag. Well, Uncle Jim, what do we do with these kids now? Can't let 'em go, can we?'

'No, we can't,' agreed Johnson, frowning. 'Wretched brats – what a pest! We'll have to change our plans and get them out of the way, if we want room to move freely.'

'Keep them prisoner, you mean? Or what?'

Anne began to cry, quietly. Dick smiled at her to encourage her. 'Cheer up, Anne,' he whispered. 'They're thieves, but not murderers!'

George looked at her cousins and Tinker. 'I say – I'm awfully sorry I dragged all of you into this!' she said, with her usual straightforward honesty.

'You kids shut up!' Johnson told them roughly. 'I've got to think what to do about you!'

Keeping his gun pointed at them, the caretaker began talking to his nephew. They had lowered their voices, but it was a still night, and the children could hear most of what they said.

'We might do best to clear out straight away,' suggested Gary.

'Can't do that – we've got to wait for Potter to come back, bringing word from his London friend, and that'll be another couple of days yet!'

'But meanwhile what'll these kids be up to? If we let 'em go, they'll make a beeline for the police and tell them all they know!'

'We'll have to keep them somewhere,' grunted Johnson.

'Yes, but where? Not in your cottage – much too risky, and the police may search it again. The same goes for Wistaria Lodge, even if the Mandevilles don't come home – and they could, any time!'

Gary stopped to think for a moment. Suddenly he uttered a triumphant exclamation.

'I know, Uncle Jim! I was riding my motor-bike round the place one day when I spotted a little island off the coast. It's a small place, and uninhabited – that's the bit that makes it so suitable! I reckon nobody ever sets foot there. It's got some ramshackle old ruins on it, and that's all! We can take these nosy parkers over and leave 'em on the island, with a few blankets and some food. When Potter arrives, we'll be off – leaving a message behind to say where the kids can be found. How about that?'

Johnson thought his nephew's idea was a good one. 'Let's get a move on, then!' he said. 'I'll get the Mandevilles' motor-boat out. Come on, you kids!'

Julian reluctantly obeyed – there was nothing else to be done. Dick gritted his teeth. Tinker and Anne were holding hands as if to cheer each other up, and Mischief was huddling close to his master. But George, one hand on Timmy's collar, stepped briskly forward with a funny little smile on her lips. Suddenly, Johnson stopped.

'I've been thinking!' he told Gary. 'We don't want to work too fast, and maybe do something stupid. There are more precautions we ought to take – let's go into the greenhouse and talk things over.'

So Gary shepherded the children into the greenhouse. His uncle was no fool – Johnson had thought of several details that might spoil his plans, as he now explained. First, once she realised the children were missing, Professor Hayling's housekeeper was bound to worry. Jenny would raise the alarm!

'So we must make her think everything's okay,' the caretaker said. 'Otherwise she'll go to the police and the kids' parents! But I have a plan. Gary, take this cord and tie our prisoners' hands behind their backs – yes, that'll do!'

Gary carried out this task very efficiently, while

Johnson kept the gun aimed at his prisoners. George and the others felt furious, but they had to stand still and let Gary tie their wrists together. When all five of them were helpless, the caretaker at last lowered his gun.

'Right!' he said. 'Now, you wait here for me and guard them, Gary. I won't be long!'

'What are you going to do?'

'Run back to my cottage as fast as I can. I'll phone that housekeeper, what's her name – Jenny – and make out I'm Mr Kirrin telephoning from Kirrin Cottage!'

George bit her lip. Johnson was very crafty! He'd obviously taken the trouble to find out just who they were and where they came from.

'You're crazy!' exclaimed Gary. 'The old girl must know Mr Kirrin's voice – you'll never be able to fool her!'

'Oh yes, I will! I'll talk in a hoarse tone, making out I've got a cold. I won't speak to her for long, either, just say the kids have gone over to Kirrin Cottage and I'm keeping them there a couple of days, so she's not to worry!'

'Good thinking, Uncle Jim! Well done!' said Gary admiringly.

The children exchanged miserable glances. They felt cut off from the rest of the world in this dark greenhouse, lit up only by their captors' torches. 'That awful Johnson has thought of everything!' George told herself. 'And Jenny's so trusting, she'll swallow his story and never suspect! Oh, how I wish I hadn't been so careless!'

Johnson wasn't gone long. 'That went off very well!' he told his nephew, smiling. 'Now, follow me, you lot! I've got the boat out.'

'You haven't brought any food or blankets for them,' Gary pointed out.

'I've thought better of that! They can do without. I told you just now I'd been thinking – well, one thing that struck me is this island of yours may be deserted, but who's to say tourists don't land on it to picnic there? So if we leave the kids loose, they'll only have to tell their story to anyone who happens by, get brought back to the main-land, and then we'll be in real trouble! No, I've got a better notion. You told me there are some old ruins – there's sure to be a cellar or such-like there. Old places like that always had cellars.'

'It was a castle, I think,' said Gary. 'Could be there are dungeons.'

'Even better! Well, we'll find somewhere in the ruins to leave our young friends shut up – they'll have shelter there from the night air, and as for food and drink, a forty-eight hours' starvation diet won't hurt 'em – ha, ha! Come on, kids, start moving!'

As George had told herself, Johnson really *had* thought of everything — and yet she was still smiling in a mysterious way, although the other children were looking very downcast.

Johnson and Gary took the children down to the beach, where the Mandevilles' boathouse stood, and made them get into Mr Mandeville's motor launch. Gary started the engine. George noticed which way he was going, and began to smile again. Just as she'd thought!

Dick noticed her smile, but he was sensible enough not to ask any questions. And sad to say, it was soon to be wiped off her face anyway — because when Gary thought he was far enough out from shore, he bent down and without any warning took hold of Timmy and threw him into the water. Then, before the children had even recovered from their amazement, he snatched Mischief away from Tinker and threw him into the sea too, after Timmy!

'You brute!' cried George, in horror. 'Get my dog out again — you can't do a thing like that!'

Tinker was shouting indignantly too, but Gary just laughed.

'Can't I just! That dog might give away the place we're going to hide you in by barking — and for all we know, the monkey may be well trained enough to untie you. I hope the nasty creatures

Suddenly Gary threw Timmy into the water.

drown!'

Well, George knew that Timmy wouldn't do that – he was a good swimmer, and could easily get back to the shore, and Mischief was intelligent enough to cling to his stronger friend. But she didn't want her dog to tire himself out by following the boat – and that was just what he was doing! Seeing him swim after them, Johnson threatened him with an oar. In the moonlight, George saw Timmy give her a sad look, and then he swam away. Her eyes filled with tears. This was one of the very few times her cousins had ever seen her cry!

A few moments later the boat came ashore on the island Gary had seen from his motor-bike – and now the others knew why George had been smiling so mysteriously as they boarded the boat! It was none other than Kirrin Island, George's very own property, where the Five had often been to camp!

Of course George had guessed at once where they were being taken. She knew the local countryside inside out, and there weren't any *other* uninhabited islands close to Kirrin. Julian, Dick, Anne and Tinker were feeling a little better now they were on familiar ground. As for the dungeons where the crooks planned to shut them up – well, those dungeons held no terrors for the Five.

'Come on, move! Faster!' growled Johnson. 'My

word, this path's steep!' he added to his nephew. 'Ah – there are those ruins of yours!'

Uncle and nephew had to search about for a few minutes before they found the way down to the dungeons. George had a mad impulse to call out and tell them where to look, but she restrained herself! At last Johnson moved aside the stone over the entrance. 'Here we are!' he cried. Then he shone his torch down the dark way into the dungeons, and said roughly, 'In you go, kids! Two days in the dark with your hands tied, waiting for someone to come and let you out, and without anything to eat – that'll cure you of wanting to poke your noses into other folks' business! Come on, Gary! Let's go! I tell you what – I've just had another idea too. We'll leave the treasure on this island as well, buried in the castle courtyard. There couldn't be a safer place for it! And when Potter's back, tomorrow or the day after, we'll come over to collect our property!'

Chapter Eleven

ON KIRRIN ISLAND

The two criminals went off, taking no more notice of their prisoners. 'Well, what a couple of idiots!' laughed Dick, when they were out of earshot. 'They were afraid *Timmy* would bark, but they forgot to gag *us*! And they must have thought we were deaf or something, talking about the treasure so freely in front of us!'

'They know we can't get out of here,' Tinker pointed out. 'I'm tied up so tight my arms feel numb already.'

George was still furious with the men for the way they'd treated Timmy, and she certainly wasn't going to admit herself beaten, not on her own island! 'Who says we can't get out of here?' she asked. 'You saw what they did to Timmy and

Mischief — well, they're not getting away with that! And this is *my* island! I bet you the stones of these ruins themselves will help us!'

She was making her way over to one of the dungeon walls. When she got there, she turned her back to the wall and began rubbing the cord that tied her hands against the rough stones. She hurt her hands, but she didn't mind that. She just *had* to get free!

Following her example, the other children tried rubbing through their bonds. It took ages — but at last they did it. George and Julian were free first, and they helped Dick, Anne and Tinker. Then they all went back the way they had come, and soon they were back at the stone which hid the entrance to the dungeons. They all pushed together, and it swung aside. They were free!

The children ran out into the open. Day was already dawning in the east, over the mainland. Suddenly George let out a cry of delight.

'Look — it's Timmy! Timmy's swimming out to join us!'

She was right. Under the golden rays of the rising sun, they could see the good dog swimming bravely through the waves. And he wasn't alone! Mischief, clinging to his neck, was having a ride on his back. It was Tinker's turn to shout with glee now.

'Mischief! Timmy's brought Mischief with him!'

The children began dancing and jumping for joy. A moment later, Timmy and his 'rider' were shaking themselves on the beach. The dog bounded up to George and began licking his face.

'Timmy dear, you've come at just the right moment. Now you can help us – and get your revenge on those horrible men for throwing you into the sea!' she said.

Tinker and Mischief were dancing about on the sand. Julian, Dick and Anne were laughing at the sight, forgetting how scared they had been not so long ago.

'And there's something else we must do,' cried Dick suddenly. 'Come on, let's hurry – we must get the treasure back!'

That was not very difficult. They hurried off to the castle courtyard, and Julian soon spotted a piece of ground which looked as if it had been dug quite recently. It was rather clumsily covered with three big stones. The children found a stick to dig with, and they soon unearthed the casket of treasure.

'Let's hide it in our larder,' suggested George. 'We can't be too careful!'

The 'larder' was a useful secret recess in one of the ruined castle walls, where she always kept

Julian found some newly dug ground which had been covered with stones.

reserve supplies of tinned food, sugar and salt, and other provisions that wouldn't go bad and that the children could use when they came to camp on the island. George liked a bit of mystery, and had hidden her provisions as carefully as if they were treasure. So the real treasure would feel quite at home in its improvised safe, and the emergency provisions were going to come in very useful!

Now the five friends were holding all the trump cards! They had escaped from their dark prison, they had recovered the treasure, and they were on their own home ground again.

'George, how do you think we can get our own back on those dreadful men?' Anne asked her cousin.

'We'll discuss that in a minute,' said George. 'But first let's have some breakfast! I'm starving. There's tinned milk, chocolate, and cocoa powder in the larder. No bread, but we've got plenty of biscuits! Get the little spirit stove out, Dick – and you run off and fetch some water from the spring, Tinker!'

It was rather a funny breakfast, but it tasted wonderful. The children felt much better with some food and hot cocoa inside them. After their meal, they talked the situation over.

'There's no problem about staying on the island,' said Julian. 'We can perfectly well camp out here until Johnson and his friends come back – we've often camped here before, so we shan't feel marooned at all! I wish we could get a message to Uncle Quentin, though.'

'Well, so we can!' said George. 'I'm a very strong swimmer. I can easily swim over to the mainland and raise the alarm.'

'Oh no, you don't!' said Julian firmly. 'This may be *your* island, George, but *I'm* the eldest, and I say you're not to do anything so dangerous. It would be rash and stupid!'

George knew he was right, really. She went rather pink in the face, and shook her head. 'Oh, very well, if you say so!' she agreed. 'But anyway,' she added, with a slightly mischievous smile, 'that wasn't what I'd actually planned to do! We can deal with those men ourselves, you know – we don't need help.'

'How do you mean?' asked Tinker, his eyes shining.

'Well, here's what I've been thinking. When Johnson, Gary and their friend Potter get here, we'll have all sorts of booby-traps waiting! They won't be expecting anything like that, and I bet we can drive them off that way – and into the hands of the police. So now, let's start thinking of some really good booby-traps!'

Dick burst out laughing. 'Good idea, George!'

he said. 'Ha, ha! Those men don't know what's coming to them!'

'And we'll have the advantage of surprise on our side,' Julian pointed out. 'They won't know we're free — they'll think we're still tied up in the dungeons.'

'They don't know Timmy and Mischief are safe and sound and have joined us, either,' added Tinker.

'*Or* that they've lost the treasure!' said Anne happily, smiling.

'Now to draw up a plan of action, then,' said George. 'We must keep careful watch, taking turns. We don't want *them* taking *us* by surprise when they come back.'

So the five friends spent most of the morning working out what Dick described as their 'anti-Johnson strategy'. Then they made themselves lunch from the reserve supplies. What a good thing George had laid in plenty of tins of baked beans and sausages at the very beginning of the holidays! There were tinned peaches too, and Anne found a packet of lemonade crystals in the 'larder' and made lemonade with the fresh spring water — delicious! After their meal, they went on with their planning, preparing a fine reception for Johnson, his nephew, and their accomplice Potter.

When dark fell that night, they fetched the old

blankets that they always kept in the only room in the castle that still had a roof on it. The blankets stayed nice and dry in there. The children rolled up in them and went to sleep. It wasn't by any means the first time they'd slept in the ruins of the castle – they didn't have their sleeping bags, as usual, but it was quite a mild night.

George took the first night watch. She sat at the top of the path which led down to the little beach for two hours, with Timmy beside her, watching the sea. Then Dick relieved her. After that it was Julian's turn, then Tinker's, and finally Anne took over at dawn. But the thieves did not appear. The children went on keeping watch until evening – they felt sure it wouldn't be long before Johnson and the others came back now.

In fact, it was exactly nine o'clock that evening, and dusk was falling, when Tinker, who was on watch at the time, called out to the others.

'Here we are!' he cried. 'I can see a motor-boat making this way!'

'I'm sure that's them!' cried George, getting very excited. 'Good! Come on, then – and find out what's waiting for you!'

Chapter Twelve

THE TREASURE IS SAFE

Yes, it was Johnson, Gary, and Potter all right! Lying flat on their stomachs on top of the cliff, the children saw them get out of the boat. It was getting dark quite fast now, but the moon was rising, so they had quite enough light to see by. Potter was a stocky, rough looking man.

'Okay, then!' he told his companions in a hoarse voice. 'If this is where you left that treasure, better get it back quick, ready to hand over to the fence, Tracy. He's expecting us tomorrow, remember!'

'I'll go ahead with a torch,' said Gary. 'By the way, what are we going to do with those kids? I don't suppose *they'll* be feeling very chirpy after two days down there in the dark!'

'Them?' said Johnson, callously. 'Oh, a phone call to their parents once we're in London will do! Interfering brats – serves 'em right for all the trouble they've given us!'

'And we're going to give you some more trouble, too!' muttered George between her teeth. 'For a start, take this!'

With a perfectly steady hand, she neatly tossed a pebble over the cliff. It fell – and hit Johnson, down below, right on the head.

'Ouch!' cried Johnson, putting a hand up the crown of his head. 'What was that?'

'Only a pebble falling off the cliff-top,' said Gary. 'Don't make such a fuss, Uncle Jim!'

At that very moment, he himself fell heavily to the ground. The shock of the fall broke the glass of his torch into tiny pieces.

'What's up with *you*?' said Johnson. 'Can't you keep your footing?'

'I slipped on something,' grunted Gary. 'Goodness knows what!'

Dick could have told him! He was the one who had carefully poured the contents of a whole bottle of cooking oil over the stony surface of the path. It made a big, slippery puddle – it was not surprising Gary had slipped and fallen!

He got up – and then it was Johnson's turn to go sprawling. When Potter came over to help him up, *he* slipped too. Gary stood there laughing at the pair of them. 'So you two can't stay on your feet either!' he said.

Cursing, the two men scrambled up, and made their way up the steep path, slipping and sliding wherever Dick had poured the oil. Meanwhile the children, Timmy and Mischief had set off for the castle again. Soon the three crooks reached the courtyard.

'It's over here!' said Johnson, stopping beside the spot where he had buried the casket containing the treasure. 'Dig here, Gary!'

Gary moved the stones, and began scraping away the crumbly earth with his bare hands.

'Here it is!' he announced happily, digging up a plastic bag. 'Now – just take a look at this, Potter!'

Potter took the bag, put his big hand inside, and brought out the casket. Eyes gleaming with greed, he opened it – and let out a cry of disgust. Instead of the gold and jewels he was expecting to find, he was looking at the skeleton of a large seagull which the children had found on the beach. They had put it in the casket and filled up the space with pebbles.

'Is *this* your treasure?' he shouted angrily.

The astonished Johnson raised his torch for a better look – but as he did so it was snatched away from him by a strange little creature which seemed to have appeared out of nowhere, and which ran off towards the castle doorway with the torch.

'What was that?' shouted the caretaker. 'It looked like a monkey – but how could there be a monkey here? Catch it, Gary!'

Gary set off after Mischief the monkey as fast as he could go. Mischief kept stopping, as if to wait for him, and then running on again – he was leading Gary into the ruins.

The young man ran after him – and stumbled over a string stretched across the doorway. Carried on by his own impetus, he fell head first, knocked his head on a big rock, and lost consciousness.

Silently, the children emerged from the shadows where they had been hiding. They picked Gary up, carried him away, and put him down out of sight behind a wall.

Johnson and Potter, who were still outside the ruins, heard a miserable voice, amplified by the echoing castle walls, shouting, 'Help, Uncle Jim! Help!'

'You stop here,' said Potter to Johnson. They had no idea it was really Julian speaking. 'I'll go and see what's up.'

In his own turn, *he* ran to the doorway, and fell over the same piece of string. He wasn't as lucky as Gary, who was only stunned – he fell with one leg folded awkwardly under him.

'My leg!' he yelled. 'I think I've broken it!'

In the shadows, George smiled. She was pretty sure he had only sprained an ankle, but what a fuss he was making! 'Well, that's two of them out of action!' she whispered to her cousins and Tinker. 'Now for the third!'

'Woof!' barked Timmy, as if he were taking part in the conversation.

'Hear that?' said Dick. 'Sounds as if Timmy wants to join the fun!'

'Well, he certainly deserves to!' said George. 'I expect he'd like his revenge – go on, then, good dog! Get him!'

Timmy didn't need to be told twice. Before Johnson had time to come to Potter's aid, he found he was being attacked by a furious creature who rushed at him fangs bared!

'That dog!' he thought in amazement. 'So he didn't drown after all!'

And then his instinct for self-preservation sent him running away, as fast as he could.

'Now!' cried Julian. 'To the boat, everyone!'

George, Julian, Dick, Anne and Tinker ran down the path, carrying Mischief and the treasure, which they had taken out of the casket and wrapped carefully in pieces of blanket. They took great care not to step on the patches of oil, and jumped into the motor-boat. Then George whistled to Timmy, who stopped watching

Johnson – the man had climbed a tree to get away from him – and ran to join the others.

Three minutes later the Mandevilles' motor-boat, carrying the happy children, was making for the mainland and Kirrin Cottage. Soon they could see the lights of the house itself.

'Uncle Quentin and Professor Hayling must be hard at work as usual!' said Julian. 'What a surprise they'll get! Hey, George – why are you changing course?'

'Er . . . well,' said George, 'I think the best thing to do is go to Kirrin village first and tell the police, like good citizens!'

Dick couldn't help laughing. 'I see!' he said. 'You think your father won't be so cross with us in front of a few policemen! I must admit we've run rather a lot of risks during this adventure – and Uncle Quentin *does* tend to lose his temper when we go running risks!'

The men on duty at Kirrin police station were very surprised when the children turned up, carrying the treasure, and told them what had been happening. They soon realised, however, that they would get lots of very good publicity in the newspapers if they arrested the men who had gone off with the Mandeville inheritance!

'I believe Mr Mandeville got home this very evening,' said the Sergeant. 'There were lights on

The happy children were soon making for the mainland.

in Wistaria Lodge when I was passing just now.'

Then a great many things happened all at once. Tinker telephoned Jenny, George telephoned her father, and the police telephoned the Mandevilles, while several men went off to get the police launch and go out to Kirrin Island to pick up the crooks. Mr and Mrs Mandeville were astonished to hear of all that had been happening while they were away in London, and Mr Mandeville came straight round to the police station.

'Has someone gone to arrest Johnson and his friends?' he asked. 'Good! A nice catch for you – and you'll owe it all to these children, you know! As for me, *I* owe them even more!' he added, smiling.

It certainly was a good catch that the policemen brought back from Kirrin Island! Johnson was furious and disappointed, Gary had a bump as big as a duck's egg on his forehead, and Potter was wailing and moaning that his leg was broken. Johnson and his nephew were taken off to prison, and Potter was sent to the hospital, under police escort. The Kirrin police had phoned Scotland Yard to tell them the name of the fence, Tracy, and he was being arrested too. He was already known to the London police force as a very shady character, and when they searched his flat they got all the proof they needed of what he did for a living.

Next day, Mr and Mrs Mandeville invited the

children, their parents and Jenny to lunch at Wistaria Lodge. It was a very cheerful meal – though interrupted several times by radio reporters who had found out where the children were, and were calling to ask them to say a few words. They even asked Timmy to bark for the listeners, too! Mr Mandeville told George and the others that he was going to use part of the treasure to build a modern Children's Home in the country near Kirrin.

Mrs Mandeville said she thought the Five and Tinker ought to have a reward themselves – and she gave each of the children two of the gold coins from the treasure, dating back to the time of King Charles I. 'As a souvenir of your adventures!' she said, smiling.

George was very relieved that she hadn't been scolded by her father, and she was delighted with her two coins. 'Oh, thank you!' she said, and she added, with a mischievous smile, 'Actually, it was high time you and Mr Mandeville came home to take possession of Lady Mandeville's treasure. If you'd been away much longer, I've a feeling it might easily have vanished again. It's a kind of disappearing treasure – now you see it, now you don't! You'd better keep it well locked up, in case it gets away once more!'

And the festive meal ended in gales of laughter.

If you have enjoyed this book, you may like to
read some more exciting adventures
from Knight Books:

A complete list of new adventures
about the FAMOUS FIVE

KNIGHT BOOKS

KEITH MILES

SKYDIVE

On location with their father, the film stunt-man, Max Rawson, Nick and Jenny find themselves involved in some daring and dangerous action of their own. Caught up in a case of international espionage, they fall into the hands of two ruthless Welsh criminals, who seek to imprison them high in the Snowdonian mountains, with no chance of their being rescued.

But, when it comes to getting out of difficult situations, it isn't only Max Rawson who can perform the stunts . . .

Stand by for action and adventure!

KNIGHT BOOKS

KEITH MILES

SEABIRD

The Gulf of Mexico is a marvellous setting for a film location and when Nick and Jenny Rawson hear the legend of the ghostly Italian pirate who haunts the islands looking for his treasure, they go to investigate on a nearby Key. But once there, they stumble upon a secret plot. And the evil perpetrators have no intention at all of allowing them to spoil it.

Stand by for action and adventure!

KNIGHT BOOKS

Prehistori

22

Prehistoric England

GRAHAME CLARK

B. T. BATSFORD LTD LONDON

First published 1940
First paperback edition 1962

Revised edition © Grahame Clark, 1962

PRINTED AND BOUND IN DENMARK BY
F. E. BORDING LTD, COPENHAGEN AND LONDON
FOR THE PUBLISHERS
B. T. BATSFORD LTD
4 FITZHARDINGE STREET, PORTMAN SQUARE, LONDON W. I

Preface

It is my aim in this new, as in former editions, to describe within the narrow limits imposed by deficiencies in our present knowledge the manner in which our forefathers lived before the dawn of history – how they earned their daily bread, what kind of houses they lived in, the arts they practised, the way they mined, quarried, traded and travelled, the means they took to defend themselves, what steps they took to care for the dead and what sacred structures they erected in the course of religious observance.

Prehistoric archaeology is advancing rapidly and, since this book was originally published, many new discoveries and several major revisions of opinion have been made. The opportunity has been taken to write an entirely new Introductory chapter and substantial portions of the text of other chapters have been re-written. Although it has been necessary to reduce the number of plates for this edition, more than half those included are introduced to this book for the first time. Only a few of the old line drawings have been omitted, but a number of new ones have been added and important new finds have been added to the map.

Cambridge, 1961   GRAHAME CLARK

5

Acknowledgment

The Author and Publishers wish to thank the following for permission to reproduce the photographic illustrations in this book:

Aerofilms and Aero Pictorial Limited for figs 37, 43, 47 and 50; Mr Derek Allen for figs 28 and 29; The Ashmolean Museum, Oxford, for figs 3, 4, 32 and 40; Professor R. J. C. Atkinson for figs 44 and 46; the Trustees of the British Museum for figs 2, 12, 22 and 31; the late Dr A. Bulleid or figs 17 and 18; Cambridge University Museum of Archaeology and Ethnology for figs 1, 26 and 30; Dorchester Museum for fig. 19; Sir Cyril Fox for fig. 41; Mr St G. Gray for figs 17 and 48; the Controller of H. M. Stationery Office and the Director-General, Ordnance Survey for figs 8, 9 and 34; Liverpool Libraries Museums and Arts Committee for fig. 21; the Ministry of Works (Crown Copyright Reserved) for fig. 39; the National Museum of Wales for figs 11, 20 and 23; Norfolk News Co., Norfolk, for fig. 35; the Nottingham Journal Ltd for fig. 27; the Prehistoric Society for fig. 24; Dr J. K. St Joseph (Crown Copyright Reserved) for figs 6, 14-16, 25, 36 and 42; Walker's Studios Ltd, Scarborough, for figs 5 and 13; Mr Wykes for fig. 33.

Acknowledgment is also due to the following for permission to reproduce the line-drawings:

Archaeologica Cambrensis for the illustration on page 55; the Trustees of the British Museum for pages 16, 19, 81 and 111; the late Dr A. Bulleid for pages 66, 71 and 117; Cambridge University Press for pages 22 and 153; Liverpool University Press for page 88; Messrs Methuen & Co., Ltd for pages 18, 105, 140, 150 and 181; National Museum of Wales for page 92; the Prehistoric Society for pages 38, 67, 87, 148 and 176; the Society of Antiquaries of London for pages 59 and 69; Messrs Thames & Hudson Ltd for page 68; *The Mariner's Mirror* for page 128; *The Victoria County History* for page 91.

A number of the line-drawings originally prepared for the first edition are the work of the late Mr L. D. Lambert.

Contents

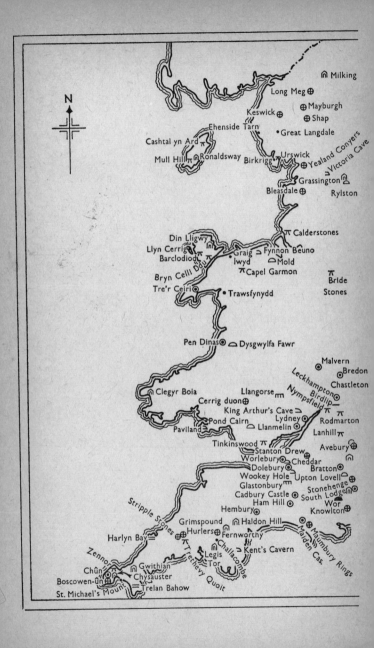

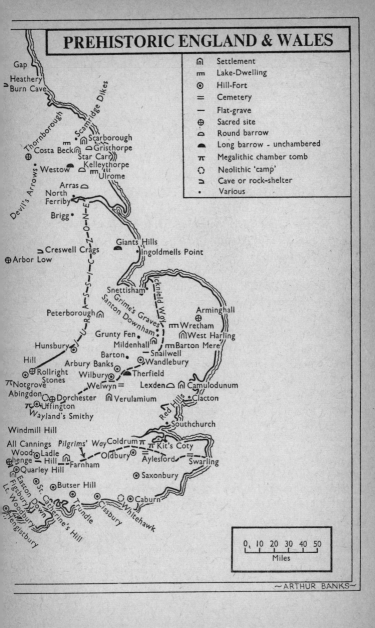

PREHISTORIC ENGLAND & WALES

⌂	Settlement
⋒	Lake-Dwelling
⊙	Hill-Fort
=	Cemetery
—	Flat-grave
⊕	Sacred site
⌒	Round barrow
⬣	Long barrow - unchambered
π	Megalithic chamber tomb
◠	Neolithic 'camp'
⌐	Cave or rock-shelter
•	Various

Gap
Heathery
Burn Cave

Scamridge Dikes
Thornborough
Scarborough
Costa Beck Gristhorpe
Star Carr
Kelleythorpe
Westow Ulrome
Devil's Arrows
Arras
North
Ferriby
Brigg

Creswell Crags
Arbor Low

Giants Hills
Ingoldmells Point

Snettisham
Grime's Graves
Santon Downham
Peterborough Icknield Way Arminghall
Wretham
Grunty Fen West Harling
Mildenhall Barton Mere
Hunsbury Barton Snailwell
Arbury Banks Wandlebury
Hill Wilbury Therfield
Rollright
Stones Welwyn Lexden Camulodunum
Notgrove
Abingdon Dorchester Verulamium Clacton
Uffington
Wayland's Smithy Red Hills

Southchurch

Windmill Hill
All Cannings Pilgrims' Way Coldrum Kit's Coty
Wood Ladle Oldbury Swarling
henge Hill Farnham Aylesford
Quarley Hill
Easton St. Catherine's Hill Butser Hill Saxonbury
Flagbury Trundle Caburn
Lt. Woodbury Cissbury
Hengistbury Whitehawk

0 10 20 30 40 50
Miles

~ARTHUR BANKS~

List of Illustrations

THE PLATES

11

1

Introductory

IT is salutary and topical to reflect that, though we are islanders and owe much of our character and achievement to this fact, we are also in a very real sense marooned inhabitants of Europe. This is true even in a geographical sense. During much of the Ice Age, for instance, when vast quantities of water were locked up in extended ice-sheets, the Thames was a mere tributary of the Rhine and the eastern lowlands formed an integral part of the North European Plain that stretched as far east as the Ural mountains. Indeed the final insulation of Britain, brought about as ice-sheets melted during the more genial conditions of the Post-glacial period, does not seem to have taken place more than eight or nine thousand years ago, when the rising sea flooded over the North Sea bed and severed the land connection between south-east England and the European mainland.

From a human point of view, also, we have to remember that Britain must originally have been peopled from the mainland and that since then it has received innumerable infusions both of blood and culture from the same quarter. During the remoter periods, before men had learned to cross the open sea in boats, contacts could only be renewed or maintained during peninsular phases. From Neolithic times onwards the sea has of itself imposed no insuperable obstacle, even if since the Norman conquest the islanders have always been strong enough to repel invasion. The position of Britain at the north-west corner of Europe, on the one hand forming a detached portion of the North European Plain and on the other projecting into the Atlantic, invited ingress not merely from contiguous parts of the Continent, but ultimately from Central Europe, Scandinavia and the Mediterranean basin. Thus, Cornwall and Wales thrust peninsulas athwart the western seaways that linked Biscayan France and Iberia with Ireland and perhaps with western Scotland; Christchurch and Southampton Water were ports of call from northern France; the rivers of East Kent, the Thames estuary, the creeks of Essex and Suffolk, the Wash, the Humber estuary and the mouths of the Tees and the Tyne offered ample means of acces from a range of the Continent extending from Flanders and the Lower Rhine to Denmark. And beyond this encircling arc, a variety of routes, traversing the Carcassonne Gap by way of the Biscay coast and following the amber routes across Germany to the Adriatic, penetrated to the relatively civilized world of the Mediterranean. The multifarious and often far-reaching contacts which Britain's geographical position invited affected far more than ports of entry, since numerous slow-moving and comparatively navigable rivers gave easy access to the interior.

Although there was doubtless some unevenness in the degree to which different parts of the country were immediately affected by foreign influences, it is no longer widely believed that there was any clearly defined difference in this regard between lowland Britain and the highland zone north and west of a line running approximately from the Severn to the Tees. While it is of course true that the lowland territories of southern and south-eastern England, being more nearly contiguous to the continent, were more likely to serve as refuges or attract conquerors, the fact remains that since the insulation of Britain all exotic influences had necessarily to come by sea and that it was not so difficult for traders or even invaders to make land-fall even on remote coasts. Although the southern part of the country may have borne the brunt, there seems no doubt that widely separated parts of the highland zone received direct impulses from the continent whether across the North Sea or by way of the Irish Sea.

Those who ventured to Britain found fertile lands in the south-east and rich sources of mineral wealth in Cornwall, and parts of Wales and northern Britain, not to mention Ireland. As a rule they were more advanced in civilization than the indigenous peoples and no doubt, whether as traders or settlers, they must often have taken advantage of their superior knowledge and power. Yet, however harsh their impact may have been and whatever their motives, traders and invaders alike brought rich increments of blood and ideas to the island population; and this gain has been no less in modern times when trade and communication flow so much more easily and successive victims of oppression have streamed in from the mainland. The very diversity and multiplicity of exotic influences have alone sufficed to prevent the country falling under the spell of any single one. Again, the sea that has divided us from the continent, while providing a highway for foreign influence, has promoted a certain independence and continuity and given us the chance to assimilate and digest alien peoples and new ideas. Although at times the pace of new arrivals and contacts has noticeably quickened, the British peoples have been able to profit from their insularity, accepting only such new ideas and techniques as seemed appropriate, at times undergoing rapid change under the impact of stimulus from the outer world, but all the while carrying on and perfecting their own millennial traditions.

The earliest (or Lower Palaeolithic) traces of human occupation consist almost entirely of flint implements. These are confined to the parts of England south of the Trent

15

basin and to a small enclave in south-east Wales. Two main groups are represented. The most abundant is chiefly represented by tools shaped to a more or less regular edge by flaking down nodules or thick flakes on either face: these were probably held directly in the hand and made to serve a variety of purposes. Industries of this kind were first systematically studied at St Acheul in the Somme Valley of

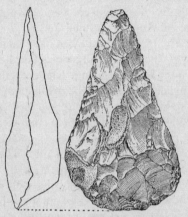

Acheulian hand-axe (1:3)

northern France, but is it now almost certain that they were first evolved in east-central Africa, where notably from successive beds in Olduvai Gorge all transitional forms have been found between crude pebble-tools and well made hand-axes. It is interesting to reflect, as one examines hand-axes from the river terraces of southern England, that closely similar tools were used by Lower Palaeolithic man over the greater part of the then occupied world as far south as the Cape and as far east as India. The other main industry, one in which emphasis is laid on flakes and on the

16

cores and chopping-tools from which they were struck, is well represented from an old channel of the Thames at Clacton, Essex, a site which has lent its name to similar assemblages found elsewhere on the northern fringe of the Lower Palaeolithic world in northern France, Belgium and Germany. To judge from the rear portions of a skull recovered from deposits of an earlier phase of the Thames at Swanscombe, Kent, the hand-axe makers had brains well within the range of modern man, even if one may suspect they had the heavy jaws and teeth and the massive browridges common among more primitive forms of hominid like the Pithecanthropians of the Pekin caves.

In southern England, as over all the northern parts of the occupied world as far south as north Africa and southwest Asia, the onset of the Late Pleistocene was marked by a shift in emphasis from hand-axes to flake-tools. The localities of Crayford and Northfleet in north Kent have yielded particularly rich flint industries of the type generally named after the French locality of Levallois, a suburb of Paris, and qualified by some prehistorians as Middle Palaeolithic. The tools were struck by a single blow from the upper convex face of cores carefully prepared by radial flaking and shaped somewhat like a tortoise, with a relatively flat base. The platform at the butt end of the flake was normally facetted as a result of shaping the core and this must have made it easier to hold the tool in the hand. Although hand-axes became less important, they persisted far into Late Pleistocene times and small examples formed an element in the flint industries of the lowest levels of British caves, industries named after the rock-shelter of Le Moustier in the Dordogne and commonly associated in parts of Europe with Neanderthal man. The Mousterians adapted themselves to withstand colder conditions by wearing skin clothing and seeking the shelter of caves. As a result they were able, even

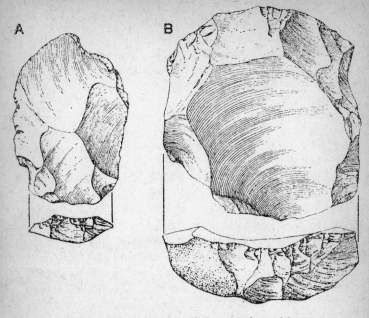

Levallois Technique: A. Flake with faceted butt
B. Tortoise core (1:3)

though they were living during the onset of the last major
glaciation, to extend the range of settlement in Britain as
far north as Creswell Crags, Derbyshire, and as far west as
Paviland in Gower.

During the last glaciation, or more accurately during
episodes of less extreme climate known as interstadials, parts
of Britain were occupied, probably intermittently, by bands
of Advanced Palaeolithic hunters. Although sparse and
marginal these people introduced the elements of a more
advanced hunting technology and meagre though the
evidence for this from Britain may be—an awareness of
aesthetic values expressed in personal ornaments and repre-

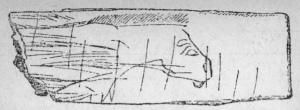

Engraving of horse's head on bone, from Creswell Crags (1:1)

sentational art. Like their immediate predecessors they were fond of caves and we find numerous traces of them in the limestone areas of Mendip and Devon, Creswell, Gower and Pembrokeshire: open sites were also inhabited, though apparently this was rare. Finds from caves in the Vale of Clwyd in North Wales and from Yorkshire at the Victoria Cave, Settle, and from an open site at Flixton, near Scarborough, testify to a further expansion of settlement during the Late-glacial period. There appear to have been two phases of Advanced Palaeolithic settlement, an earlier one by people whose culture combined Advanced Palaeolithic (Aurignacian) and Mousterian elements and a younger one, named after Creswell, contemporary with a late phase of the Magdalenian culture of France and Belgium, but with a distinct flint industry combining microliths with convex and trapezoidal points. The Creswellian flints recall those found on surface stations in the Low Countries and North Germany rather than in the Magdalenian deposits of French caves and it is suggestive that a Magdalenian harpoon-head of reindeer antler from Aveline's Hole, Mendip, can be matched most closely from a Belgian site. Even more direct pointers to the North European Plain, of which Britain still formed a peninsula, come from an open station on Hengistbury Head, Dorset, which yielded tanged points of a type found on Late-glacial sites in Denmark.

The Post-glacial period began in north-west Europe with the final retreat of the Scandinavian ice-sheet about 10,000 years ago. The most important factor in the environment of Post-glacial times has been an increase in temperature, sufficient to produce major changes in vegetation and animals and so in the conditions of life for early man. The curve of temperature since the Ice Age has not been an even one and it is convenient to distinguish three main phases: to begin with we have an Anathermal phase during which temperatures rose from arctic and sub-arctic levels towards those obtaining to-day; then during an Altithermal phase summer temperatures rose appreciably above those obtaining in the same region to-day and temperate Europe passed through what is sometimes termed the Post-glacial Climatic Optimum; and, finally, they receded from this peak and with minor fluctuations reached their present levels. Alongside these went changes in other aspects of climate: thus, Anathermal climate was continental or Boreal in character with relatively contrasted seasons, whereas Altithermal climate was more equable and moister, Atlantic in type; again, the drier Sub-boreal climate with which Medithermal times opened gave place to a wetter and colder Sub-atlantic one. A more or less parallel sequence has been established for vegetation. The broad effect of the change to Post-glacial conditions was that forests replaced the open arctic-alpine flora, but well-defined stages can be noted in the development of these: at first only trees like willow and birch, capable of withstanding cold conditions, could spread, but as temperatures rose these were joined by pine, which in due course dominated forests; in late Boreal times hazel frequently formed extensive scrub and the deciduous trees began to grow in importance, until during Atlantic times they dominated the landscape; throughout Sub-boreal times alder, oak, elm and lime continued to be the most important trees, but farming, introduced at a late stage of Atlantic times, was beginning to make inroads on the forests; and Sub-atlantic times were marked by the expansion of beech (already present since Atlantic times), an increase in pine, an intensification of the effects of farming and in certain areas a widespread expansion of bogs. Changes in vegetation on this scale were bound to have a profound effect on wild animals and we find that creatures like the reindeer adapted to an open landscape were replaced by ones suited to a forest environment, such as red deer, roe deer, elk, bear, wild pig, wild ox and beaver.

The effect of all these changes was enough to upset the established routine of human life. At first and for some 5,000 years, the land continued to be occupied exclusively by hunter-fishers, but the culture of these people differed sufficiently from that of their predecessors to be classified as Mesolithic. By and large the new aspect of the hunter-fisher communities of north-western Europe was the product of various kinds of adaptation to the new forested environment. This involved important changes in the quest for food, favouring the use of the bow and so indirectly the popularity of microlithic flints used to barb and tip arrows; and by diminishing open hunting-grounds encouraged fishing in lakes and rivers and strand-looping activities on the shore. In order to utilise the abundant timber some groups developed axes and adzes for felling trees (5) and working wood, which in turn increased the use of composite tools and made possible the adoption of dug-out boats for inland navigation. The pervasive nature of the forest doubtless helped to encourage more permanent settlement, whether by lake, river or sea-shore, and this in turn made it easier to adopt the more settled mode of economy introduced by the Neolithic invaders. Again, the northern extension of temperate climate made it possible to colonise territories previously unoccupied, including the northernmost counties of England, Scotland and Northern Ireland.

The earliest traces of Mesolithic occupation from England belong to the Maglemosian culture that takes its name from the great bog *(magle mose)* near the Danish locality of Mullerup where it was first recognised. As we are reminded by the trawling of a fine antler spearhead from a

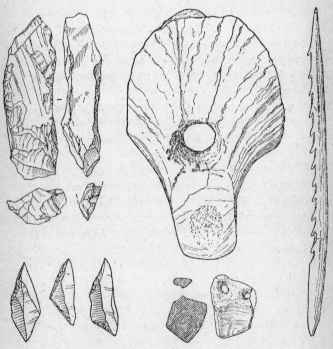

Star Carr: flint axe, microlithic arrowtips, elk antler mattock, amber bead and stag antler spearhead (1:3)

depth of 19-20 fathoms between the Leman and Ower Banks in the North Sea, some 19 miles from the Norfolk coast, the Maglemosian culture flourished while eastern Britain still formed part of the North European Plain. Precisely in what part of this wide region the Maglemosians stemmed from their reindeer-hunting predecessors is still uncertain, but in the lakeside settlement of Star Carr near Scarborough we can see how the culture appeared in Britain in its primitive form at the close of Pre-boreal times. Finds of Maglemosian character from the full Boreal period mainly occur in the region east of a line between Hartlepool and Southampton Water with concentrations in Holderness and the Thames valley, but there are signs of penetration as far west as Devon and Pembrokeshire and some indications of a thrust through the Midland Gap to Northern Ireland.

A markedly different type of Mesolithic industry occurs mainly in the regions of older rocks in south-west England, Wales, northern England and the Isle of Man (not to mention eastern Scotland), but also well within the Maglemosian province on the sandy soils of north Lincolnshire and the eastern margin of the Fenland. In these industries the microlithic component is strongly developed often with minute geometric forms and the macrolithic element correspondingly reduced, axes and adzes for example being absent; moreover, on the few sites where bone has survived it has been used only for the simplest forms of awl or bodkin. In the few instances in which it has been possible to date these microlithic industries by modern methods they have been shown to date from the close of Boreal or from Atlantic times. Their late date and the uncertainty whether Britain was occupied at all during the final phase of the Late-glacial period, makes it difficult to derive these industries from the native Creswellian. Alternatives are that they spread in the south, from France or Belgium, or that they developed locally from the Maglemosian.

South of the Thames a well-defined culture of undoubted Maglemosian antecedents flourished during Atlantic times in a territory centered on the Weald of Kent, Surrey, and Sussex, but extending into Wessex. In this Wealden culture the microlithic element included small geometric forms and a type of asymmetric, hollow-based point first recognised from the area of Horsham; and the axes and adzes, while still made by basic Maglemosian techniques, were on the whole larger and either more celtiform or pick-like in character. One of the most interesting aspects of the Wealden people is that, to judge from the hollowed-out floors of clusters of huts at Abinger, Farnham and Selmeston, they occupied settlements which seasonally at least were comparatively stable.

Yet the real beginning of settled life as we know it came with the introduction of mixed farming based on the growth of cereal crops and the breeding of domesticated livestock. The Neolithic way of life must have been introduced by immigrants from overseas who brought their women with them as well as seed corn and cattle. It is now reasonably certain, thanks to radio-carbon analysis of charcoals from archaeological sites and of samples from levels in peat-bogs giving evidence of deforestation, meadows and cultivation, that they reached us around 3000 B.C., if not earlier. It is particularly interesting that closely similar dates have been obtained from widely separated parts of the British Isles from the East Anglian Fens to Cumberland and even as far west as County Sligo, suggesting that farming spread rapidly over the country. On the other hand the Neolithic farmers only took up a very small proportion of the lighter, better drained and more easily worked soils, comprising in southern Britain mainly chalk, limestone, sand and gravel;

24

and it is likely that in many areas the hunter-fisher population continued their old way of life.

The new way of life must have reached us from overseas, since few of the species on which neolithic economy depended are found wild in this country. Moreover it is most unlikely that the polishing of flint axes, the manufacture of pottery and the construction of megalithic tombs, found with farming over much of western Europe, were separately invented in this country. The precise sources from which elements of Neolithic civilisation reached us can still not be closely defined. It is reasonable to think that the idea of building collective chamber tombs reached the west country by the Atlantic route, since close analogies for the tombs in the Cotswold—Severn area are known from the Biscayan region of western France (see p. 146); even so a small group in the Medway valley of Kent point to either Denmark or the Netherlands. The earliest pottery, notably that from Hembury, Maiden Castle and Shippea Hill, typically lacks decoration and is too simple to link easily to specific groups on the continent: an obvious source of our south-western pottery is France; but some of the eastern wares may be related to the Michelsberg pottery of the Rhineland or even conceivably to the funnel-neck beakers of northern Europe. It is suggestive that the closest analogues for the enclosures with causewayed ditches, typified by Windmill Hill, Wiltshire (14), but occuring also on the chalk of the Sussex Downs and the Chilterns, as well as in the Thames Valley at Abingdon and Staines and in the south-west at Hembury, are associated with the Michelsberg culture in the Rhenish area. The suggestion that the earthen long barrows of England owed their inspiration to Kujavian graves of Poland seems less well founded (see p. 154).

The twelve hundred years or so during which our Neolithic period lasted gave ample time for indigenous development. Among the many features native to Britain may probably be numbered the earthen long barrows, including the remarkable crematorium barrows of Yorkshire, and certainly the 'henge' monuments (see pp. 171-86), possibly the most distinctively British of our prehistoric monuments. Native development also made itself felt in flint-work and in pottery. The Middle Neolithic phase was marked by the emergence, alongside plain vessels (1), of bowls with carination, hollow neck and thickened rim, having scored, incised or impressed decoration. Distinctive regional styles include those from the Sussex enclosures; from the neighbourhood of Mildenhall, Suffolk; from the Middle Thames and Chilterns and from Ebbsfleet in the south-east. The last two of these were found in the ditch silting of the Windmill Hill enclosure alongside decorated wares apparently local to the site.

The Late Neolithic was marked by the appearance of coarser pottery, by a number of new flint-forms, including polished knives and lop-sided arrowheads and by the development of elaborate flint-mines in the chalk of East Anglia, Sussex and Wessex, probably in competition with metal. Pottery was of two main kinds. That which takes its name from Peterborough (2) or Mortlake, though coarser in ware, shows a development from the thickened rim and hollow neck of the Middle Neolithic vessels mentioned above; decoration in the form mainly of zig-zag patterns impressed by whipped cord, shell-edges and the articular ends of small bones is commonly applied to the rims and the whole or almost the whole of the body, reminding one on the one hand of that found on Sub-neolithic wares over large tracts of Eurasia, but nearer home comparing with wares of comparable age in Ireland. The other kind, named after Clacton and mainly found east of a line from Scar-

26

borough to Portland, differs in nearly all respects. It is flat-based and has straight, flared sides. Cord impression is absent and the usual techniques include grooves, stabs and plastic relief. Common designs include multichevrons, dotted triangles and lozenges, a variety of running and cable patterns in plastic relief, and rusticated surfaces made by pinching up the surface.

It was into this milieu that newcomers began to penetrate from the Continent, bringing with them the custom of making beaker-shaped pots decorated by horizontal bands of geometric design impressed by finely toothed stamps. This was evidently part of a series of widespread movements that affected almost the whole of Europe from Iberia to Bohemia and the Rhineland at the close of Neolithic times. To judge from basic regularities in the form and decoration of pots, in armanent (bows and arrows, wrist-guards and tanged daggers) and in dress-fasteners (buttons with V-perforations made by boring into the under-surface from two directions) the spread of Beaker people must have been rapid. Almost certainly they were after sources of copper and it is significant that their advent was soon followed by the beginning of metal-working.

The idea of making beakers was introduced by several movements. Beakers (group B1), having a smooth profile (4) and decorated by a toothed stamp in the style traditional among the bell-beakers of Europe, reached Wessex from the Rhineland. From the Netherlands came three distinct groups, barrel-shaped beakers with everted lip (B2), beakers with zoned decoration made by impressing a cord (B3) and, crossing directly to northern Britain, ones (C) with a short but well-defined neck. The beaker tradition established in Britain was a very mixed one and it is hardly surprising that fresh departures should have occurred in the new territory, notably the appearance of a distinctively British

27

form (A) having a tall, flowering neck (3) and decoration enriched with deep panels of saltire designs. Although they continued to rely mainly on flint and stone for tools and weapons, the beaker-using peoples of Britain, as elsewhere in Europe, began to employ copper. Analysis of copper artefacts found with B 1 beakers in Wessex shows that whereas some were made from central European ores, the majority indicate the use of Irish ones. The beaker people, who thus initiated copper metallurgy in Britain, made simple flat axes with expanded working edges, daggers and even halberds mounted at right-angles to the shaft. In addition they hammered alluvial gold into a variety of ornaments.

Like other parts of temperate Europe richly endowed with copper, gold and above all tin, Britain was in due course brought within the range of Mycenaean trade. It was as a result of this that decisive advances were made in metallurgy, including the manufacture of tin-bronze and the use of valve moulds that made possible more complex castings and consequently more elaborate tools and weapons. The importance of overseas markets and the fact that our mineral resources were concentrated in the highland zone explains how it was that wealth was concentrated in the hands of Wessex middlemen athwart routes from Ireland, Cornwall, Brittany, the Lower Rhine, Denmark, Central Europe and ultimately the Mediterranean. Much of what we have learned about the forces behind the rise of our native Early Bronze Age has been gained from a study of the grave-goods buried with the leaders of the day, since these were often made of materials imported in the course of trade and in their technique of production they sometimes show traces of exotic contacts. Most of the richest of these are found under round barrows in Wessex with an important concentration in the Stonehenge area, but outlying groups occur in the south-west, in South Wales, on the Sussex Downs and in East Anglia. The form of their daggers, at first flat with numerous small rivets on either side of a very short tang (Bush type) and later with mid-ribs defined by grooves on either face of the blade and a few large rivets (Camerton type), and the shapes and ornamentation of rather specialised kinds of pottery cup (grape cups covered with bosses and Aldbourne cups standing on a hollow foot and ornamented by dotted triangles and chevrons) show clearly enough that a close relation existed between Wessex and Brittany, another important source of tin in the ancient world. Abundant amber, used for crescentic necklaces, cups and other things, suggests that the Wessex people were rich enough to divert Jutish amber from the routes that flowed south across Germany to the Mycenaeans and there are other clues that point to contact with northern Germany and even central Europe. The abundant gold came in the main from Ireland, but the fashion of using it in sheets, often for covering base materials, and other tricks of gold-smithery, point to the East Mediterranean, as do even more emphatically the exotic faience beads of segmented form traded by the Mycenaeans and found in upwards of thirty Wessex graves.

The Middle Bronze Age was one of uneventful, insular development, but the increased use of bronze and the wealth of gold objects, now worked from bars rather than in sheets, testify to a certain quiet prosperity. The rite of cremation now universal was neolithic in origin and had been growing in popularity during the Early Bronze Age. The collared urns used to contain the ashes were derived in large measure from Peterborough-Mortlake prototypes, the collar itself represented an enlargement of the heavy moulded rim of the Neolithic ware and the lavish use of cord impression for ornamentation stemming from the same source; but a tendency to zone patterns horizontally may owe something to beaker traditions. Most of the basic bronze types, such as dirks, socketed spearheads with small leaf-shaped blades, and palstaves (axes slotted on either face of the butt), were introduced at the beginning of the period from Germany; but the native smiths modified these, sometimes radically as when they added loops to spearheads, but more often by relatively minor nuances that were yet sufficient to impart a distinctively British or even local aspect.

The Late Bronze Age was marked by widespread changes in the types of bronze tools and weapons, by a significant increase in the bulk and turn-over of metal evidenced by large and numerous hoards both of new objects and of scrap, and by an abrupt departure in metallurgical practice through the inclusion for the first time of significant proportions of lead as an alloy of copper. Already before this innovation exotic types had begun to intrude upon a Middle Bronze Age background: knobbed sickles and various ornaments, including twisted torcs, ribbed bracelets and coiled finger-rings, came in from Germany; and from the central Rhineland came two forms of leaf-shaped swords (Hemigkofen and Erbenheim), insular versions of which formed an important element in the armament of the British Late Bronze Age. Again, although certain kinds of palstave continued in use, most of the important tools of the period were introduced, notably the socketed axe and in due course such things as the winged axe, socketed knife, chisel and gouge. Another feature of the period was the introduction of sheet bronze for shields and various forms of container; buckets were imported from central Europe and cauldrons from the Mediterranean, but both were modified by the native craftsmen, particularly in regard to their handles. Changes in metalware need not in themselves imply more than trade or the movements of artificers, but there are signs, particularly from Sussex and Kent, that complete families, displaced by the thrust of Urnfield people expanding from central Europe, crossed over from northern France.

Already during the last phase of the Late Bronze Age Britain was beginning to feel the impact of the earliest iron-using culture in temperate Europe, named after the cemetery of Hallstatt in Austria. By 600 B.C., and probably earlier, bronzes and a number of iron objects in the Hallstatt style, many of them locally made but all based on exotic prototypes, began to appear on a broad front from south Wales to north-east England. One result of this was that old links with the metal-producing areas of highland Britain were severed and the inhabitants of the lowlands had to meet their need for socketed bronze axes by importing them ready-made from Brittany. About the middle of the sixth century the first iron-using colonists began to come in mainly from the Low Countries, but partly from France north of the Loire. The immigrants established settlements as far apart as Scarborough, West Harling, Eastbourne, Hengistbury and possibly even Castell Odo at the extreme south-west tip of Caernarvonshire. To begin with their culture (Iron Age A) was of devolved Hallstatt character, but before long it began to show influence from the style that developed on either side of the Rhine in the fifth century B.C. and takes its name from the Swiss site of La Tène. La Tène features are present for instance on some of the pottery from All Cannings Cross, Wiltshire, and Long Wittenham, Oxfordshire, in a number of brooches from different parts of the country and in a group of dagger-scabbards mainly from the Thames and East Anglia.

During the second period of the Early Iron Age the original culture persisted, though in a modified (A2) form, the swan-neck pins of Hallstatt type for instance giving place to native ones with ring-heads and pottery acquiring La Tène

31

traits like ring-feet and cordons. The role of immigrants in the British Iron Age is subject to debate. According to the still prevailing theory, fully developed La Tène culture (B) was introduced to southern England around 300 B.C. by immigrants from the Marne basin of north-east France; these were soon followed by groups that impinged on Lincolnshire and the East Riding, represented by loose finds from the Witham and chariot burials from Arras; and lastly by others reaching the south-west from Brittany or beyond. The archaeological finds from this period reflect well the aristocratic nature of Celtic society. It is this which helps to explain the existence among comparatively primitive people of schools of exquisite craftsmen, exempt from base labour and free to devote themselves to the production of conspicuous rather than merely useful articles; the existence, though by no means on the scale of the continent, of richly furnished burials; and the emphasis on chariots, parade armament and hill-forts. Moreover, it makes it easier to credit the numerous invasions suggested by the archaeological evidence, if we think of at least some of these as intrusions of scattered groups of nobles and their retinues.

The La Tène Iron Age B culture continued to flourish over the greater part of the country down to the Christian era and in some parts down to the Roman conquest itself; indeed it was precisely during the third phase of the Early Iron Age that a distinctively British style of engraved decoration appeared first on swords and scabbards and then in a more developed form on bronze mirrors. Yet, so far as south-east England was concerned, the decisive factor was growing Germanic pressure on the Marnian territories. As early as 150 B.C. Gallo-Belgic coins began to reach the Thames in quantity, imported perhaps by individual refugees. Although the Belgae stood up well to the Cimbric and Teutonic incursions of 111-110 B.C., it was probably the sense of insecurity engendered by this event that led to folk movements across the Channel at the close of the century. The areas immediately affected lay on either side of the Lower Thames, extending over the present counties of Kent, Essex and Hertfordshire. The Belgic invaders brought with them a comparatively advanced technology and made their pottery on the wheel, a sure sign that specialisation of function had proceeded some distance. The use of coins and the extensive systems of dykes guarding their strongholds, suggest that politically they were organized in larger units than their predecessors, even if it was not until the last two or three generations of the prehistoric period that inscribed coins, making it possible for us to chart the fluctuating boundaries of the various realms, were taken into use.

The later history of the Belgic province in the south was one of growing expansion and sophistication. The extension of Belgic territory as far as Suffolk, Cambridgeshire, Gloucestershire and Dorset was accomplished partly by expansion overland but partly also by overseas movements into Sussex and Hampshire, almost certainly by refugees at the time of Caesar's campaigns in Gaul. Although Gaul was constituted a Roman province in 51 B.C., it was not until the time of Tasciovanus (15 B.C.-A.D. 10), the first Catuvellaunian ruler to inscribe his name on coins, that there is evidence for close or intensive trade relations. No doubt it was political memories that held back a development which, when it came, brought such luxuries as wine, silver vessels, fine pottery and so on from Gaul and even from Italy to the tables of the ruling class in Belgic Britain.

Despite their exposure to Roman luxury and civilization, it was the Belgic tribes that gave the Claudian legions the greatest trouble in the initial phase of the conquest. In this respect the stout resistence indicated by signs of massacre at Oldbury, the Caburn, Maiden Castle and Hod Hill contrasts with the complaisant attitude of non-Belgic tribes like the Regni of west Sussex or the Iceni of East Anglia. Even so, the Claudian invasion was very different in character from Caesar's incursions of 55-54 B.C. and the disciplined weight of Roman arms was bound to prevail. By A.D. 47 it was possible for the governor Ostorius Scapula to stabilise a provisional frontier running from the Trent to the Severn estuary, and within another forty years Agricola's campaigns had reduced the north of England and Wales and so brought their prehistoric phase to an end.

PRE-ROMAN IRON AGE	Third	150 B.C. – A.D. 43/85
	Second	350 B.C. – 150 B.C.
	First	550 B.C. – 350 B.C.
BRONZE AGE	Late	900 B.C. – 550 B.C.
	Middle	1400 B.C. – 900 B.C.
	Early	1650 B.C. – 1400 B.C.
COPPER AGE		1850 B.C. – 1650 B.C.
NEOLITHIC	Late	2150 B.C. – 1850 B.C.
	Middle	2600 B.C. – 2150 B.C.
	Early	3000 B.C. – 2600 B.C.
MESOLITHIC	Late	5000 B.C. – 3000 B.C.
	Middle	7200 B.C. – 5000 B.C.
	Early	8000 B.C. – 7200 B.C.
ADVANCED PALAEOLITHIC		30,000 B.C. – 8000 B.C.
LOWER (& MIDDLE) PALAEOLITHIC		4/500,000 B.C. – 30,000 B.C.

Major chronological divisions: Prehistoric England & Wales

2

The Food-Quest

LIFE in prehistoric Britain was moulded more by the exigencies of the food-quest than by any other factor. Then, as now, the whole structure and tempo of society was governed by the nature of its economic life. For all but a tiny fraction of our history—a mere week-end in the year of human experience—man has lived as a parasite on nature, hunting and gathering his food and collecting such materials as he required for his handicrafts. Yet farming, although a comparatively recent innovation, which only reached these islands around the beginning of the third millennium B.C., was the sole key to human advancement and emancipation, giving man for the first time some measure of control over his food-supply over and above what was possible through the storage of wild products.

The immediate predecessors of man in the evolutionary succession were vegetarian, and it seems, therefore, reasonable to assume that wild vegetable food entered largely into the diet of the earliest men. It can be taken for granted that the people who made the Lower Palaeolithic flints found in the drift deposits of southern England exploited to the full the plant life of the genial interglacial epochs during which they roamed these northern latitudes. Roots, shoots, nuts, fruits, and berries were gathered each in their due season by small bands comprising one or two families, who wandered over familiar trails their own well-recognised territory, visiting at appropriate times localities favoured by the various species. If it were only possible to recover their vocabulary we may be sure that it would reflect an accurate and intimate knowledge of the plant world. Of the receptacles used to contain the natural harvest or of the digging-sticks needed to grub up the roots no trace has survived, though from Mesolithic times until the Bronze Age we have digging-stick weights in the shape of quartzite pebbles with hour-glass perforation, resembling those used by the modern Bushman of South Africa. Among the earliest traces of vegetable food are the carbonised hazel-nut shells from the Farnham pit-dwellings and other Mesolithic sites. Wild vegetable food continued to supplement diet throughout prehistoric times, and the sloe, haw, and blackberry, collected by the Glastonbury lake-dwellers, are not despised by country folk in our own day. Wild plants of different kinds also produced various raw materials of value to primitive farming communities. Moss was used by prehistoric carpenters for caulking bevel-and-groove fittings and plugging cracks in wooden huts. Ferns and bracken were gathered for bedding, hair-moss and osiers for basketry, and certain fungi for tinder. Birch bark was stripped for making receptacles and possibly even canoes. Caraway and poppy seeds were used to add interest to cereal foods, and certain plants, for example the weld, were taken to provide natural dyes for textiles.

To judge by analogy with modern primitive peoples, insects must from the earliest times have contributed their quota to the food supply. Succulent grubs, snails, and above all the sweet honey of wild bees, were eagerly gathered and relished to relieve the monotony of the diet. Bees' wax would also be used for many purposes, in later times for casting bronze.

The gathering of wild vegetables and insects was largely relegated to women and children. Hunting game and fur-bearing animals was a man's work. The methods employed varied at different periods. In Lower Palaeolithic times the horse, various cervids, and such giant fauna as elephant, rhinoceros, and hippopotamus were the chief quarries. They must have been caught in fall-traps set by trails leading to watering places, or driven over precipices, though, as the point of a fire-hardened lance of yew-wood from the Clacton Channel shows, hand-weapons were also used. Great masses of mammoth bones found at some continental sites suggest that by such means numerous victims were caught and butchered close to where they fell. After a kill it can be imagined that everyone ate to repletion, not knowing when another opportunity might occur. The alternation of gorging and enforced fasting, bred of an uncertain food supply, is one of the characteristics of existing hunting peoples which strikes travellers most strongly.

Hunting from a distance by means of missiles was introduced by Advanced Palaeolithic people. The cave-dwellers of Creswell and Paviland killed their reindeer, wild horse, and bison with flint, bone or ivory headed lances propelled from spear-throwers. The chase now played a dominating part in life, the appetite for animal food being sharpened by the rigours of a Late-glacial climate. The extent of this preoccupation with wild animal life is reflected in the content of the art of this time as displayed on the walls of the caves and rock-shelters of the Dordogne or the Pyrenean region, or on carved objects from the deposits resting on their floors. From the meagre British Advanced Palaeolithic material it is possible to cite only a few engraved bones, among them a broken piece of rib-bone with a rather crude delineation of the forepart of a horse from Robin Hood's Cave, Creswell (see p. 19).

In Mesolithic times, as the finds from Star Carr so well showed, the character of the fauna changed. Temperate forms like the elk, red deer, roe deer, wild pig, and aurochs became the chief food quarries. The lance was replaced by

37

the bow and arrow, the latter tipped by tiny microliths. The antler masks (12) from Star Carr suggest that stalking played an important part in hunting stags. The dog was the only domestic animals the Mesolithic people had.

With the coming of agriculture hunting declined in importance, although it continued to supplement the food supply throughout the prehistoric period, as it does today. The elk had disappeared by Neolithic times, and the

Barbed and tanged flint arrowhead. Early Bronze Age (1:1)

aurochs by the Bronze Age, but wild deer and boar survived until recent times. As for fur-bearing animals, the Glastonbury lake-villagers hunted the fox, wild cat, otter, and beaver. It is interesting to note that in the course of the Bronze Age the bow and arrow gave way to the spear as the chief projectile. The sling seems to have appeared in the Late Bronze Age in restricted areas, and to have spread more widely in lowland Britain during the Early Iron Age. Although certainly used in warfare, at witness the dumps of pebbles at Maiden Castle, Dorset, the sling was also used in hunting. At the peaceful village settlement of Glastonbury clay sling-pellets were evidently a home product, many of those found being still unfired. Probably they were used to shoot birds, remains of which include pelicans, cranes, swans, and ducks. It is unlikely that hunting had developed as a sport prior to the emergence of pronounced class distinctions during the Early Iron Age. Possibly the use of wild boar designs as helmet crests or shield decorations may be one reflection of a love of the chase. A Belgic prince's idea of sport would probably have been to assist at a battue of animals stampeded into nets by dogs and horsemen.

Evidence of ancient fishing is not always easy to come by, but there is no doubt that the art was practised by Advanced Palaeolithic man: representations of fish are not uncommon in cave art and fish-bones have been found in cave deposits. The discovery of fish-shaped bone lures and pointed gorges shows that the line was used. When the fish swallowed the gorge a sudden tug would cause it to swivel and the points to pierce the gullet. The hook was not introduced until Mesolithic times on the continent, and it remained barbless until the spread of metal. Net fishing, an integral part of the Maglemose culture, must have been carried on in Eastern England away back in Mesolithic times, though the earliest evidence we can yet adduce for it in this country is from the Glastonbury lake-village, where lead net-sinkers were quite common. The villagers caught roach, perch, trout, and shad. Large fish, notably pike and salmon, were sometimes speared. The inland fisher-folk of Mesolithic times commonly used leisters consisting of two or more barbed prongs of wood or bone lashed to a wooden handle. Isolated bone prongs have been dredged from the Thames and from the old inland fishing and hunting grounds on the present North Sea bed, and others have come from ancient mere beds in Holderness. Iron fish-spears, their form modified by the possibilities of the material, were in common use in parts of Britain until comparatively recent times. A late eighteenth-century observer throws an interesting sidelight on the methods used, when he tells us of the River Dyfi, that it 'abounds in salmon, which are hunted in the night, by an animated but illicit chase, by spear-men who are directed to the fish by lighted whisps of straw'. The most primitive method of catching fish, and one that would leave little or no archaeological trace, is the use of various forms of trap. Three distinct kinds of eel trap are used in the Fenland today.

Fishing from boats in the open sea is likely to have been a late development, though it is by no means improbable that the curraghs seen by Caesar off the south coast were sometimes used for this purpose. On the other hand, the resources of the sea-shore, notably shell-fish and an occasional seal, were fully appreciated in early times. Strand-looping was especially common in Mesolithic Europe. It can be assumed that shell-middens from this period must have accumulated along many stretches of the contemporary coastline of southern Britain, since covered by the rising sea. Neolithic middens have been lost to us from the same cause. Beaker sherds were found in a midden at Cataclews, near Harlyn Bay, but the majority of the middens in this part of Cornwall date from the Early Iron Age. To this period belong those heaped up along the shores of the meres at Southchurch, Essex, among which oyster, cockle, mussel, periwinkle, and whelk are represented. The only shell middens available for study in southern Britain, in fact, date from a time when the collection of shell-fish had long become an ancillary occupation. The Romans were quick to recognise the virtues of British oysters, which soon established themselves as delicacies in Rome itself.

· During the Early Iron Age the sea-shore produced a commodity of outstanding economic importance among primitive communities, namely salt. There is no evidence that rock-salt was mined in prehistoric Britain, as it was in Austria, and the sea was the natural alternative source. It is strongly suspected that the 'Red Hills' of the Essex coastal strip acquired their characteristic colour through burning associated with the extraction of salt from sea water. Quantities of burnt briquetage in the form of bars and stands are associated with the sites, which cluster on the estuaries of the Colne, Blackwater and Crouch and neighbouring marshes. It is possible that these were arranged in stacks and heated, sea water then being poured over them and the resultant salt removed by scraping. Similar briquetage, which is known to have been associated with salt production in the lower Rhineland, one source of our Iron Age A culture, has been recorded from the East Anglian Fenland, from the Lincolnshire coast at Ingoldmells Point, and at Hook, near Warsash, Hampshire, where it was found with fired clay platforms.

The type of farming practised in prehistoric Britain was a mixture of stock-raising and agriculture. In Neolithic times and for the greater part of the Bronze Age—and indeed over much of the highland zone throughout the prehistoric periods—crops were subsidiary to herds. To begin with wheat was the main crop, mainly emmer, but including einkorn or small spelt and bread wheat; in the course of the Bronze Age barley rose from small beginnings to be the most important cereal; and in the Iron Age wheat, which now included spelt, regained importance, and oats—and in due course rye—began to enter the picture as cultivated crops. Before crops could be sown existing vegetation had first to be cleared and, as most of this was forest, it is easy to see why flint and stone were in demand in Neolithic times and how much urgency there was to secure the best materials for axes even if this meant mining, quarrying and extensive trade. It is likely that fire also played a part both in clearing the ground and in enriching the soil with phosphate. Indeed the signs are that to begin with the grain

41

was sown in small temporary clearings, possibly being merely raked among the ashes by tree boughs. The systematic tilling of fixed fields probably did not come till the introduction at some time during the Bronze Age of a light form of wooden plough or ard drawn by a couple of yoked oxen. In the Mediterranean zone, where it first developed, the main object of cultivation was to pulverise the surface and conserve moisture in the sub-soil and this purpose was admirably served by working the ard at right angles in alternate directions, a process which resulted in fields of squarish shape.

Once the turf was removed from the chalk slopes, ploughing and the processes of natural erosion tended to induce a certain terracing, the upper margins of the field cutting into the hillside, the lower ones being raised in height through accumulation of soil working downwards. The system of horizontal banks or lynchets, formed in this way, can be quite prominent even when viewed from ground-level, especially when the sun is casting long shadows. From the air, in conjunction with the lower banks formed where the plough turned on its course along the slope, they reveal the Celtic field system almost as clearly as a map (6). A main drawback of the light plough or ard was that its use was virtually confined to the more easily worked soils, which formed a primary area of settlement, notably gravels, sands, chalk and limestone. At first this constriction was no hardship, but as the primary areas began to fill up, it became necessary to break up the stiffer, but potentially rich, loam and clay lands, by using a heavier type of plough with wheel and coulter and requiring a larger plough team. There are signs, though there is not yet conclusive proof, that this innovation may first have been introduced, even though on a limited scale, by the Belgae. The fields cultivated by such heavy ploughs were long and narrow like the strip fields of the Medieval open-field system. The new plough made possible the cultivation of heavier and richer soils and vastly increased the cereal output of south-eastern England. The old 'scratch agriculture', however, persisted on the poorer soils throughout Belgic times. Indeed, during the Roman occupation the heavy plough appears to have been confined to the farms of the villas, the Romano-British peasants carrying on in their old style of agriculture. Most of the Celtic fields of the Sussex Downs are known to have been cultivated during the Roman era, and some may even have been formed at this time. The strip field did not spread over the lowland generally until the Teutonic invasions.

Among the commonest traces of prehistoric agriculture are the sickles used for reaping, though it may be emphasised that of themselves they do not necessarily imply the practice of agriculture, being equally adapted for cutting wild grasses. Although a few flint flakes showing traces of the lustre caused by friction with the silica in corn storks have been found, we have no evidence of the kind of handle in which these were mounted and nothing comparable with the wooden reaping-knives having flints inset into a groove, such as are known from the Swiss lake-villages. From the close of Neolithic times and the earlier half of the Bronze Age, however, we have numerous flint sickle blades, sometimes crescentic in form, but often with a more pronounced curve at the tip. Their blunted or constricted butts show that they were hafted at right-angles to their wooden handles. Their use as sickles is suggested by the diffuse lustre of the kind just mentioned, which is sometimes to be found covering a zone half an inch deep on one edge. During the Middle Bronze Age single-edged metal sickles, reinforced by one or more ridges and secured to the handle by a knob, came into fashion. The two-edged socketed sickle was a

43

British invention of the Late Bronze Age, and a few specimens were traded to France and Switzerland. It is notable that the great majority of sickle blades, whether of flint or bronze, both knobbed and socketed, have been found in East Anglia and the Thames Valley. This need not imply that corn growing was concentrated in these regions, because the sickles may well have been used for other purposes such as lopping foliage for feeding livestock; in any case imprints of cereal grains, accidentally caught up in making hand-made pots, show that corn-growing was widely practised even in Neolithic times.

Querns for grinding the gain are other material evidences for early agriculture. The earliest querns, introduced by the Neolithic immigrants but continuing in use well into the Early Iron Age, were operated by rubbing an upper stone against a lower one, culminating in the shapely saddle-quern with its bolster-like topstone. Rotary querns comprising two circular stones, the lower one conical with a socket for the spindle on which the upper one revolved, were apparently introduced by Iron Age B people.

Of the domesticated food animals of our earliest farmers the ox, a robust variety with a broad skull and large horns, was by far the most numerous. Next came the pig. Goat-horned sheep (*Ovis aries palustris*) and the goat itself were at first less common. The domestic animals of the Iron Age people differed in more ways than one from those of their predecessors. Oxen continued to be numerous, but they were of a smaller type *(Bos longifrons),* having short horns and long narrow foreheads. Forest clearance evidently favoured sheep and goat at the expense of swine. At Glastonbury and All Cannings we find that the sheep was second only to the ox. Moreover, the sheep were of a different type (*Ovis aries studeri*), slender, large horned creatures resembling the somewhat deer-like sheep of the island of Soay

44

near St Kilda. Goats and pig were less numerous. Only scanty traces of horses have been found in British Neolithic contexts and it seems likely that these belong to wild ones hunted for food. There is no evidence for the domestication of the horse in Britain until towards the end of the Bronze Age. The animal kept by the Iron Age A people was small in size, standing $11^{1}/_{2}$-$12^{1}/_{2}$ hands, and slender-limbed, recalling the ponies of Exmoor. Remains of dogs have been found in each of our Neolithic 'camps' tested by excavation, and may therefore be presumed to have played an important role, most probably helping in the herding of animals. Dog droppings commonly survive owing to their high content of calcium salts, due to a diet of gnawed bones. Although the skull of a wolf-like dog has been recognised from Star Carr, the oldest reasonably complete skeleton from Britain must be that excavated from the ditch of the Neolithic 'camp' on Windmill Hill, Avebury. While not resembling closely any existing breed, it recalls in certain respects a largish fox-terrier. Long-legged, short-backed and small-headed with an exceptionally wide thorax, it belongs to the sub-species *Canis familiaris palustris*, first recognised from the Swiss lake-villages. Later dog remains from prehistoric Britain seem to conform to the same general type.

The introduction of a farming economy did not for some time result in the development of settled life as we understand it. Our Neolithic forbears—and those of the earlier stages of the Bronze Age—were essentially pastoral nomads, who supplemented their food-supply by cultivating temporary plots, and by hunting, fishing, and the collection of wild plant products. The 'camps' or enclosures of the type best known from Windmill Hill, Avebury, were probably centres to which men who lived in small groups foregathered at some special season to conduct ceremonial activities, effect exchanges and so on (14). Their leading feature today is the concentric rings of discontinuous ditches with low internal banks. The character of the ditches shows them to have been in the nature of quarries, while the banks built from the excavated material were themselves too slight to be of defensive value. It is probable that their chief purpose was to hold in position concentric palisades set at intervals. Entrances into the inner area are marked by gaps in the banks and ditches. The total area of the Windmill Hill enclosure is about 23 acres. The one at Whitehawk on Brighton racecourse covers $11^1/_2$ acres, the innermost of the four rings enclosing rather less than two acres. The herdsmen appear to have squatted in stretches of ditch in which they lit fires and discarded rubbish, bones—mainly animal, but including a few human ones, perhaps indicative of cannibalism—broken pots, chipped flints, and a few fragments of rubbing stones. Other camps of this kind which have been excavated include one destroyed by gravel diggings at Abingdon, Berkshire, and others on the sites later occupied by the Iron Age hill-forts of the Trundle, Goodwood, Maiden Castle, Dorset, and Hembury, Devon.

Settled farming based to a major extent on husbandry came in with the plough. Already from the Middle Bronze Age one can recognise in certain limited parts of southern England a number of farmsteads, in some instances integral with systems of Celtic fields (6). The farms consist of embanked compounds enclosing timber huts, of which postholes are today the sole remaining trace. Many of those first explored are in Sussex, including those on Park Brow and New Barn Down, near Worthing, and two on Plumpton Plain, Brighton. From Wiltshire one may cite another recently excavated on Thorny Down, Winterslow. During the Early Iron Age people seem to have lived either in single farms or in small hamlets. Of the latter, in most respects merely aggregations of individual farms, but with rather more scope for specialised activities such as smithing and potting, very little is known. Their exploration constitutes, indeed, one of the major desiderata of British archaeology. Thanks in the main to the highly intelligent excavation of a site known as Little Woodbury (8) in the parish of Britford, Salisbury, we are much better placed for the single farms. The mental picture we are enabled to form about them as the result of digging is all the more remarkable that as a rule there are no surface traces other than crop-marks, and that nothing other than post-holes remains of their timber structures. Both Little Woodbury and the analogous site on Meon Hill, near Stockbridge, Hampshire, were discovered from the air.

The main activity of the Little Woodbury people was the cultivation of their land by the light two-ox plough. The farm was probably about 20 acres in extent, although probably a half of this would be fallow land. At harvest the corn would be reaped, brought into the farm enclosure, and dried on frames, pairs of stout posts set 6-8 feet apart with numerous cross pieces, similar to those used in damp climates in some parts of Europe to-day. The grain was then husked in an oblong hollow, scooped out of the ground and probably provided with a rough shelter to keep off and rain. Some would be set aside for seed and stored in a small rectangular granary raised from ground level on wooden piles. The bulk, however, would be roasted in preparation for storage in subterranean silos, circular pits, perhaps from 3 to 5 feet in diameter (7), and sunk anything up to 8 or 9 feet in the chalk, lined with some kind of large receptacle, probably of plaited straw. The silos must have been entered by ladders, either runged ones like that recovered from the Glastonbury lake-village, or notched timbers resembling those found in old iron-mines in the Forest of Dean. Since the silos were rendered stale by bacteriological action in a matter of five years or so, they had to be discarded and new ones cut at frequent intervals. Disused storage-pits would be filled with spoil from newly excavated ones, mixed with rubbish of all kinds, old meat bones, potsherds, and debris from the grain-roasting, crackled flints, fragments of clay ovens, charcoal, and ashes. Sometimes, even, they would be used for a burial. Their interpretation as 'pit-dwellings' is surely one of the strangest aberrations of archaeology! While not actually engaged in cultivating the ground or dealing with the crops, activities must have centred on repairing and making implements, weaving and plaiting, wood-turning, and the maintenance of buildings, drying-frames, palisades, and the like. The conservatism displayed in the maintenance of the farm, the same drying-frame being rebuilt up to ten times on the same spot, for example, implies a long era of peace, although there is evidence of a short spasm of anxiety when the site was hastily and incompletely defended. Further work alone can prove definitely whether this phase of defensive preparation coincides with troublous times in the third century B.C. when bands of Middle La Tène warriors supposedly crossed the Channel.

Tangible traces of pastoral activities are afforded by the linear banks and ditches and the associated quadrilateral enclosures found on the downlands of southern England. The best known of the enclosures, which are generally interpreted as cattle kraals, is South Lodge Camp on Cranborne Chase, Dorset. Others have been excavated in Somerset, Wiltshire, and Sussex. The travelling earthworks probably served both to define tracts of grazing ground and as drove-ways for herding cattle and sheep. In origin the system appears to date from the Late Bronze Age, although it persisted, except where encroached upon by cultivation, into the Early Iron Age. The junction of a number of such ranch boundaries can clearly be seen on the air-photograph

1　Neolithic bowl of plainware

2　Bowl of Peterborough type

3 Necked beaker and flint dagger

4 Bell beaker, archer's wrist-guard and copper dagger and knife

5 Star Carr, Yorkshire: birch trees felled by
Mesolithic man

6   Celtic fields at Grassington, Yorkshire

7   Maiden Castle, Dorset: storage pits

8   Little Woodbury, Wiltshire: Iron Age farmstead

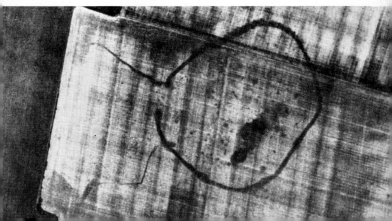

9 Quarley Hill, Hampshire: hill-fort and ranch boundaries

10 Creswell Crags, Derbyshire

11 Paviland Cave, Glamorganshire

12   Star Carr, Yorkshire: stag-antler mask

13   Star Carr: part of the brushwood platform

of Quarley Hill, Hampshire, within the oval hill-fort (9). The system of parallel banks, up to 17 in number, at Scamridge, Yorkshire, probably relates in some way to early pastoral activities—possibly as barriers to cattle raiders.

It is likely that during the Early Iron Age in southern England herds were mainly in the hands of folk who dwelt in villages close to water and rich pastures, rather than in those of the dwellers in isolated upland farms. Examination of discarded meat-bones on early sites shows that cattle were slaughtered all the year round, but they were probably thinned out with the approach of winter because of the difficulty of providing fodder.

There is a close relation between the abundance, and above all the certainty, of food supply and the density and grouping of population, vital aspects of ancient society about which we know disappointingly little. Thus a food-gathering economy implies a low density of population and an organisation in small scattered groups. Conditions in Upper Palaeolithic Britain must have resembled those recently obtaining in the waste lands of northern Canada. The population is unlikely to have been greater than two or three hundred. Under the more genial conditions of Mesolithic times, when the withdrawal of ice-sheets had increased the area open to settlement and strand-looping offered an additional source of nourishment, it is possible that the population density approximated to that of Alaska, giving a total of perhaps from three to four thousand for England and Wales. It can rarely have happened that more than 15 persons met together, save at times of tribal gatherings, when for a few days, coinciding in all likelihood with the ripening of certain wild fruits, scattered bands of food-gatherers congregated to express their solidarity in dancing and feasting. On such occasions we can imagine that hunters and fishers of outstanding ability, natural leaders of their bands, extolled their prowess in boasting song and that all rejoiced in momentary freedom from the quest for food.

The stage of semi-nomadic pastoralism and garden plots must have allowed a considerable increase in population—perhaps as much as tenfold by the Middle Bronze Age. In daily life social groups would still have been small, though here again we must allow for seasonal gatherings at centres like Windmill Hill and sacred 'henges' such as Avebury, Stonehenge, and Arbor Low. It is likely that society was organised on a patriarchal basis, a clue to which is perhaps afforded by the burials in the earthen long barrows. The conclusion that certain members of society excercised functions of a priestly character seems irresistible in the presence of the great sanctuaries.

The adoption of settled agriculture not only brought a further increase of population, but by making settled life in larger communities practicable it made for economic progress in a variety of ways. Iron Age A society was pre-eminently one of peasant equals. This would explain the ease with which comparatively small bands of well-armed Iron Age B warriors established themselves in different parts of the country, reducing the native population to the status of hewers of wood and drawers of water. On the other hand there is evidence in the defensive earthworks thrown up against invaders or rivals that danger may have stimulated leadership and enhanced the cohesion of social groups, although one has the impression that these were still comparatively small at the time of the hill-forts. The predominant impression remains that of peasant communities easily dominated by warrior leaders, among whom it is worth noting that women were able to attain the highest rank. It was the immense improvement in agricultural methods in Belgic Britain, typified above all by the intro-duction of the wheeled plough with mould-board capable of turning a furrow, that provided the economic basis for political organisation on an altogether larger scale, and helped to intensify disparities in wealth among different sections of the population. When the Roman conquerors came they found princes wielding authority over extensive tracts of country, minting coins, and maintaining at their courts schools of craftsmanship, together with a large class of well-to-do people able to import quantities of goods from Gaul and even from Italy herself.

3

Dwellings

THE most ancient dwellings discovered in Britain are the natural rock-shelters and caves inhabited by Upper Palaeolithic man during the long winters of Late-glacial times. The most carefully explored are the caves which open on to Creswell Crags (10), a ravine in the limestone near Worksop, Derbyshire—notably Robin Hood's Cave, the Church Hole, Mother Grundy's Parlour, and the Pin Hole. Langwith is another cave in the neighbourhood which has yielded traces of Upper Palaeolithic man. Further north the Victoria Cave, Settle, has produced a few objects of reindeer antler which may be of similar age. Ffynnon Beuno and Cae Gwyn on the north side of the gorge opening into the Vale of Clwyd, near St Asaph, have given definite evidence of the presence of Upper Palaeolithic hunters in North Wales. Richer traces are found in the south-west in the carboniferous limestone of South Wales (Cat's Hole, Paviland (11), and Hoyle's Mouth), the Wye Valley (King Arthur's Cave), and Mendip (Aveline's Hole, Gough's Cave, Wookey Hole, and Uphill), and in the Devonian limestone of South Devon (Kent's Cavern and Bench Cavern). Leaving on one side La Cotte de St Brelade, Jersey, which at the time of its occupation by Middle Palaeolithic man formed part of the French mainland, Kent's Cavern and the Pin Hole, both of which have yielded quantities of Mousterian implements, have the best claim to be the most ancient dwellings yet discovered in Britain.

The idea of sheltering in the mouths of natural caves or under the cover of overhanging rocks was not confined by any means to Upper Palaeolithic man. Mesolithic people sheltered in the Victoria Cave and at Creswell. Many Derbyshire caves have yielded sherds of Peterborough ware, proving occupation by late Neolithic man. The most famous associated group of metal objects of the British Bronze Age came from Heathery Burn Cave, Co. Durham, to which a well-to-do family had evidently retreated, perhaps in the troubled times which heralded and accompanied the arrival of iron-using peoples. The high-water mark of cave dwelling in Britain, judged by the actual number of troglodytes at any one time, came in the second and third centuries A.D. Down to the present day quite a number of caves, walled across the entrance, are inhabited in the limestone regions of France.

The term 'Cave Dweller', applied to Upper Palaeolithic man, is not very apt, because men have tended at all times to avail themselves of natural rock shelters, and Upper Palaeolithic man himself only lived in caves during the winter months, spending the summer in light artificial dwellings of the type illustrated in the French cave art. Further, in regions like the loess belt of South Russia, where caves are absent, he built himself winter houses, sinking the floor below the surface of the ground to eliminate draughts and provide material for a low wall.

The oldest artificial dwellings yet discovered in Britain are those of the Mesolithic food-gatherers. The most famous Mesolithic settlement yet explored in this country, namely Star Carr, Seamer, near Scarborough, was situated on what had been the shore of an extensive lake. Excavation showed that the inhabitants had built a rough platform (13) on the water's edge by throwing down quantities of birch stems weighted down by glacial pebbles and lumps of clay. From the remains of this quantities of food debris and equipment were recovered. The small size of the platform ($c.$ 18 × 16 yards) shows that no more than three or four families can have lived there together. Since no traces were found of any substantial frame-built structure—and the stumps of uprights would surely have survived—it can be assumed that any shelters took the form of skin tents or of light structures made of reeds or twigs. High up on the Pennines we find traces of summer shelters, generally in the form of more or less circular patches of flint chips with perhaps a hearth close by, but occasionally with the added testimony of burnt birch branches and ling. In the south of England evidence for some form of light shelter has been recovered by excavations at Downton near Salisbury in the form of pointed stakeholes driven into the sub-soil, some vertically, others at oblique angles. On the other hand within the territory of the Wealden culture in the south-east there are signs of more permanent structures. One of the best-known settlements was grouped around a spring-head at Farnham, Surrey. Here were uncovered the foundations of a group of huts in the form of irregular hollows scooped out of the gravel. Although they may seem inhospitable as we see them to-day, when banked around with soil from the original excavation and roofed with branches and possibly turves, these semi-subterranean earth-houses must have been quite snug in their time. There is no evidence in the form of postholes to suggest that our Mesolithic people understood the principle of frame construction; the nearest approach was the placing of a post at the entrance of one of the Farnham dwellings, presumably to give head clearance.

Very little evidence is available about the nature of the houses or settlements occupied by our earliest farmers. In this respect the contrast is very marked with the indications from south-east Europe and over the whole territory of the 'Danubian' people from Central Europe to the Low Countries, where we have evidence, a thousand years older than the earliest Neolithic in Britain, of houses up to 50 yards or more in length, grouped in villages comparable in size with modern ones. No doubt this reflects the greater importance of pastoral activities in Britain, where our farmers did not begin really to settle down until fairly well on into the Bronze Age. The commonest and often the only structural indications of Neolithic settlement are clusters of basin-shaped hollows which are presumed to have been lined, probably with basketry, for storing cereals and possibly other foodstuffs. Such have been recognised particularly clearly at the Middle Neolithic settlement at Hurst Fen, Mildenhall, but the series begins with the early 'pre-camp' phase at Windmill Hill and extends over a broad territory from Hazard Hill and Hembury in Devon to Risby Warren

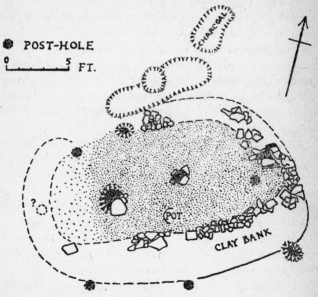

Plan of Neolithic house, Clegyr Boia, near St David's

in north Lincolnshire. Yet, since the excavations carried out on Haldon Hill, a prominent and commanding site a few miles south-west of Exeter, we have been able to infer that the Western Neolithic folk were acquainted with timber frame construction. The arrangement of the post-holes shows that we have to envisage a dwelling of quadrilateral form, some 20 feet in length, but tapering in plan, one end being $14^{1}/_{2}$ feet, the other 17 feet in width. At the northern corner of the broader end was the entrance, at the southern corner the basin-shaped cooking-place made of baked clay. Spreads of stones were found along the outer walls and also dividing the cooking-place from the interior. The stones may have served as footing for timber or wattle walls. The internal post-holes strongly suggest that the roof was gabled, as indeed one might expect of a house of this shape. Confirmation of this has since come from two sites in Wales—Clegyr Boia near St David's and Mont Pleasant, Glamorgan—and from Ronaldsway in the Isle of Man.

Extremely little is known of the houses or settlements for much of the Bronze Age. Among the few plans recovered are those of the rectangular houses from a layer at Gwithian in Cornwall attributed to the latter part of the Middle Bronze Age.

In general the evidence for ancient houses tends to be more abundant in the highland than in the lowland zone of Britain, though even here not all that might be desired. The properties of the stone which made it desirable to the ancient builders made it equally so to the setter-up of stone hedges, for whom the aggregations of material incorporated in ancient structures appeared as convenient quarries. In contemplating the hut-circles of Dartmoor and North Wales, therefore, one ought always to remember that they represent only a fraction of what was visible even a century or two ago. Again, these stone monuments of the highland zone should remind us of how much we have lost in the richer lowlands, where there must once have stood busy farms and hamlets in place of the meagre post-holes revealed by the excavator to-day.

The most numerous stone-built huts of the prehistoric period in England occur on Dartmoor. Significantly, nearly all of them occur above the present limit of cultivation at *c.* 1000 feet and few are found about 1400 feet. Of two main groups, the earlier, dating from Neolithic times and from the earlier half of the Bronze Age, is found on the southern and western fringes of the Moor between the Avon and the Tavy, whereas the younger, beginning in the Late Bronze Age but mainly belonging to the first phase of the Early Iron Age, is concentrated on the south-east margin. The earlier huts, which seem to have belonged to pastoralists who cultivated nothing more than small plots, sometimes occur on the open moor, like the seventy or more (not necessarily occupied at once) on Standon Down above the Tavy. Others are enclosed by stone-walled 'pounds', like Grimspound near Moreton Hampstead and Trowlesworthy Warren (16) on the upper Plym, which were doubtless used for herds. Individual huts are usually between 10 and 20 feet across inside. The single entrance, formed of two stone uprights and a lintel, was narrow and low, rarely exceeding $2^1/_2$ by $3^1/_2$ feet, and sometimes the interior was further kept snug and warm by the addition of a shelter wall to screen the doorway from the prevailing west wind. The walls composed of turf or loose stones retained by facings of vertical slabs are generally between 4 and 6 feet thick, and seldom, if ever, more than 4 feet high. The roof, probably of branches covered with turf, was supported by the walls and the central post which rested either in a hole or on a stone slab. The floor was of beaten clay, sometimes with a stone paving. Drainage was provided for by siting the huts on sloping ground. At the highest part of the interior, generally on the right of the entrance, there was often a low stone dais or bench, which, covered with fern or heather, served as a seat by day and a bed by night. On the edge of Dartmoor, where wood was more easily to be obtained, the benches were made of timber, only a few retaining stones remaining in position. As a rule each hut has a hearth sunk in the floor. Generally these are associated

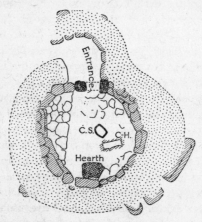

A Dartmoor hut (*c.* 1:120)

with heaps of fire-crackled pebbles, showing that pebbles heated in the hearth played an important part in cooking and in boiling water. From one hearth in a hut at Hay Tor nearly two barrow-loads of charcoal were removed, the fuel including stunted oak, alder, and peat. At Legis Tor a round-based crock was actually found in position in one of the stonelined cooking-holes, having inside it a fire-cracked flint. The younger settlements, found on what is now the drier side of Dartmoor, belonged to people who, to judge from the attached Celtic fields, relied to a greater extent

58

on agriculture. Yet the small areas of the fields, around one acre for each hut, show that they must still have depended largely on stock-raising. Sometimes the hut circles relate to individual or small family holdings with from one or four huts. Agglomerations also occur, as at Kestor where upwards of twenty huts were found in quite a small area; these did form a street to be sure, but stood at the corners or edges of adjacent fields. The huts were often 30 or more feet in internal diameter, and the hut roofs were sometimes carried on a ring of posts set round one at the centre.

A second class of dry masonry dwelling found in the highland zone is the courtyard house, in which more than one room opens on to a central unroofed courtyard. Possibly the best-known examples are those at Chysauster in western Cornwall (15), where we have eight arranged along a street, four aside, each with terraced garden plots attached. House 5, of which a plan is given, shows most of the characteristic features, namely an asymmetrical courtyard rather larger on the left as one enters, a circular room with a hollowed slab to carry roof post straight ahead, and on the right a long narrow cell which may have sheltered

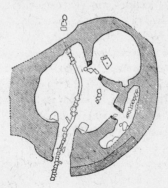

Courtyard house at Chysauster (*c.* 1:500) (*cf.* Figure 15)

cattle. The walls at Chysauster, which at one point still stand to a height of $5^1/_2$ feet, are built of dry masonry with facings of heavy blocks and a core of earth and rubble. The courtyard presumably was left open, but the compartments were roofed with timber and turf. A system of drains, consisting of shallow gullies covered by stone slabs, is a feature of the main room of many courtyard houses. As a rule they are designed to carry away water, but in at least one instance at Chysauster they acted rather as a conduit to bring it in.

There is some doubt as to when courtyard houses were first constructed. In North Wales, where they occur on both sides of the Menai Strait and down the coast of Merioneth, the only dated examples have been assigned to the mid-Roman period, and have generally been regarded as a product of the *Pax Romana*, locally enforced from Segontium. Recently excavated examples include two at Caerau, Clynnog, Caernarvonshire, which, though perhaps more evolved in form, nevertheless belong to the same general class as Chysauster. In western Cornwall itself the courtyard houses at Porthmeor, Zennor, have been shown to belong to the second to fourth centuries A.D. Yet the excavators of Chysauster were convinced of the pre-Roman age of that site. One can in any case by fairly sure that the type is a native one, and has not, as some have argued, been inspired by the many-roomed Roman villa. The same general idea in house design is common not only to Cornwall and North Wales, but also to the Hebrides, where it is embodied in the wheelhouses, and the Shetlands, where at Jarlshof it can be traced back to the Late Bronze Age. The prehistoric origin of the type can hardly be doubted: whether particular examples are of Roman or pre-Roman age can only be determined by excavation.

A third type of stone-built dwelling-place is the enclosed

hut village of North Wales and the northern counties of England. The enclosures themselves, which tend to be of basically rectangular form with rounded corners, consist of low walls with stone facings and rubble cores, designed to contain rather than to defend the community within. Near the middle there is usually one hut rather larger than the rest, presumably that of the chief man. Other huts are often placed near the entrance or even outside the enclosure. The enclosed area, which varies in extent from less than one-half to more than one and one-third acres, is subdivided by interior walls, probably to facilitate the penning of cattle or sheep. The 'Celtic' fields, which are generally to be found either adhering to, or in the close neighbourhood of, the enclosures, show that agriculture as well as pastoral activities contributed to the well-being of the inhabitants. The huts themselves are mostly circular in plan, but sub-rectangular forms are quite common.

Enclosed villages of this kind are difficult to date. In Cumberland and Westmorland where such sites abound, over fifty being known from the latter county alone, a few have been attributed to the pre-Roman period. Urswick Stone Walls has somewhat rashly been relegated to the first, if not to the second, century B.C., on the strength of a decorated bronze fragment, while the way in which the Roman road swerves to avoid the Ewe Close village shows that this may at least mark the site of a pre-Roman settlement. However, it must be admitted that most of the sites competently investigated in the northern counties have been proved to be Roman and specifically of second century date. To this time must be assigned the recently excavated example at Milking Gap, Highshield, Northumberland, which together with others in the region flourished under the protection of Hadrian's Wall. Further south the characteristic enclosed village site at Grassington in the West Riding of Yorkshire has been shown to belong to the same period. In North Wales villages and hut-groups of similar type have been proved to date from even later times. Din Lligwy, Anglesey, a polygonal enclosure with two circular and several rectangular structures within, has been dated to the fourth century, while Pant-y-Saer in the same island is not earlier than the sixth century. Yet, late as many of the enclosed hut-groups and villages undoubtedly are, they, like the courtyard house, have their roots in a prehistoric past.

In lowland Britain knowledge of houses contemporary with the stone-built ones of the west and north has to depend on excavation, since being timber-built they leave little or no trace on the surface. At a rule even the spade can do no more than reveal traces in the form of post-holes or drainage trenches. We have little to compare with the crannogs of Ireland and Scotland, or the lake-villages of Switzerland and south Germany. Moreover, the English material is not only scarce, but also disappointing in that only the foundation platforms have been recovered. The most ancient marsh structures yet discovered in England are those near the village of Ulrome in Holderness, a region which in early times was covered by a net-work of lakes. Here at two sites, West Furze and Round Hill, timber and brushwood platforms were found during modern drainage operations, each dating from the Late Bronze Age, with suggestions, especially strong at Round Hill, of an earlier and quite possibly Neolithic stage. Unfortunately there is no definite information about the dwellings themselves. The platforms consisted of about $1^1/_2$ feet of brushwood laid on a foundation of tree-trunks packed with loose twigs. It was observed that the foundations of the upper platforms were more skilfully constructed than the lower ones; instead of being laid promiscuously the trunks were sometimes crossed, and piles were driven in to ensure their stability, the outer ones being inclined at an angle. The Late Bronze Age platform at West Furze measured 50 by 72 feet. It was placed with the long side across the marsh, and from either end there were causeways to the dry land. Sites apparently of the same general type are known from the Vale of Pickering, for example on the banks of the Costa Beck. The few finds suggest that the sites were occupied from some time in the Early Iron Age until about A.D. 70.

The Cambridgeshire and Lincolnshire fens, which might be expected to have produced useful evidence, have in fact proved curiously barren. The meres of East Anglia have been slightly more fruitful. Traces of piles and timber were found in the beds of West and Mickle Meres, Wretham, while the stone and piles which came to light during drainage works at Barton Mere, near Bury St Edmunds, seem to indicate an artificial island or crannog. Several bronze spearheads and rings show that it was occupied during the Late Bronze Age. A comparable but undated structure was found in Llangorse Lake, near Brecon.

Far and away the best explored are the marsh villages of Glastonbury and Meare in Somerset, which between them throw a flood of light upon life in the Early Iron Age. At the present day the Glastonbury village consists of a group of low mounds barely visible above the general level of the marsh, bounded to the east by a natural watercourse known as the 'Old Rhyne', which in early times was a broad sheet of water affording added protection as well as access to the site. The village, which occupied a triangular area some three or four acres in extent, was enclosed by a palisade formed of piles up to 12 feet long, bound together by intertwined timber, brushwood, and hurdle work. Within was a massive substructure varying in character in different parts of the site: its margins were formed of heavy logs laid parallel to the palisade with offsets at right-angles, the interstices being filled with brushwood, peat, and clay; in the interior it was most strongly developed under the actual sites of huts, where it was sometimes three beams thick, each layer being laid at right angles to the last. The foundation

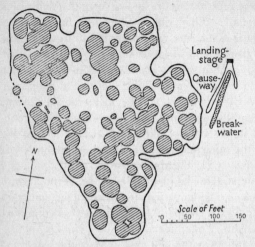

Glastonbury lake-village: general plan

of the village was held together partly by the border palisade, into which new rows of piles had frequently to be driven to replace those pushed outwards by pressure of the huts within, and partly by the mortising of horizontal beams to uprights driven into the underlying peat.

The hut-floors, of which there were at least 61 and possibly 15 more, were circular in plan, ranging from 18 to 28 feet in diameter, with small vestibules projecting from the entrance. An oak door, $3^1/_2$ by $1^1/_2$ feet, found in the peat outside the settlement had pivots cut from the solid and two holes about half-way down near the opposite edge, presumably for a handle or a fastening device. It probably formed half of a double swing door. In some parts of the village individual huts were linked by means of pathways of sandstone rubble. Floors were made of clay paved with split wood flooring-boards from 6 to 8 inches wide, arranged either concentrically or across the hut from side to side. The weight of the huts compressing the underlying marsh frequently made it necessary to throw down fresh layers of clay. Sometimes as many as ten floors accumulated in this way in one hut. To help counteract the tendency for the huts to sink and spread, piles were driven in at the edge in much the same way as they were around the whole settlement. The heaping on of new floors, which was nevertheless necessary, involved the driving of more piles, several concen-

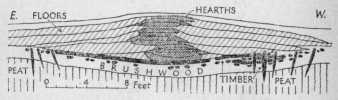

Glastonbury lake-village: hut foundation

tric rows of which were found under some mounds (17). Hearths were of baked clay or occasionally of lias slabs arranged to form a circular paved area. Since they were normally near the centre of the hut they tended to need replacement even more frequently than the floors, as many as thirteen being found superimposed. Dome-shaped clay ovens were also found at Meare. Apart from an occasional central post, which no doubt carried a conical reed-thatched roof, no trace of the super-structure of the huts was recovered. Thus, much as we have learnt of their foundations, we know little of the huts themselves, save that they were circular in plan, with vestibules and conical roofs. Nor unfortunately do we know how many of huts were inhabited at any one time.

For actual plans of the farmsteads occupied by the plough-agriculturalists we have to rely upon the excavation of sites on chalk or gravel, at which little more than arrangements of post-holes can be expected to survive. From a study of these it has been established that the Late Bronze Age farmers lived in family groups with two or three dwelling-houses and a number of ancillary structures for cooking, storage and working, fenced off in compounds and approached through the encompassing Celtic fields by narrow hollow ways. The houses had thatched roofs supported on circular settings of timber uprights and the existence of

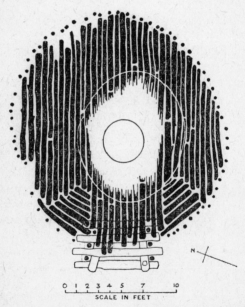

0 1 2 3 4 5 7 10
SCALE IN FEET

Glastonbury lake-village: hut foundation (*cf*. Figure 17)

porches suggests that the walls were low, if indeed the roofs were not in some cases completely conical. Among the best explored farmsteads of this type are those on Itford Hill and Plumpton Plain on the Sussex Downs, but as we know from Shearcliff Hill, Dorset, and from confused traces on Thorney Down, Winterbourne Gunner, they also appeared in Wessex.

It is striking fact and one that underlines continuity with the preceeding phase of British prehistory that the dwelling houses of Early Iron Age Britain seem to have been almost exclusively round or at least curvilinear, even though rectangular houses were normal in those parts of the continent from which our earliest iron technology was derived. Already in the first phase of the Iron Age there was considerable diversity in plan. At Micklemoor Hill, West Harling, Norfolk, one of the two round houses was supported by a simple circular setting of posts, but the larger of the two was apparently penannular in plan, enclosing a circular yard approached by a causeway across the encircling ditch and itself entered by a porch. Simple round huts with porches were found at Staple Howe, Knapton, in the East Riding. At Cow Down, Longbridge Deverill, Wiltshire, on the other hand, a large structure 50 feet in diameter was carried on three concentric rings of posts.

Even more elaborate in construction was the larger of the two houses, some 50 feet across, found during the excavation of a farmstead at Little Woodbury, near Salisbury, belonging to a devolved stage of the A culture and dating from the second phase of the Iron Age. In this case the roof was carried on two concentric rings of posts with, in addition, a square setting of really stout ones in the middle; a well developed porch suggests that the roof sloped down close to the ground.

The size of the house is impressive and raises tantalising

Reconstruction of farmhouse of the first phase of the Early Iron Age, Micklemoor Hill, West Harling, Norfolk

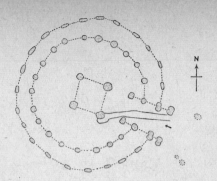

Iron Age farm at Little Woodbury, near Salisbury (*cf*. Figure 8)
(Max. diam. *c*. 50 feet)

questions relating to social organisation. It seems unlikely
that the farm could have been run by one family alone, or
that so large a dwelling would be required, unless servants
or possibly another family shared the accommodation,
though some space would of course have been required for
domestic animals. No sign of a hearth survived, but this
would probably have been within the area defined by the
four central posts. The part between the two rings may well
have been subdivided radially to provide stalls and sleeping
accommodation. Such a house plan has been interpreted
as, in origin, a dwelling house and outbuildings brought
together under one roof. It was noted at Staple Howe and
Cow Down that weaving looms had evidently been set up
in the main house. Remains of clay baking ovens, resembling
more complete ones from the Meare Lake village, and
Maiden Castle, Dorset, remind one of another of the important activities carried on indoors.

The full measure of our ignorance of prehistoric houses
in England is brought home by the reflection that we know
practically nothing of those of Belgic times, the most pros-

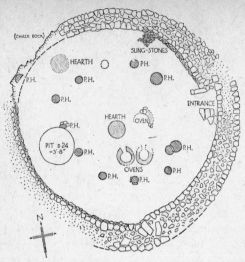

Iron Age hut at Maiden Castle (*c.* 1:130)

perous in our prehistory. The small circular hut with central post at Salmonsbury, Bourton-on-the-Water, recalls most closely those described for the Late Bronze Age in Sussex; and a little round shack was found under the Roman villa at Lockley's, Welwyn.

At Camulodunum (Colchester) and Prae Wood, Verulamium (St Albans), we have dykes and loose finds—at the former even dirty patches which may have marked the sites of dwellings—but of the nature and range of the houses at these capital centres we know nothing. Yet we should learn much if we could but measure the floors of Cunobelin's palace against those of his headmen and his humbler subjects.

4

Handicrafts

PREHISTORIC man was a craftsman who by the work of his hands fashioned his tools and his weapons, his means of transport, his dwellings and his tombs, and all those externals by the study of which archaeologists attempt to reconstruct the social life of the past. In other chapters the products of his hands are considered functionally as they illuminate certain broad aspects of his existence; here an attempt will be made to appraise them as indications of his capabilities as a craftsman.

Many of the handicrafts practised in prehistoric times have survived unchanged or with slight modification down to recent times, a few even to the present day. When one remembers how crafts were transmitted from master to apprentice, often enough from father to son, the survival of methods of construction or of manufacture for centuries, and sometimes millennia, is to be expected: only some drastic break in cultural tradition, like the Industrial Revolution, would be sufficient to disturb relations harmoniously established between men and material through the ages. It is more difficult to appreciate this continuity in England than in most countries because economic change has here been all-pervading; yet a visit to the Bygones Gallery in the National Museum of Wales or to one of our all too rare folk-museums, like those at York and Cambridge, will often help. Many of the exhibits, dating from the days before machine-made objects had displaced the products of village craftsmen to anything like the present extent, might have come from a prehistoric settlement where conditions of preservation had been exceptionally favourable; conversely much of the wood and iron work and baskets from the Glastonbury lake-village could easily have been made a century ago, or even in some cases at the present day. In the more outlying parts of Britain the picture is naturally clearer: indeed, up to a few years ago a traveller in the Hebrides or some of the remoter parts of Ireland could experience conditions approximating broadly to those of the Early Iron Age. He could study at first hand primitive dwellings and a whole series of handicrafts from spinning and weaving to potting and quern-making which archaeologists have laboriously to reconstruct from such evidence as remains.

Bill-hook from Glastonbury lake-village (1:6)

In any review of prehistoric craftsmanship it is inevitable that attention should first be directed to flint which has played a more vital role in the evolution of human culture than any other material available to the archaeologist. Although it is true that its enduring qualities have caused flint to survive where other materials have disappeared and so to bulk unduly large in our picture of early craftsmanship, this fact of itself makes it of unique importance for the deciphering of the earliest chapters of human history. Moreover, the degree to which flint and allied materials combine tractability with toughness made them peculiarly acceptable to early man, while the diversity of forms into which it can be worked and the variety of techniques employed provide at the same time the clues most useful to archaeology. It is not for nothing that we speak of a Stone Age.

The technical possibilities open to a worker in flint are surprisingly numerous. He can vary his angle of flaking, employ different instruments and in all manner of subtle ways control the effect of his blows. Simple flakes with rather deep bulbs could be removed by rounded pebbles or hammerstones impacting at a single point or by bashing the core against a heavy stone anvil. For detaching the shallower flakes needed in making slender hand-axes of smooth outline the Acheulians had already devised the ingenious system of applying indirect force by striking down on a rod held against the point of fracture. Yet a certain roughness of surface is bound to result from even the most skilful flaking, since the intersection of flake-scars is of the essence of the technique. To obtain an absolutely smooth surface it was necessary to grind away the traces of flaking on a stone rubber, a technique which, originally evolved in the working of bone, was first applied to stone by Mesolithic, and to flint by Neolithic, man.

No greater mistake could be made than to suppose that the working of flint was confined to the Stone Age: on the contrary, it reached it apogee during the earlier stages of the Bronze Age, when metal was still too rare to satisfy the demand for more advanced forms, and persisted even when new materials had become more generally available. Quite a distinctive flint industry has been recognised in lowland Britain for the Late Bronze Age and flint-working was still carried on, albeit with greatly reduced standards, during the Early Iron Age. The subsequent survival of the craft was due to properties of flint which in prehistoric times were of secondary importance, namely its ability to produce sparks and its suitability as building material. The Romans certainly dressed flint for buildings, although little is known of its employment for other purposes during the occupation. From Saxon times onwards, however, its use as a component of the strike-a-light is well attested. With the adoption of firearms gun-flint manufactories grew up in most af the cretaceous areas of England. The pedigree of the modern industry may not be as straightforward as some have argued, but in some sense the Brandon knappers must embody a tradition of craftsmanship almost as old as man. Watching them turn out gun-flints for West Africa until a few years back, one could not but be impressed by the speed at which they worked—an average worker would produce from 5,000 to 7,000 flakes and up to 2,500 gun-flints a day—and by the high proportion of waste resulting from their activities. Both are points to be borne in mind when interpreting ancient working floors. Again, let those who marvel at the flaking on, say, the hand axes used by Lower Palaeolithic man, reflect that modern workers can turn them out in a few moments. Prehistoric man must have been every bit as expert.

What has been said about flint applies equally to certain other stones which share its essential properties, such as augite granophyre, sarsen and various kinds of chert. Rocks which could not be flaked had to be pecked into shape and smoothed by grinding. Unlike flint, however, they could be perforated for hafting without undue difficulty. Already in Mesolithic times we find quartzite pebbles perforated by the junction of hollows worked from opposite faces, resulting in holes of 'hour-glass' section. Direct perforation of stone appears to have been introduced to England by Beaker people. During the Early Bronze Age some very shapely axe-hammers were made in southern England. It is quite possible to perforate hard stone by hand, using a solid wooden drill and abrasive sand, but much quicker to employ a tubular drill rotated by a bow. Probably both methods were employed in prehistoric Britain.

The introduction of copper and its alloy, bronze, opened

up new vistas to the prehistoric craftsman. Two main ways of shaping his material were open to him; he could exploit its relative softness by cold hammering, or take advantage of its low melting-point by casting it in moulds. The evolution of casting methods went hand in hand with improvements in form. Flat shapes could be cast in an open mould. More elaborate forms having surface relief required valve moulds composed of two or more parts. Finally, the adoption of the ingenious *cire perdue* process greatly widened the scope of the worker in bronze. The procedure was as follows. The craftsman would begin by making a wax model of the object he desired to make, sometimes by means of a mould. Then, first dipping it in a liquid solution, he would coat it with a stout envelope of plastic clay. Slowly baking this over a fire, he would simultaneously harden the clay and expel the wax, leaving room for the molten metal which could then be poured in and allowed to solidify before being broken out of its mould. By suspending a clay core it was a simple matter to cast sockets or even bronze vessels by this process. The hammering technique was used for beating up flanges on the sides of flat axes and sword hilts, for toughening cutting edges, spreading rivet-heads and flattening and shaping sheet metal, such as was needed for the shields and cauldrons of the Late Bronze Age. The hammer was also used in conjunction with the tracer or chisel-shaped punch to produce 'incised' decoration on metal objects. Repoussé decoration on the other hand, such as can be seen on the Mold cape or the shield from Moel Siabod (23), Caernarvonshire, could be wrought by hammering around pieces of hard wood, bone or metal held inside the sheet.

In working gold the smith took full advantage of the softness of his material. During the earlier part of the Bronze Age ornaments made of gold sheet hammered to the thinness of a visiting card were the vogue, prominent among them being the lunulae and twisted ribbon torcs of the highland zone and the famous gold beaker from Rillaton Manor. The metal was used even more sparingly at this time in Wessex, where it was applied in the form of plating to bone and bronze discs and shale cones and in the form of lozenge and rectangular shaped plaques attached to a backing, probably of wood or leather. The thin gold leaf applied to the wooden bowl from Caergwrle illustrates in its concentric circle ornament the accuracy with which the old goldsmiths were able to use compasses on the soft metal. By the Middle Bronze Age the supply of available gold had increased sufficiently for them to strive for a richer three-dimensional effect by using the metal in bars. Sometimes, as in the plain penannular bracelets with simple or expanded terminals, the appeal of the ornament depended upon its smooth massive appearance. A richer effect was produced by the wreathed torcs of Tara type, like that from Grunty Fen, near Ely, the twisted flanges of which were designed to catch the light. It was at one time supposed that these were fabricated from two, three or four ribbons of gold twisted together and reunited at either end to form the characteristic tapered terminals, but in fact they were produced from a single bar. The smith began by cutting grooves along the whole length stopping short only as he approached the two ends; next he hammered or punched each of the members so defined into a flat flange; then he annealed the whole and twisted it into a screw pattern; finally, he shaped and bent the terminals. Sometimes, however, as in the torc from Yeovil, he cut right through the bar, reducing it to four strips united only by the unworked terminals; after they were flattened the individual flanges were reunited by a gold and copper alloy—the earliest known use of this process in Britain.

During the Early Iron Age and up till Tudor times, when

the blast furnace was introduced, iron was produced exclusively by the primitive bloomery process. The ore, which had to be used in a rich form, was heated on a charcoal fire intensified by bellows. By hammering out the cinder impurities from the resultant mass only small quantities of wrought iron could be produced at a time, but it was ready for immediate hand forging. In working the iron the craftsman went through the two stages of 'mooding' and 'smithing', the former covering the moulding of the heated bar to approximately its desired shape, the latter the drawing and final finishing of the object. It is probable that the iron 'currency-bars' found in the province of the Iron Age B people were primarily sword 'moods', although this by no means precludes their use as currency. The most famous find of such objects was that made in Wayland's Smithy, a megalithic tomb on the Berkshire Downs. The legend, according to which 'a traveller whose horse had cast a shoe on the adjacent Ridgeway had only to leave a groat on the capstone, and return to find his horse shod and the money no longer there', lends colour to the currency theory, though we cannot yet associate the invisible smith with the tomb earlier than the Compton Beauchamp charter of A.D. 955. In the final stage of his work the smith sometimes showed an astonishing mastery of his material. If we look, for instance, at the terminals of the Barton fire-dog, we cannot but marvel at the assurance and withal the economy with which the head was beaten into shape, the eyes and nostrils indicated by a few deft blows. By comparison the Capel Garmon example (20) is commonplace, although not without interest for comparison with modern wrought-iron work.

Potting is another craft which, thanks to the persistence of fired clay, is well represented in the material available to archaeological enquiry. The wide range of possibilities open to the potter makes the choice of particular styles and methods of outstanding significance. It is important, also, to bear in mind that in prehistoric times pottery was essentially a domestic product, which, unlike metal, was rarely traded far afield. Of pottery it can truly be said that it bears the plastic imprint of culture, though its physical composition illustrates that we have also to take account of the influence of locality. Again, the minor differences, revealed by petro-logical examination, between sherds of the same ware from different parts of the country often reflect no more than varying geological endowments; indeed, when checked by examination of natural deposits, it may sometimes allow one to detect importation of raw material or possibly of finished pots.

It is probable that the simpler forms of Neolithic pottery were modelled from a single lump, but some at least of the shouldered bowls were built up from two pieces. The more elaborate coil method by which the pot was built up from the base by the addition of successive rolls of clay, or spirally as in coiled basketry, was practised by the Peterborough people and persisted throughout the Bronze Age in food vessels and native cinerary urns, serving to emphasise their community of tradition. Both the leading Neolithic wares were round-based, flat bases making their first appearance in Clacton ware and Beakers. The device of raising the base of the pot on a hollow foot or pedestal was apparently introduced comparatively early during the prehistoric Iron Age, though it did not become common until spread over the south-eastern counties by the Belgae. The possibilities of rim treatment are too numerous to follow out in detail, but without going into the matter more closely one may say that the prehistoric potter ranged from tapering to flattening, everting, inbending, thickening, rolling and vari-ously moulding the rims of his pots. Spouts, on the other hand, have yet to be found on British prehistoric pottery.

Handles are poorly represented. True handles are confined to the rare class of handled Beaker, to a small series of more or less contemporary cups from Wessex, to biconical cinerary urns dating from various stages of the Cornish Bronze Age and to a few globular vessels of the Late Bronze Age in Sussex. Ledge handles are found on a few Late Bronze Age cinerary urns and on certain Iron Age bowls. The lug is the only common form of handle. In its plain and vertically perforated forms it occurs on Neolithic pots of the Western culture and on Late Bronze Age cinerary urns. Horizontally perforated, it is found on grooved food-vessels, on Cornish cinerary urns, on exotic pottery from Late Bronze Age settlement sites and on certain Early Iron Age vessels.

Among the methods of improving the appearance of her vessels the prehistoric potter resorted to surface slips, burnishing and various kinds of decoration. Apart from the haematite-coated pottery of the Iron Age A people and a single Hallstatt vessel from near Eastbourne, showing concentric black lozenges on a red haematite ground, there is no evidence for the painting of pottery in early Britain. The commonest types of decoration were incision, grooving and scoring with a blunt tool, pricking, surface roughening or rustication, moulding by pinching up, the application of plastic strips and pellets, and finally impression by diverse means, including twisted cord, bird-bones, finely toothed stamps and the human fingertip or nail. Certain incised or impressed decoration, it should be added, was made more prominent by the rubbing in of a white filling. There is little evidence that the colour of the finished pot was deliberately influenced by the final process of firing in the kiln.

The prehistoric potter was often guided by traditions emanating from non-ceramic sources. Thus the simpler rounded bowls of the Neolithic culture are clearly based on leather bags, while the more ambitious carinated bowls look back to the same simple container stiffened by withy hoops inserted at shoulder and lip. Such a derivation is supported by the decoration found on vessels of the Abingdon variety, on which diagonal scoring on rim and shoulder recall the stitching by which the hoops were sewn to the leather and vertical scoring on the neck brings to mind the puckering which would naturally occur where the leather was constricted. The mode of manufacture of Peterborough ware, on the other hand, together with certain elements in its decoration, argue for its derivation from coiled basketry. Wooden vessels were another source of inspiration. The well-known handled Beaker from Bottisham, Cambridgeshire, for instance, is not only 'wooden' in form, but the decoration on its base suggests such growth rings as would be visible on a wooden mug cut from the solid. The shallow tub-like pots from the Caburn and from Glastonbury are likewise influenced by wooden prototypes, such as, indeed, were found on the latter site. During the Early Iron Age the potter was frequently inspired by metal vessels: thus, the angular shouldered pots decorated by finger printing, common during its earlier stages, recapitulate the riveted bronze buckets of Italian origin, which spread over western Europe with the Hallstatt culture; pedestalled La Tène and Belgic pots can be traced to bronze beaked flagons of Graeco-Italian origin, by way of such vessels as those from the Waldalgesheim grave; and bead-rim bowls of the type found at Maiden Castle are almost certainly modelled on bronze bowls like those from Glastonbury and Spettisbury. The appearance of metal was sometimes imitated by surface treatment of pottery; thus, the glow of copper might be rendered by the rich red of haematite paint.

So far we have dealt with materials which have survived in bulk, the flints and stones, metal work and pottery which form, as it were, the bony framework of archaeology. An

14 Windmill Hill, Wiltshire: Neolithic enclosures

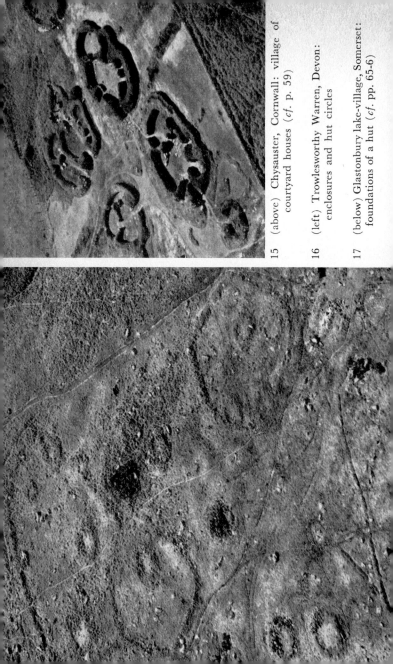

15 (above) Chysauster, Cornwall: village of courtyard houses (*cf.* p. 59)

16 (left) Trowlesworthy Warren, Devon: enclosures and hut circles

17 (below) Glastonbury lake-village, Somerset: foundations of a hut (*cf.* pp. 65-6)

18 Osier basket-work from Glastonbury lake-village

19 Impression of wollen textile on bronze axe

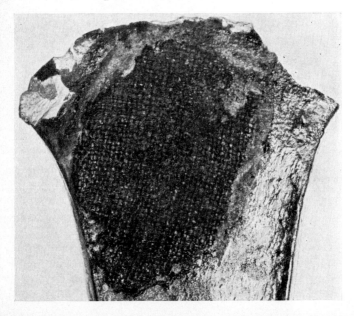

20   Iron fire-dog from Capel Garmon, Denbighshire

21   Bronze tankard from Trawsfynydd, Merioneth

22 Iron Age helmet from the Thames

23 Bronze Age buckler from Moel Siabod, Caernarvonshire

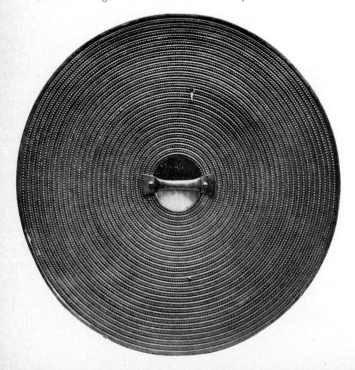

24 Grime's Graves, Norfolk: miners' picks resting against
the flint seam

25 Grime's Graves: flint-mines from the air

26 Hoard of metal scrap from the Late Bronze Age

27 Sterns of dug-out boats, from the Trent of Nottingham

even greater part was played in contemporary life, however, by substances of organic origin, which have seldom come down to us. Of these wood was perhaps the most important. The felling of medium-sized timber such as would be required for house frames or palisades was doubtless accomplished by axes, even polished flint ones having been proved effective by experiment. For the extra large trunks needed for the uprights of 'henge' monuments, dug-out canoes or coffins the process was sometimes assisted by fire. Saws played no material part in prehistoric carpentry. For splitting timber wedges were much used, as indeed they were for hollowing out canoes or coffins: holes would be bored at intervals and the intervening wood splintered off by wedges until the walls were reduced to the right thickness, after which the ends would be dressed smooth by an adze. Before specialised types of metal tools were available the wood worker had to content himself with simple forms —shafts and handles for implements and weapons, bows, shields, paddles, bowls and tubs cut from the solid and the like. The earliest wooden objects turned on a rotary lathe so far discovered in England are the tubs and axle-hubs from Glastonbury and the Belgic bowls from Harpenden. The simple pole lathe surviving in parts of Wales is more likely to be a cheap substitute for than a forebear of the rotating lathe. There is evidence that the device of the

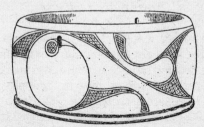

Wooden tub from Glastonbury lake-village (1:6)

tenon and mortise was known already by the Early Bronze Age. Metal gouges and chisels made it possible during the Late Bronze Age to cut grooves into which boards could be inserted with sufficient accuracy to fit canoes with separate stern boards and tubs with separate bases. It was not until the Early Iron Age, however, that it became practicable to build tubs out of staves held together by metal bands; added security was given by dowelling neighbouring staves by wooden pegs. At this time also we have evidence, in the form of oak and ash loom frames from Glastonbury, of the use of heated metal for burning holes in woodwork and tracing simple decorative patterns.

In classical times Britain was famous for her basketry—as witnessed by Juvenal and Martial—but little concrete evidence has survived. The material most commonly used was osier. Substantial portions of wicker baskets interlaced on ribs arranged alternately in pairs and triplets were recovered from the Glastonbury lake-village (18), in the neighbourhood of which osier baskets are still plaited. Wicker-work must have been used for many purposes, including the sides of carts and wagons, the framework of coracles, fish traps, frames for leather shields and panniers for pack horses. A similar method of plaiting applied to split saplings was used for the hurdling required for the walling of pens and houses and the revetting of earthen banks. Fine baskets were made from hair-moss (*Polytrichum commune*). An unfinished specimen was recovered from the ditch of the older Roman fort at Newstead (*c*. A.D. 80), but was almost certainly native work. The collections at Kew include a basket from Northumberland, brooms from Sussex and Westmorland and a hassock from Yorkshire, as modern examples of similar work. Pieces of charred plaited material from an Iron Age store pit at Worlebury may come from a coiled basket. Vegetable fibres of different kinds, twisted into string, were used for lines, nets, snares and for all manner of purposes. Although little in the way of actual string or cord has come down to us, we are constantly reminded of its importance to the men of the time by the frequency with which it was used for impressing decorative patterns on Bronze Age pottery. One of the few recorded finds was that made under Silbury Hill by Dean Merewether, who speaks of 'fragments of a sort of string of two strands, each twisted, composed of (as it seemed) grass, and about the size of whipcord'. Excavating a Bronze Age round barrow at Garton Hall in the East Riding, Mortimer found 'fragments of string or fine rope, a little thicker than coarse worsted, made of two strands, each being of a fine fibre resembling flax, and well twisted' under a woman's skull—probably the remains of a hair-cord.

Animal products provided another rich source of raw material for the craftsman. Bone was worked into buttons and toggles, combs, needles, potters' tools and hilt-plates. Antlers, cut short and with all but the brow tine removed, served as quarrying implements, roots were mounted as hammer-heads, and tines blunted and perforated, made excellent cheek-pieces for bridles. Horn must have been used for many purposes; a ladle of this material, for instance, was found in a Beaker at Broomend, Aberdeenshire. The bark vessel from an Early Bronze Age oak coffin burial at Gristhorpe, Yorkshire, described as 'curiously stitched with the sinews of animals', illustrates the use of a product which must also have been required for stringing bows. The importance of animal skin is emphasised by the ubiquity and abundance of the flint scraper, though the only direct evidence for its use comes from burials like that at Gristhorpe in which it was wrapped round the body. Leather objects found in neighbouring countries make it likely that the same material was employed here for scabbards and sheaths, shoes, shields, pouches, harness and all kinds of belts and straps. Hides, of course, were one of Britain's staple exports to the Roman world before the conquest.

Weaving must have been one of the leading handicrafts in prehistoric Britain, but it has left few traces. Indirect evidence in the form of spindle-whorls and loom-weights—the latter not easily distinguished from thatch-weights—is common for the Early Iron Age and at Late Bronze Age sites like Park Brow and Plumpton Plain, Sussex. Weaving combs, which have by some been alternatively interpreted as implements for removing hairs from skins, are a common feature of the Early Iron Age. As it happens nearly all traces of the textiles themselves come from the Bronze Age and most of these from the earlier phase during which inhumation was the rule. The excavators of a round barrow at Rylston, Yorkshire, found the body in a hollowed tree-trunk enveloped from head to foot in a woven fabric. Other finds from the same period make it likely that the dead were buried fully clothed, as we know they were in the famous oak coffin burials from Denmark where the garments are almost perfectly preserved. Carbonised traces from among the ashes of cremated burials of a later phase of the Bronze Age suggest that corpses were burnt while still clothed. Again, when bronze or copper axes and daggers placed with the dead were wrapped in textiles, as they often seem to have been, the threads may survive in fossil from, having been replaced by metal oxide (19). Several examples of this are known from burials of the Wessex Early Bronze Age, for instance from the Normanton Bush and Lambourne barrows. In every case where the threads can be tested the Bronze Age textiles have proved to be of wool, though there are some indications that linen may have been used. During the Early Bronze Age the thread was fine, ranging from 20 to more than 40 to an inch, and the weave was invariably plain or tabby. Twill weave seems first to have appeared in the British Isles during the Late Bronze Age and our only example comes from Island MacHugh, Co. Tyrone. The indications are that upright looms were in use, certainly from the Late Bronze Age, and these seem to have been set up in the dwelling houses.

One of the attractive features of prehistoric archaeology is that one is concerned all the time with products of individual craftsmen. It is true that the metal-worker, wood-carver, or potter, conformed to prevailing styles and largely inherited his techniques; yet, even so, one can sense individual creative energy as one handles objects made from first to last by particular men. Artefacts were shaped to meet definite needs, but it would be wrong to imagine that even during prehistoric times these were only material. Social emulation, religious feeling and aesthetic satisfaction were each, and often in combination, of decisive importance. Even when objects were intended strictly for use they might be finished to a point beyond, and sometimes far beyond, what was strictly necessary. This applies even to such a primitive tool as a hand-axe. Refinement of form made, it is true, for economy of material and greater ease in use. Yet the craftsmen who made some of the finest Acheulian hand-

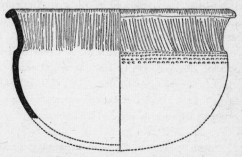

Bowl of Mildenhall ware from Hurst Fen (1:6)

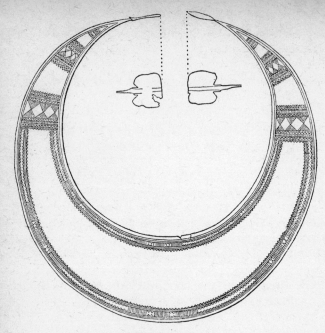

Gold lunula (1:3)

axes were surely moved by feelings akin in some measure to that of the artist; they rejoiced in their mastery over flint and in their ability to produce forms which still delight the eye of the connoisseur.

In marked contrast to the hunting peoples of the Late-glacial period, whose traces in Britain are so sadly meagre, but who in France and Spain decorated the walls and ceilings of caves and rock-shelters with representations of such passing realism, the simple pastoral farmers of the Neolithic and Bronze Ages practised an art of geometrical ornamentation or, in the sphere of cults, of schematic or symbolic representation. In ornamenting artefacts, whether metal

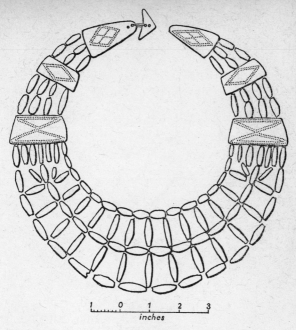

Jet necklace

objects or pots, men and women alike drew upon a comparatively simple stock of patterns—herring-bones, zig-zags, chevrons, triangles, lozenges, saltires and the like—varying only in emphasis and combination according to cultural and regional groupings. An interesting commentary on the poverty of invention of this art lies in the tendency to skeuomorphism, the recapitulation in ornament of the appearance of objects made in different materials. We can see this for instance in the way the makers of Abingdon and Mildenhall pottery suggested by the nature and disposition of its ornament the puckering and sewing of leather prototypes; or, again, in the scoring on gold lunulae, flat moon-shaped

Engraving of spiral and schematic figure, Barclodiod
passage grave (1:10)

neck-ornaments, of patterns reminiscent of the spacer-plates used to keep apart the strands of multiple crescentic necklaces of amber or jet during the Early Bronze Age.

Among cult representations pride of place goes to those pecked on stones forming part of megalithic passage-graves. Although this art focusses in the British Isles mainly on eastern Ireland and specifically on county Meath, there are interesting examples almost due opposite on Anglesey and the Mersey estuary. Both the main elements of the passage-grave art, namely the schematised human figure and the spiral, occur this side of the Irish sea, the former at Bryn Celli Ddu and Barclodiod, and the latter at the last-mentioned and on what must be remnants of another megalithic tomb, the Calderstones at Liverpool. The Calderstones also bear traces of a second group, comprising human feet and weapons, examples of which recur over a wide extent of England in an Early Bronze Age setting. A human foot recurs on the inner face of a stone cist at Harbottle Peels, Northumberland, and no less than six are present, this time with a number of cup-marks, rounded depressions an inch or two in diameter and sunk a fifth of an inch or so in the rock surface, on a slab from West Harptree on Mendip. The weapon shown on one of the Calderstones was a halberd. Daggers and axes, connected possibly with thunder-worship, are depicted on a stone in a round barrow at Badbury, Dorset, and on sarsen uprights at Stonehenge.

A radical change came with the introduction during the Early Iron Age of La Tène art. Now we find ourselves in the presence of an art produced by full-time craftsmen working to embellish the persons and enrich the favoured possessions of a small class of warrior chieftains and their women. In its continental homeland the art arose from the impact of Classical Greek motives, mainly through the medium of vessels associated with winedrinking, on the vigorous barbarian genius of Celtic-speaking people, whose craftsmen responded by creating a style that holds a secure place in the history of decorative art. Although only introduced here in its mature form during the third century B.C., La Tène art as practised in Britain during the last two or three centuries of our prehistory was far indeed from being purely derivative. Few examples of British La Tène art could be mistaken for continental productions. And in a number of fields, for instance in the style of decorating the backs of mirrors and in the development of enamel-work, British artificers made signal contributions. Insularity is of course a general explanation for divergence, but the vitality may stem in part from the school of metal-working, testified to by early La Tène daggers from the Thames as having been established west of London as early as the fifth century B.C.

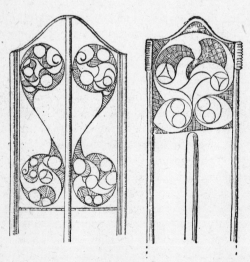

La Tène sword-scabbards from Hunsbury (*left*) and Meare (1:2)

It is only by handling their products that one is able fully to appreciate the skill of the metal-smiths in rendering designs so tenuous and yet overall so firm. They achieved their effects partly by hammering or casting to obtain relief, partly by incision with chasing for contrast, and partly by the use of colour. This latter was first obtained on the continent by the use of Mediterranean coral, a technique exemplified from Britain by, among other pieces, a fine engraved brooch from Newnham Croft, Cambridge. Coral was in due course replaced by red enamel. At first this was applied to roughened surfaces, but in order to cover more extensive areas it was necessary to cut into the surface more deeply to give a greater purchase to the enamel. The *champlevé* process, in which the British craftsmen excelled, is well exemplified by the harness-mounts from Santon Downham, Suffolk, one of which is reproduced on the cover of this book.

In its essence La Tène art was non-representational. Naturalistic elements from Greek art, notably the palmette, were transmuted into magical patterns of curves and scrolls.

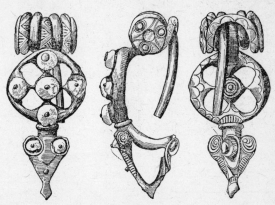

La Tène brooch with coral studs, Newnham, Cambridge (1:1)

Such may be seen on plastic renderings like those on the Witham shield and the Trawsfynydd tankard sword-mount (21), the horned helmet from the Thames at Waterloo Bridge (22), or the gold bracelet and torc from Snettisham (hoard E) (35) or, incised on scabbard mounts **or**, more flamboyantly, on the backs of bronze mirrors dating from the last quarter of the first century B.C and the opening half of the first century A.D. It was only during the final phase of the prehistoric Iron Age, at a time when the Birdlip and

Engraved mirror from Colchester (1:3)

Desborough mirrors were receiving their voluptuous roundels and scrolls, that the artists of Belgic Britain were influenced and to some degree corrupted by the crude naturalism of Roman art. Yet even so there is still some Celtic feeling in the bronze boars from Hounslow, the fish-head spout from Felmersham or the ox-head terminals of fire-dogs like those from Capel Garmon (20) or Lord's Bridge, Barton. The probability is that the White Horse of Uffington, stylised but still recognisably equine, was first cut into the chalk slope that overlooks the Vale of that name at this time. This noble animal, it is well to remember, can only have survived through frequent scouring of the chalk, a very symbol of continuity between the prehistoric past and the present day.

5

Mining and Trade

BROADLY speaking, there were two important differences between the organic and the mineral materials of which early man availed himself. Whereas the former could be obtained locally in the normal course of farming or food-gathering, the latter had often to be mined or quarried, and, being of more restricted occurrence, had to a greater extent to be diffused by trade. The degree to which mining and trade were able to develop were themselves conditioned to some extent by the general economic level. Thus we can trace two distinct stages in the relation of Stone Age man to his principal raw material. When as a food-gatherer he moved about in small groups in pursuit of fish, game, roots and berries and other natural produce, he collected his flint in the same way, here gathering it from surface spreads left behind by eroded chalk or boulder-clay, there utilising nodules taken from an old river gravel; where no other source of supply was available he searched the beach for likely pebbles, as we have all done at the seaside.

Neolithic man on the other hand, used to raising a large proportion of his food by his own efforts, was fully capable of undertaking the disciplined work of mining necessary to assure himself of a supply of flint direct from the chalk, its primary source. Mined flint had many advantages. It occurred in larger pieces than beach pebbles and most gravels, and was free from the flaws acquired by nodules in their manifold adventures since leaving the parent chalk. For many purposes derived flint was adequate, but for the blades of the axes and adzes used in felling and dressing timber, a task of immense importance among primitive communities, the extra toughness of the mined material was highly valued.

Certainly early man found it worth while to acquire mined flint, because we find traces of his burrowings as far apart as Portugal, Sicily, South Sweden, Denmark and Poland, not to mention regions outside Europe. Nowhere in our continent do the mines cluster more thickly than on the chalk of northern France, of Belgium between Mons and Liège and of southern England. Those at Weeting, Norfolk, which pass under the rather sinister name Grime's Graves, were among the first to be explored and have received more attention than any others in England. Sussex can boast four mining sites tested by excavation, the famous ones enclosed by the ramparts of the great Iron Age hill-fort of Cissbury, on the downs above Worthing, Harrow Hill and Blackpatch a few miles to the west, and Stoke Down behind Chichester. The mines on Easton Down, near Salisbury, are the only ones yet investigated in Wessex. North of the Thames flint-mines are so far unknown apart from Grime's Graves and other Norfolk examples.

Making allowance for their meagre equipment our Neo-lithic forbears solved with remarkable success the eternal problem of mining—how to obtain the best return for the smallest outlay compatible with a reasonable degree of safety. They adapted their methods skilfully to suit local conditions. Thus, where, as at Peppard, Oxfordshire, the flint seam they wished to exploit outcropped or came very close to the surface, they extracted it by open workings. Where it occurred at a certain depth they tapped it by means of shafts undercut at the base. Only when the depth of the shaft involved a substantial amount of dead work did they find it necessary to drive radiating galleries and so compensate by extracting a larger quantity of flint. Working such galleries must have been dangerous, as the discovery of a miner's skeleton crushed with antler pick in hand at the Belgian site of Obourg illustrates, but on the whole we can admire the judgment of the old miners who were generally careful to leave sufficient chalk intact to ensure their safety.

From the surface it is impossible to obtain any idea of what the mines were like. At most they reveal themselves as hollows caused by the gradual settlement of their infilling (25). The shallow ungalleried shafts are frequently quite invisible. To explore a galleried mine cleared of its rubble infilling, as one can do at Grime's Graves, is an unforgettable experience. Descending the shaft, one cannot but be struck by the assurance of the miners who dug through 10 feet of sand and boulder-clay and quarried 20 feet of chalk, including two layers of inferior flint, the 'topstone' and 'wallstone', before reaching the coveted 'floorstone'. When one remembers that this shaft is one of several hundred at this single site and that for acres the chalk has been honeycombed by a network of galleries, one begins to understand how attractive must have been the flint and how well organised the miners.

All this is the more remarkable for the poverty of their equipment. The actual work of quarrying was mainly done by means of red deer antlers with beams cut short and all but the brow tine removed. Such implements, although usually described as 'picks', would hardly have been effective wielded in the way suggested by this term. It is much more likely that they were held in the left hand, the right being used to hammer behind the brow tine, the tip of which was applied to a line of weakness in the chalk. Holes of the kind which this would make, if for some reason the operation was not carried to its conclusion, were observed at Blackpatch and Harrow Hill, while a high proportion of the antlers from Grime's Graves were battered on the beam immediately behind the brow tine, which itself was

GRIME'S GRAVES

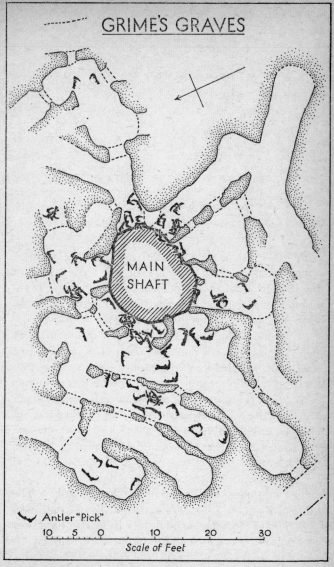

⌄ Antler "Pick"

10 5 0   10   20   30

Scale of Feet

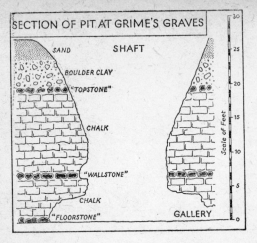

SECTION OF PIT AT GRIME'S GRAVES

SHAFT

SAND

BOULDER CLAY

"TOPSTONE"

CHALK

"WALLSTONE"

CHALK

"FLOORSTONE"

GALLERY

Scale of Feet

usually broken short or at least showed signs of wear. A flashlight photograph of antlers as they lay against the flint seam (24) in a gallery abandoned for 4,000 years, and a close-up of finger-prints impressed on the chalk caked on one of the handles, bring us close to those in whose hand they were once held. Some of the hardest quarrying work at Grime's Graves was done by tough stone axes. Loose material was handled by shovels, sometimes provided with blades formed of ox scapulae, sometimes no doubt entirely of wood. The volume of material removed from the deeper shafts at Grime's Graves must have been considerable: of the three cleared the depth ranged from 30 to 40 feet and the diameter at the mouth from 28 to 42 feet. Spoil from the subterranean workings was mostly dumped in disused galleries, so as to avoid unnecessary labour. Both rubble and flint must have been hauled up the shaft in baskets. The chafing of ropes or thongs was noticed above the entrances to galleries at Grimes Graves and the joist marks of a timber cross-beam were seen at the head of one shaft. The miners themselves doubtless climbed in or out by means of ladders or notched timbers, no chalk-cut steps having been observed in the English galleried mines. One fact borne in upon anyone who wriggles along the ancient galleries to-day with a torch and (if he is wise) with a spare candle and matches is that the miners must have required artifical light for their work. Actually they used open lamps, generally of chalk, but sometimes of pottery, in which a wick doubtless floated on animal fat. They were certainly smoky, because at Harrow Hill original soot-marks were found over gallery entrances.

How the mining was organised we have little information, but it is probable that the miners concentrated on one shaft at a time, exhausted it and then refilled it with the rubble excavated from the next. This explains how fresh and un-weathered even the entrances to the galleries appeared to their modern explorers. Graffiti scratched on the chalk walls of galleries at Grime's Graves and Harrow Hill may have been tallies for reckoning loads, but how many men were necessary to operate a mine and how the work was regulated we do not know.

Everything we have learnt goes to show that the miners were expert at their work. It seems, therefore, more than likely that we can envisage communities of miners, supplying flint to a large surrounding area. The existence around the shaft heads of heaps of waste flakes and axes broken in the making suggests that, besides actually extracting the flint, the miners roughed out the forms of implements, although the polishing process seems to have been carried out else-where. This is quite what one might have expected, since flint is a weighty substance, the proportion of waste is high and means of transport in Neolithic Britain were exiguous. How far and by what means the flint was traded we do not know, but it is evident that mining sites were focal points to which different groups were in the habit of repairing. Among the pottery recovered from Grime's Graves both the leading Neolithic wares are represented, and what is more interesting some of the sherds show evidence of hybridisation.

For some purposes Neolithic man preferred materials other than flint for his axes, even in the siliceous areas of southern England; elsewhere he was constrained to use them in the absence of flint of sufficient size. Since most of the older rocks were too tough for flaking, they were sought in the convenient form of pebbles or small pieces detached by glacial action or normal weathering. Thus we find neither mines nor open quarries for obtaining such materials. On the other hand close-grained rocks suitable for flaking were commonly obtained in the form of scree on mountain slopes as on the high crags of Graig Llwyd, Penmaenmawr, or on Great Langdale in the Lake District; occasionally, as at Mynydd Rhiw in Caernarvonshire, localised seams might even be quarried by opencast workings. Other important factories were in the north of Ireland at Tievebulliagh and Rathlin Island, Antrim, and at various localities in Cornwall, since submerged by the sea. The extent of the stone axe trade has been proved by systematic comparison of samples from stone axes all over the country with those from the source areas. The great concentration of axes made from exotic rocks on Salisbury Plain drawn from many remote areas, emphasises the importance of this region in the life of prehistoric Britain during the third and early second millennia B.C. On the other hand it is no less striking to find axes from Antrim in Kent and on the Dorset coast or from North Wales in Lothian or East Anglia. Precisely how the trade was organised we do not know. The extreme variety of polished axes at the quarries suggests that this finishing process was carried out elsewhere. It is possible that, as among native tribes in central Australia, parties visited the sites to replenish their supplies each season, either quarrying the rock themselves or obtaining axes from the owner of the quarry. On the other hand it seems inconceivable that we can account for the widespread nature of the distribution in such terms. Presumably axes passed through several hands before finishing up at their final destination.

The coming of metallurgy to Britain early in the second millennium B.C. created new demands, even though at first the competition of metal led flint-workers to exert themselves as never before. Thus the demand for the finest flint axe-blades stimulated flint-mining which reached its peak around 2000–1800 B.C.; and the flint daggers used by the Necked Beaker people were the finest artefacts ever made from this material in Britain. Even so the future lay with metal and, primarily, with copper.

We have no counterpart in Britain to the elaborate copper mines of the Tyrol and it must be assumed that the ores were won by open cast workings. Study of the trace elements in the earliest copper objects from southern Britain suggests that the first native sources exploited were those of Ireland. It seems likely that sulphide ores were worked and that these were obtained as much as possible from zones where they had been enriched by the deposition of copper and other minerals from the oxidized zones. Quite a complex series of operations was needed to win the copper. After extracting the ore the next process was to concentrate it, removing as much as possible of the sulphur. The concentrated ore was next roasted in heaps, care being paid to keeping the temperature fairly low and ensuring an even distribution of air. The roasted ores were then smelted and this process had often to be repeated with intervening roastings in order to separate the iron. It is possible that further refining took place while the metal was being resmelted in the crucible in preparation for casting, since impurities would oxidize during exposure to blast and could then be removed as scum. Before, therefore, the smith could get to work on his metal this had to be won from the ore by a series of long and complex processes, to which others were added when he required alloys for more complicated castings. One of the most important alloys of bronze was of course tin. The only certain native source in the British Isles was Cornwall, from which the metal was also almost certainly exported to the Continent. The activities of the ancient Cornish tinners have therefore more than ordinary interest. Prior to the middle of the fifteenth century, when shaft-mining became common in the county, the ore was obtained either by 'streaming' or by burrowing in the face of cliffs. Whether prehistoric man practised the last method we may never know, because the sea must have eroded most of the evidence. In any case we may be certain that he obtained the bulk of it from tin streams fanning out from parent lodes higher up the hillside. Sometimes these are found 30 or 40 feet below ground surface, but it can be taken for granted that the early tinners worked those most easily accessible. They must have set about their work in much the same way as their successors of historical times. Clearing away the overlying soil they would shovel some of the tin 'bed' into a sloping wooden waterway or 'tye'; then by vigorous stirring they eliminated the lighter waste, leaving as residue the heavier ore in the form of sand and lumps of tin-stone. The former was ready for smelting, but the latter had to be crushed, the smaller pieces ground like grain in a quern, the larger broken by hand on rocks, which thereby acquired cup-like hollows.

There appear to have been two phases of main intensity in the exploitation of Cornish tin, an earlier at the dawn of the Bronze Age, and a later dating from its close and from the Early Iron Age, the evidence for the latter of which is the more conclusive. At first the chief centre of metallurgy in the British Isles was in Ireland, which owing to its wealth in alluvial gold stood temporarily in the van-guard of civilization in north-western Europe. Yet, although well supplied with copper, Ireland had to import all her requirements of tin, most of which must have come from Cornwall. In return the Cornish seem to have acquired some of the Irish gold export; the graceful handled beaker from Rillaton was doubtless made of gold washed from Irish stream-beds, while the two crescentic gold neck-ornaments (lunulae) from Harlyn were almost certainly imported from Ireland in finished condition. Most of the gold found in prehistoric ornaments in Britain was washed from Irish and Scottish streams. Although a nugget of 22 oz. was found in Co. Wicklow as late as 1795, no more than £ 30,000 worth of the metal was obtained during the follow-ing 70-80 years, showing that the alluvial deposits were well-nigh exhausted.

With the development of a vigorous native bronze in-dustry in England, the home demand for tin must greatly have increased. On the other hand, the evidence for Cor-nish tinning at this period is slender, and it looks very much as though Brittany was an alternative source of supply. There is evidence that by the end of the Early Bronze Age the tin trade was in the hands of intermediaries who found it as easy to supply Wessex from Brittany as from Cornwall. An intriguing element in the problem is the presence in no less than 36 Wessex graves of blue faience beads of seg-mented form, the affinities of which are unambiguously Egyptian. A closely similar type of bead was found in a tomb at Abydos dated by a scarab of Amenhotep III (1412-1376 B.C.). More decisively, spectrographic analysis of

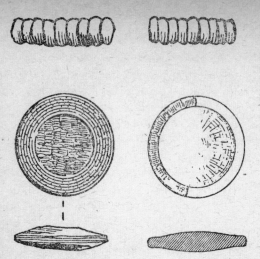

Wessex links with the Mediterranean (1:1). *Above:* Segmented faience beads from Wilsford, Wiltshire, and Tell el Amarna, Egypt. *Below:* Gold bound amber discs from Manton, Wiltshire, and Isopata, Crete

beads from Wiltshire and from Tell el Amarna (1380-50) has recently demonstrated their virtual identity in composition. The pattern of distribution of such beads in Central Europe and the Mediterranean suggests that they were traded by the Mycenaeans in return for the tin they so badly needed to feed their bronze industry. It is interesting to recall that the old antiquary, Colt Hoare, recorded a segmented bead from a disc-barrow at Sutton Veny, Wiltshire, which, while resembling the faience ones in form, was made of tin. Even more suggestive is a necklace from Odoorn in the Dutch province of Drenthe, comprising four segmented beads of faience and no less than twenty-five of tin, as well as a number of perforated amber lumps of varying shapes and sizes. We can only speculate whether the

104

tin in the Sutton Veny and Odoorn beads came from Cornwall or Brittany, but it is worth noting that both these tin-producing regions have yielded segmented beads of faience.

The Odoorn necklace introduces another substance widely traded in prehistoric Europe. A certain amount of amber is to be found on the shore of East Anglia to-day, but there is no evidence that it was exploited in ancient times. The amber lumps used for beads and handled cups in Early Bronze Age Britain were almost certainly imported from the west coast of Jutland. The bulk was attracted to Wessex, where it occurred in as many as fourteen of the graves containing faience beads. The close similarity between a gold-bound amber disc from a Wessex barrow at Manton, Wiltshire, and one from the Tomb of the Double Axes at Isopata, Crete, provides an interesting parallel between objects from either extremity of the old amber routes. The Odoorn necklace suggests that the amber was paid for by exports of tin, which went to supplement the Danish supplies, principally drawn from Bohemia, likewise in return for amber.

The importance of trade within Britain itself may be gauged from the fact that all the copper used in the developing metallurgical industries of the Middle and Late Bronze Ages must ultimately have been won from the highland zone, to which the ores are restricted. The extent to which metal was traded in the form of refined ores, metal ingots or finished artefacts and the way in which this trade was organised are topics of vital import to an understanding of the Bronze Age, about which as yet too little is known. Streamed tin could have been traded in leather bags, but it can be assumed that it would have been too wasteful, conditions of transport being what they were, to transport copper ore. One may therefore take it that the metal was traded either in the form of ingots or worked up into tools or weapons. Certainly many bronze artefacts used in lowland Britain were made in the highland zone and notably in Ireland, but even in the Middle Bronze Age we find regional styles of common bronze tools in southern England —for instance low-flanged palstaves in the east and south-east and others with strongly developed ones in Dorset, Devon and Somerset. Again, by the Late Bronze Age the amount of metal in use provided in itself a source for smiths, as we see from the founders' hoards of the period, comprising worn-out objects and cakes of metal resulting from their melting down. These founders' hoards (26) remind us that bronze was highly valuable, an alloy of substances that had often to be secured from distant sources by means of trade. From the same period we have a number of hoards of new bronzes, which many people interpret as the goods of travelling salesmen. Like the founders' hoards these merchants' hoards must have been extremely valuable and they were presumably buried in the ground during periods of insecurity.

With the immigration of iron-using peoples the exploitation of our native deposits of iron ore must shortly have begun. Knowledge of the earlier stages is still very incomplete, but by Belgic times there is plenty of evidence that Wealden iron was worked: among the miners' camps investigated may be mentioned Saxonbury, near Frant, Castle Hill, Tonbridge and the one in Piper's Copse, near Kirdford, Sussex. The fact that Caesar alluded to Wealden iron in 55 B.C. suggests that its exploitation may have been earlier than is proved by existing evidence. The vast quantities of slag available to the Romans when road making in this area at the close of the first century A.D. also argue in favour of a considerable antiquity for the industry. Incidentally, it has been recorded of one of these iron roads that when struck by lightning its course was plainly revealed by a track of blasted corn; in recent years they have largely been traced by air photography. That the qualities of Northampton ironstone were appreciated in early times is shown by the discovery of quantities of slag at the famous hill-fort of Hunsbury, when it was gutted by modern ironstone workings in the latter part of the nineteenth century. It is probable also that the iron ore of the Forest of Dean was exploited in the Early Iron Age, although positive proof is not yet available.

Another mineral exploited in prehistoric Britain was lead. Although the mines of Mendip were not worked on a substantial scale until the coming of the Romans, the alacrity with which they undertook operations, proved by the discovery of a lead pig dating from the year 49, points to some native activity before the Conquest. Such, indeed, is hinted at by Strabo's inclusion of silver as a British export and proved by the occurrence of lead rings and net weights at the Glastonbury lake-village, as well as by the finds at Hunsbury and the Caburn. The Hunsbury lead must have been traded from the south-west by way of the forest-free Jurassic zone, a principal highway of prehistoric Britain.

The adoption of iron by no means lessened the use of bronze and the consequent demand for tin, both for home consumption and for export. Indeed, it is for the later stages of the Bronze Age and for the Early Iron Age itself that the evidence for prehistoric tinning is most conclusive. In addition to the indirect evidence of ancient objects incorporated in tin streams and of imported objects concentrated in the most important tin working areas, we have proof positive in the form of ancient smelting furnaces and tin slag, such as were found in Chûn Castle, Penwith, and in the tin coinage minted during the opening decades of the first century B.C. in south-eastern England. Even more enlightening as regards trade are references in Greek and Latin authors. Disregarding the rather dubious hints of earlier voyages, that of the Greek scientist Pytheas, undertaken in 325 B.C., is the earliest recorded. The following description of tin streaming given us by the Sicilian writer Diodorus was almost certainly based on information ultimately derived from this traveller: 'the inhabitants of that part of Britain which is called Belerion (Land's End) ... prepare the tin, working very carefully the earth in which it is produced. The ground is rocky, but it contains earthy veins, the produce of which is ground down, smelted and purified.' The finished product, which, Diodorus tells us, was beaten into an astragalus form, was traded by way of Corbilo at the mouth of the Loire and the Garonne Valley to Narbonne and Marseilles. The 'certain island lying off Britain called Ictis' referred to by Diodorus is generally identified with St Michael's Mount. At low tide the island is connected with the mainland by a narrow isthmus, conforming to his statement that 'during the ebb of the tide the intervening space is left dry, and they carry over the tin in abundance in their wagons'. As one contemplates the Mount at low water it is good to think of the wagons jolting across with their precious freight to the harbour, there to be bought by foreign merchants for shipment to the Mediterranean and the Classical World.

In view of this flourishing trade it might have been expected that Cornwall would have been richer than it was in prehistoric times. Yet, even for the period when we know that intimate trade relations were maintained with centres as far afield as Marseilles, there is no evidence of any special wealth among the tinners. A few coins, some Mediterranean pottery, including wine jars from Chûn Castle, and possibly some Greek vases exhaust the list of imports from the ancient world. A number of finds of objects of Irish gold emphasise that, as earlier, Cornish tin was traded north as well as south. The Cornish tinners produced a relatively scarce but highly essential metal, yet show few signs of material wealth. But this is the common fate of primary producers, and never more so than when widely separated in civilization from the purchasers of their product. It may be true that, as Diodorus phrased it, the inhabitants of Land's End were 'very fond of strangers, and from their intercourse with foreign merchants ... civilized in their manner of life', but when it came to business the Cornish tinners must have cut poor figures by the side of the wily Greek. One must also realise that under primitive conditions the infertile region of Penwith could hardly have raised sufficient food for a numerous population of miners; the tinners must, therefore, have spent a large proportion of their income on purchasing such necessities as food and clothing. Then, again, the process by which the metal was extracted was not one to give rise to marked grades of society. Streaming required but little capital and could be carried on by small parties. The social basis for a luxury trade in the form of a wealthy upper class was, therefore, absent at any rate among the native tinners themselves.

In Britain as a whole we find no marked increase in trade until the coming of the Belgae brought south-eastern Britain within the economic orbit of the Roman province of Gaul. During the earlier centuries of the Iron Age imports were mainly confined to manufactured objects of metal, like the bronze cordoned bucket of North Italian origin from Weybridge, Surrey. Although some of our exports, notably tin and gold, were highly valuable, their bulk was small.

The great development of commerce during the century prior to the Claudian Conquest was due in large measure to Caesar's subjugation of Gaul, by which Britain became an immediate neighbour of the Roman world. This both increased the demand for the primary products which Britain was able to export and stimulated the flow of imports from the Continent. Enlargement of the Gaulish export trade was viewed with favour by the Romans because it enhanced the revenues of the province through increased dues from customs. There is little doubt, also that trade with Britain was cultivated as conscious 'Romanising', by means of which the native independence of the Britons was undermined. The growing economic wealth of south-eastern England, following upon the introduction of more advanced agricultural methods, tended to increase the surplus for export and at the same time fostered the rise of princely families able to indulge their taste for exotic imports.

Among the leading exports from Belgic Britain were minerals such as gold, tin, iron and silver and agricultural products, notably corn, cattle and hides. Organised trade in manufactured exports can hardly have played an important part at this time, though a decorated mirror and some enamelled fibulae certainly reached Holland. The discovery of individual pieces as far afield as the Fayûm, Egypt, confirms that British enamel work was appreciated in the Roman world, but these were probably soldiers' mementoes reminiscent of the brasswork brought home from India in our own day. Not the least important of our exports at this time was slaves. Tall fair young Britons enjoyed high favour in Rome and were sent to market on slave chains. A number of these have survived, notably a fine example 12 feet long and having six collars from Lord's Bridge, Barton, Cambridgeshire (30). The presence of an incomplete gang-chain of closely similar type in the great find of metal objects from Llyn Cerrig Bach, Anglesey, close to Holyhead, suggests that Ireland may have been one source of victims. Perhaps East Anglian blonds were for export only and Irishmen were imported to fill their places. An alternative theory is that the Anglesey Druids either ran out of Welshmen or found Irish imports cheaper for ceremonial slaughter. If this is felt to be unduly gruesome, let it be remembered that less than two hundred years ago European princes were glad to sell tall grenadiers for ready cash.

In return we received oil and wine and a variety of manufactured articles. Great amphorae, in which the oil and wine were once contained, were found with the well-known burials at Welwyn, Stanfordbury, Snailwell and Mount Bures, as well as loose at many sites in south-eastern England. It is impressive to think of these bulky containers with their not inconsiderable content being transported all the way from Marseilles, up the Rhone valley, across central France to the Channel ports and so by ship to Britain. The nature of the manufactured articles imported also bears witness to a very great increase in the physical volume of trade, as compared with any previous period. Luxury objects like the elaborately decorated pots fired in the kilns of Arezzo in Italy, from Barrington and Foxton, Cambridgeshire, or the silver cups and bronze masks from the Welwyn burial have earlier analogies (31); what is new is the wholesale importation of imitation Arretine ware manufactured in North Gaul. So close, in fact, did trade relations with Gaul become that the material culture of broad masses of the Belgic population of England became tinged with Roman influence, while their rulers came to approximate more and more in their mode of life to leaders of provincial society within the Empire.

One of the most striking innovations of the last phase of the Early Iron Age, one which testifies to advances in the political as well as the economic sphere, was the introduction of coinage. At first, and beginning *c.* 150 B.C., the coins

Wine amphora from Welwyn (1:24)

circulating in Britain were gold ones made in the area of the Lower Somme. It is interesting to note that these coins were based on the Macedonian Philippus of the fourth and early third centuries B.C. The models on which the Gallo-Belgic coiners worked may have reached them by way of Massilia or more directly from the Danube Valley. At first the Celtic workmen seem to have made a good job of reproducing the coins, but the Germanic penetration into Belgic Gaul caused a rapid and progressive degeneration in the course of which chariots and horses were reduced to mere blobs and the head of Philip was rendered by a crude representation of the garland (28). By c. 100 B.C. coins had begun to be struck in the parts of Britain occupied or strongly influenced by the Belgae. Coins did not begin to be inscribed by their rulers (29) in Britain until the closing decades of the first century B.C. Our oldest inscribed coinage was struck, probably between 30-20 B.C., by Commius the refugee who ruled over the Atrebates, a Belgic tribe occupying the territory from Hampshire and west Sussex to the Thames, and whose sons, Tincommius (20 B.C.-A.D. 5), Epillus (A.D. 5-10) and Verica (A.D. 10-43), inscribed their own coins in due turn. Among the Catuvellauni of Hertfordshire and Essex the first prince to inscribe his coins was Tasciovanus (15 B.C.-A.D. 10), perhaps a grandson of the Cassivellaunus who so strongly opposed Caesar, and father of the Cunobelin (A.D. 10-41), immortalised by Shakespeare as Cymbeline. Among the non-Belgic tribes the inscription of coins, when undertaken at all, as it was by the Iceni of East Anglia, the Dobunii of the Lower Severn and the Brigantes of the north, began at the dawn of the Christian era.

6

Communications

To most people of the present day, used to moving rapidly from place to place as inclination or the call of business directs, early Britain would indeed seem a dull place, if by any magic they could transport themselves 2,000 years in time. Travel in those days was more infrequent than it is easy to imagine to-day, and when undertaken must have been hideously uncomfortable and protracted. Yet it is easy to forget how many of the conditions of our daily life are the product of changes accomplished with revolutionary activity during the last few generations. Our great-great-grandfathers must as young men have experienced conditions of travel and transport more akin to those of Belgic than of modern times.

Travel, as distinct from folk movement, was in early times confined to the voyages of traders and the progresses of the great, while, in a world where food and the great bulk of the necessities of life were produced locally, transport was mainly confined to minerals and luxury articles, most of which were beyond the reach of all but a small proportion of the population. Yet it would be a great mistake to minimise the importance of travel and transport in early times, just because they were restricted in scope. On the contrary, the mere fact that under primitive conditions people do tend to live close to the soil of a particular neighbourhood only makes the more potent such interchange of goods and ideas as defective means of communication made possible; as agents of cultural change their importance can hardly be exaggerated.

Although no direct evidence for wheeled transport is known from Britain before the Late Bronze Age, it may well turn out to be a good deal older. Indications of plough furrows at Middle Bronze Age and perhaps even earlier levels at Gwithian in Cornwall suggest that the traction plough went back at least to a very early phase of the Bronze Age. If oxen were used to draw ploughs at this time, so they could have been used to pull waggons. These, being of wood, would normally vanish from the archaeological record, but it is significant that a solid wooden wheel has been found at the same level and close by a wooden trackway at Nieuwe Dordrecht in Holland and that both have been dated by radio-carbon analysis to between 1800-1900 B.C.

The earliest traces of harness were bridle-bits, dating from the Late Bronze Age and made of stag's antler, simple affairs consisting of a transverse mouthpiece inserted into cheek-pieces that were perforated for the attachment of reins. It was not until the appearance of an aristocratic form of Celtic Society during the Early Iron Age that we find elaborate traces of horse gear. It is evident that alongside weapons and jewellery, harness and chariot fittings provided the most important outlet to men given to display. Bridle-bits consisting of two rings joined by two or three links were either made of bronze or of iron plated with bronze. Some, like examples from Ulceby, Lincolnshire, and Ringstead, Norfolk, were decorated in relief or by incision, and others like an example from Polden Hill, Somerset, had enamelled roundels. The terrets through which chariot reins passed were another item singled out for ornament. Some of the finest enamelled pieces, like those from Santon Downham, Norfolk, and the Polden Hills, are usually explained as horse-brooches. Ornamentation was also applied to the heads of linch-pins used to hold chariot wheels on to their axles.

As a Celtic aristocrat rushed about on his chariot he liked to cut a figure like his counterpart in an expensive sports car—and a certain number of flashing parts, together with delicate finish of details, helped to give the desired effect.

The skill of the ancient Britons as charioteers is well known; indeed, according to Caesar, so effective were they in war that they threw 'the enemy's ranks into confusion by the mere terror inspired by their horses and the clatter of their wheels'. Their horrific aspect was elaborated by some classical writers who describe the wheels as armed with scythes for mowing down the enemy. Such reports may be discounted, not only because excavation has failed to disclose such armatures on the many chariot wheels recovered, but also because it is difficult to see what use these could have been if we accept Caesar's statement that the warriors brought up to the fray by their charioteers fought on foot, leaving the vehicle to withdraw from the action.

The Iron Age B overlords of east Yorkshire were frequently buried with their chariots, like their cousins in the Marne district of France. The most usual features to survive are iron tyres, sometimes bronze coated, bronze nave hoops, linch-pins and various horse-trappings, including bits and terrets. The Holyhead hoard included iron tyres of $2\frac{1}{2}$ and 3 feet in diameter, linch-pins, nave hoops, terrets and bridle-bits. In the famous grave group excavated at Arras in 1877 an iron mirror and the bronze ferrule of a whip shank were found together with most of the foregoing and the skeleton of a muscular woman, perhaps a warrior queen of the Boudicca type. As a rule the wooden parts of the chariots had vanished beyond recognition, but a labourer who witnessed the discovery of one near Cawthorne Camp, north of Pickering, reported wheels with four spokes and a pole 7 feet long with metal hooks and rings to engage the yoke. The metal tyres range in diameter from $2\frac{1}{2}$ to 3 feet.

Caesar's statement that the charioteers were capable of running out along the pole to the yoke while travelling at full speed suggests that the car was open in front. This is confirmed by the circumstances of one of the Marne burials in which a body laid on the floor of the chariot extended some distance along the pole. The sides of the chariots, however, were probably walled in with some light material such as wicker-work.

While it is only to be expected that war-chariots would bulk largely in the archæological, as in the literary record, we have to depend upon the merest scraps of evidence for the homely vehicles which played so much more important a part in daily life. During the excavation of the Glastonbury lake-village part of the axle-box and a spoke of a wooden wheel were found; originally it must have had twelve spokes and an external diameter of about 2 feet 10

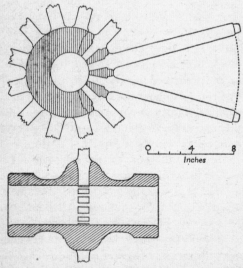

Inches

Wooden wheel hub from Glastonbury lake-village

inches. Evidently the villagers were capable of turning out wheels on the spot, because an unfinished axle-box was also recovered, while the high standard of workmanship shows that they were practised wheelwrights. From this we can infer that among the Iron Age B people, at least, wheeled vehicles were in common daily use. Wheel ruts of gauges between $4^1/_2$ and 5 feet were found in the eastern entrance of Maiden Castle and in the western entrance of Hembury, in each case to be referred to the B people. Similar ruts were recovered inside the entrance of the Belgic site in Prae Wood, Verulamium. Metal linch-pins designed to prevent the wheel slipping off the axle provide further clues to the use of wheeled vehicles. Whether, in addition to two-wheeled carts, four-wheeled vehicles were in common use in pre-historic Britain there is no direct evidence, though Diodorus tells us that tin was carried to Victis from the mainland in wagons, and four-wheeled carts were certainly used on the Continent during the Early Iron Age. It is likely that wheel-less vehicles of the *travois* type, dragged over the ground as sledges are drawn over snow, were also used in pre-historic Britain. The survival of the sliding vehicle up to modern times in Scotland and Wales, and up to the present day in parts of Ireland, argues in favour of their once having been more widely distributed in Britain. Their absence from museum material by no means argues against this, since they are easily made without metal parts. Sooner or later traces of wooden sliding vehicles are almost bound to turn up in water-logged sites. Finally, it must be empha-sised that the great bulk of merchandise carried over land routes must have been on the backs of pack-horses, as indeed it was up to comparatively modern times. Not only were early methods of harnessing horses almost incredibly waste-ful, but the roads required for vehicular traffic were vir-tually non-existent.

117

Few subjects conceal more danger to the unwary than ancient trackways. The mistake most commonly made is to seek and attempt to identify what has never in fact existed. Roads in the sense of fixed and narrowly defined ways, paved or metalled to withstand the wear and tear of constant traffic, are so much a part of our daily life that some effort is needed to envisage the countryside without them; yet all know that, save for a brief interlude under the aegis of the Roman Empire, western Europe knew no roads of this character until the middle of the eighteenth century. What is not always appreciated, however, is that the un-metalled tracks which preceded roads were not fixed but of necessity shifted over comparatively broad belts of country. It sometimes happens that by observing the alignment of a county boundary or by the study of documents it is possible to map the line of an ancient route, but such a line does not of course represent anything more than its most recent fixation.

An excellent example of an ancient cross-country route is the Jurassic Zone, a belt of light soil connecting the Cotswold country with the East Riding of Yorkshire. Sited along the line of junction between the upper part of the Lias and the lower part of the Oolite in north Oxfordshire, it expands in Northamptonshire into a belt of country as broad as twenty-four miles, only to narrow down in Lincolnshire to a bare four miles. Within this zone, which under primitive conditions must have appeared as a more or less open corridor, bounded on either side by dense forest, it is rarely possible to define more closely the route followed by early travellers, save where, as in the case of the Lincoln Edge, the topography is sufficiently marked; here, indeed, one can identify at least one version with the road, which to the north of Lincoln is known as Middle Street and to the south as Pottergate. But the fact that, apart from its course along the western rim of the Edge, the Jurassic route cannot be at all closely defined does not in any sense diminish its importance. Its existence during the Early Iron Age is not only proved by the distribution of antiquities along its course, but is positively demanded by the community of style in the decoration of La Tène metal-work in the south-western and north-eastern provinces of the Iron Age B culture in Britain.

The great through ways of the Chalk country, notably those linking Wessex with the coasts of Norfolk and Kent, are similar in general character, though they tend to be more closely defined topographically. The more northerly of the two, the western end of which is close to Avebury, traverses Berkshire as two roughly parallel tracks, one keeping the crest of the downs, the other following the lower slopes. Some have explained this reduplication as a function of the seasons, the higher one, the famous Ridgeway, being for winter use, the lower or Icknield Way coming into its own during the summer months with the drying up of springheads. The Ridgeway enters Berkshire above Ashbury and sweeping on past Wayland's Smithy, Uffington and Letcombe Castles, and Lowbury Camp makes a characteristic approach to the Thames fords by diverging forks. One version of its course is still preserved by a green track, which makes a favourite haunt for walkers (32). Mentions in Anglo-Saxon charters, the absence of Roman features in its lay-out and its alignment on a series of Iron Age hill-forts combine to suggest that the Berkshire Ridgeway was in use during the last centuries of prehistoric Britain, while indications are not lacking of an even greater antiquity. The Icknield Way follows the foot of the downs from Ashbury to Wantage and fords the Thames at Wallingford and near Goring. North of the river it carries on alone, following the lower slopes of the Chilterns. Then, joining the Cambridge-

London road at Baldock, it continues to Royston, traversing on the way the edge of Therfield Heath, where its recent tracks can be seen furrowing a zone of country a quarter of a mile in width. Maintaining a north-easterly course, the Way passes through Newmarket and pushes on across the chalk belt from ford to ford, crossing the Kennet at Kentford, the Lark at Lackford, the Little Ouse at Thetford and the Wissey at Bodney. Finally, passing Swaffham on the west, it crosses the Nar and makes for the coast near Hunstanton. Although stretches of it were used in Roman times, the Icknield Way can certainly lay claim to a respectable prehistoric antiquity. Indeed, it seems to have marked a line of movement as early as Neolithic times, if we can rely upon the siting of isolated Long Barrows along its course at Churn, near the Goring Gap, at Dunstable and on Therfield Heath. The distribution of the characteristic pottery, on the other hand, suggests that Beaker-using people, entering by way of the Wash, found their way down to northern Wessex by travelling in the opposite direction.

Another notable thoroughfare leads from Salisbury Plain to Dover. As the Harroway it crosses the Hampshire Downs, north of Andover and south of Basingstoke. Then, bearing a trifle southwards, it passes through Farnham to reach the Hog's Back and the North Downs, along the southern slope of which it crosses Kent as the Pilgrims' Way to reach the coast at Dover. The antiquity of the route is hard to establish. In Surrey it appears to have been used to some extent during Roman times, but in Kent there is definite evidence of its Iron Age antiquity; not only have numerous finds of Belgic coins been found along its course, but it actually passed through Bigbury Camp. How much earlier the route may be we have as yet no certain means of knowing.

Besides through routes there must have been in prehistoric times, as to-day, a very large number of local lines

28 Gallo-Belgic and British coins, showing progressive break-down of design

29   Inscribed Belgic coins: Tasciovanus, Cunobelin,
Verica and Epaticcus

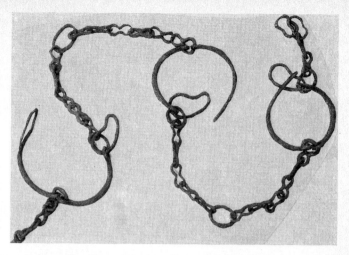

30 Slave chain from Barton, Cambridgeshire

31 Silver cup and bronze masks from a Belgic burial,
Welwyn, Hertfordshire

33   Hembury hill-fort, Devon, from the air

32   Berkshire Ridgeway from the air

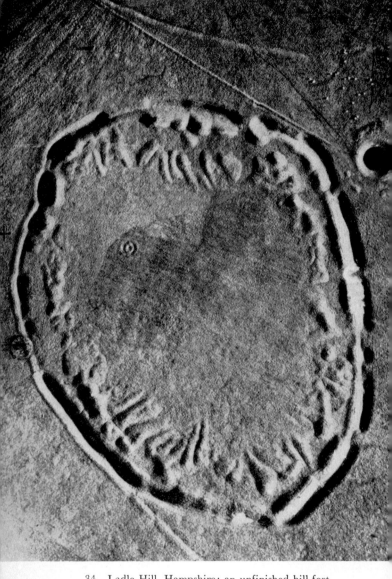

34 Ladle Hill, Hampshire: an unfinished hill-fort

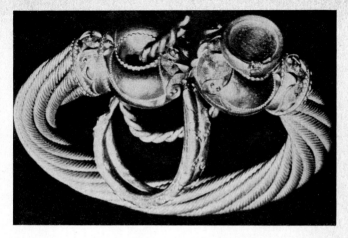

35 Snettisham, Norfolk: hoard E

36 Old Oswestry hill-fort, Shropshire

37   Maiden Castle, Dorset, from the air

of communication. In Wessex these tended to follow the crests of the downs as ridgeways, skirting the heads of streams and linking hill-forts. Thus in Hampshire two main ridgeways have been identified, one running from Winkelbury westwards, past the camps on Ladle Hill and Beacon Hill to Walbury and round to Fosbury, the other entering the county near Quarley Hill and travelling eastwards to Danebury, Woolbury, St Catherine's Hill, Butser Hill, and so to the South Downs.

More specialised and representing the only artificial lines of communication to survive from prehistoric Britain are various forms of timber and brushwood trackways. Tracks of this sort were used during the Second World War by the Germans in their efforts to advance over marshy ground with tanks towards Leningrad and it is interesting that they have modern analogues in the perforated metal sheeting used for improving airstrips or getting heavy transport over boggy ground. One object for which they could have been used in prehistoric times was for crossing the alluvium of river valleys—and it is suggestive that traces have been found in the Ancholme valley in the vicinity of dug-out canoes such as would have served as ferries. Another was to cross extensive fens and bogs and for this reason it is hardly surprising that numerous examples should have come to light in the Cambridgeshire and Somerset fens. Two main classes exist, namely light foot-ways 2 or 3 feet across and trackways sufficiently wide and solid to take wheeled traffic; whereas the former were generally made by faggots of birch or hazel stems thrown down end to end across transverse bearers, the latter were built of heavy transverse baulks of timber. Ingenious means were sometimes used in construction: for instance, two Somerset foot-tracks dating from the Late Bronze Age had transverse bearers held in position by wooden piles driven through either end; and the transverse beams of the vehicular track of Meare were secured by vertical pegs driven through mortise holes at the ends which projected sufficiently to retain stringers on either margin. Trackways of each kind have been dated to the Late Bronze Age in both Cambridgeshire and Somerset fens. Up to the present the only tracks proved by pollen and radio-carbon analysis to be of Neolithic age—those of Blakeway, Honeycot and Honeygore in the Somerset levels—are narrow footways, but the discovery at Nieuwe Dordrecht in Holland of a heavy trackway suitable for vehicular traffic and of a solid wooden wheel in close proximity, both dated by radiocarbon to the nineteenth century B.C., means that we have to keep our minds still open about when wheeled traffic first reached these islands.

So far we have confined ourselves to land transport, yet prior and probably even subsequent to the harnessing of animals this was essentially subsidiary to transport by water. By means of inland waterways traffic could pass easily through heavily forested regions, difficult to traverse on foot and impassable to vehicular traffic. Moreover, the economic advantages inherent in water transport, which repaid vast expenditures upon inland waterways by modern states, must have been even more pronounced when animal transport was either lacking or its value diminished by defects in harness and vehicles. Further, it cannot be recalled too often that the prehistory of Britain is in large measure a story of the impact of influences from the Continent which, whether ethnic or purely commercial in character, were all dependent upon boats.

As is only to be expected, it is the boats of the inland waterways that bulk most prominently in the archaeological record, and of these our information is limited almost entirely to those of robust build, canoes dug out of tree trunks. In England these are most commonly found in the beds of existing rivers or in contiguous alluvial deposits, but occasionally, as happens far more often in Ireland and Scotland, they turn up in marshes or old lake-beds in more or less close association with crannogs or other forms of lake-dwelling. Thus one was found close by the Glastonbury lake-village and another near the Llangorse crannog, but most of them come from the Fens or from such rivers as the Thames and the Trent or their tributaries.

In size dug-out canoes range from 8 feet or so to the $48\frac{1}{2}$ feet of the famous boat found at Brigg in 1886 during the construction of a gasometer on the right bank of the Ancholme. They also vary considerably in shape: they may be squared or tapered to a point at both ends, or they may have a pointed prow and a squared stern; or, again, they may be squared or rounded in section. As a rule they are made of a single piece of wood, but in a few cases, for instance in the Brigg boat, in one from Short Ferry, Fiskerton, on the Witham below Lincoln, and in two others recently dredged from the Trent at Clifton, near Nottingham, the stern has been made from a separate piece inserted into a groove caulked with moss (27). The device of fitting a stern-board was an economical one, since it allowed the use of trunks with rotten cores. The task of hollowing out a sound piece of timber, after first of all shaping out the main form of the boat, must have been a severe one. Careful study of the boat from Llangorse shows that the hole-and-wedge method described in an earlier chapter (p. 96) was employed for the main part of the work. In thinning the walls special care had to be taken to avoid causing splits. To judge from the Llangorse boat, vertical grooves were cut by means of a gouge and the intervening wood removed by a chisel. When hollowing out boats with transverse ribbing, the hole-and-wedge process must have been modified in its later stages.

Apart from a small canoe of unknown date from Astbury, Cheshire, none of the English specimens shows traces of oar-holes or thole-pins. The normal method of propulsion was undoubtedly by paddle rudder. In some dug-outs a seat was cut in the solid at the stern for the paddler, notably in those from Llangorse and from the Royal Albert Dock, Woolwich. Narrow in proportion to their length—the $48\frac{1}{2}$-foot Brigg boat was less than $5\frac{1}{2}$ feet across—the larger ones must have been difficult to manœuvre. One can imagine that balers, such as that found in the punt-like example in Whattall Moss, Ellesmere, must have been put to frequent use, even in the still water of rivers and meres. There are no certain indications of outriggers on British dug-outs, such as those used by mariners on the Indian and Pacific oceans. The small holes at intervals along the gunwale of the Brigg boat may probably be explained in terms of an extra stroke like the one found still in position on the small dug-out from Giggleswick Tarn, near Craven, Yorkshire. The occasional discovery of dug-outs in pairs reminds one that in recent times two hulls poined by cross-pieces were used in several backward parts of Europe for ferrying horses and cattle across rivers. Experiment has shown that a similar device could have served to transport the Prescelly stones from their source in Pembrokeshire, along the coast of South Wales, across the Bristol Channel and by way of rivers with only a short portage to the neighbourhood of Stonehenge.

The earliest traces of navigation in Britain is a wooden paddle from the Early Mesolithic site of Star Carr, over nine thousand years old. It is highly probable that this was used to propel a wooden dug-out like that found recently at Pesse in Holland, dating from Middle Neolithic times in that country. A few dug-out boats from England can be dated by archaeology. For instance one from the Erith marshes, Kent, is said to have had a polished flint axe and a flint scraper on its floor. Another from the Cambridgeshire fens near Chatteris is reported to have contained a bronze rapier from the Middle Bronze Age. And a dug-out boat from the Glastonbury lake-village must date from the latter part of the Early Iron Age. On the other hand, the earliest examples of the kind with inserted stern-board, those from Brigg and Short Ferry, have been shown by pollen-analysis to date from the Early Iron Age.

A boat worthy of special mention is that recently exposed on the Humber shore at North Ferriby. The basis of the vessel was a stout central plank about 2 feet wide and 43 feet long, from which it was built up by the addition of at least three thick oak planks on either side. The planks were fitted edge to edge, but in rather a special manner; the lower edge of each was bevelled to fit into a V-shaped groove cut in the top of the one below, a device for which the only parallels are found on the Gujarati coast of India. As is usual with boats of carvel type the joins were caulked with moss and covered by thin wooden battens; these were held in place by the ties of twisted yew which sewed together the planks. How the necessary rigidity was achieved is not clear, although ribs may have been tied to the knobs found projecting from the central plank. It is possible that this boat was built by people used to dug-outs in imitation of carvel-built boats they may have seen. There is nothing to suggest that it was capable of anything more than estuary and coastal work, except in the fairest weather.

Although the archaeological evidence is confined to the chance discovery of a single example in a brickyard at South Ferriby, not very far from the boat just described, it is probable that vessels built of wicker-work frames with skins stretched across played a far more important role in water transport in general than the dug-out canoes upon which attention has so far been focused. Two distinct forms

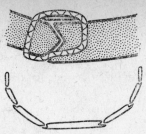

Section and detail of the North Ferriby boat

of such vessels survived up to modern times, and indeed persist locally in slightly modified versions up to the present day, namely the coracle of Scotland, Wales and the Marches, and the curragh of western and north-western Ireland. The mere fact of the survival in the Celtic fringe of the primitive wicker and skin boat, similar to those which still ply the Tigris and the Yalung river of Tibet, is enough to make probable its widespread occurence in prehistoric Britain. Fortunately the copious references to the craft in classical writings remove all doubt that this was in fact the case. It is important to realise, as a recent author has so convincingly proved, that the vessels, seen by Caesar on the coast of southern England and copied by him when fighting Pompey's lieutenants in Spain (49 B.C.), were not coracles but curraghs. Coracles were no doubt in use as river-craft, for fishing and for ferrying, a task of prime importance in the absence of bridges; but what is significant about Caesar's observation is that it allows us to envisage sea-going vessels. Indeed, Lucan, writing a century later, describes the making of a curragh and specifically comments: 'thus ... on the expanded ocean [did] the Briton sail'. Ancient Irish writings teem with references to the seaworthiness of the curragh, which from its lightness and shallow draft was capable, especially when fitted with a mast and sailing before the

126

wind, of relatively high speeds. Entirely characteristic is the tale of St. Brendan, who, early in the sixth century, is said to have sailed to Iceland in forty days, visiting the Shetlands on the way back and ending up in Brittany. Again, the Anglo-Saxon Chronicle refers to three Irish 'Scots' who landed on the coast of Cornwall from a hide-covered boat in A.D. 891, seven days out from Ireland. Testimony from a classical source is provided by the third-century writer Caius Julius Colinus, whose rather dry statement makes us view the capabilities of the curragh in a more sober light. 'The sea which separates Hibernia from Britain', he writes, 'is rough and stormy throughout the year; it is navigable for a few days only; they voyage in small boats formed of pliant twigs, covered with the skins of oxen.' Still, when all allowance has been made for Celtic exuberance, it remains a fact that by means of these frail craft communication was maintained in early historic, and by inference, in prehistoric times between Ireland, the western seaboard of Britain and Brittany. Further, if we accept the testimony of Caesar, a coastwise trade was maintained by similar vessels off southern England. There seems no reason why, under favourable conditions, journeys should not by this means have been made across the English Channel almost as freely as across the Irish Sea.

Yet we must face the fact that in prehistoric times the carrying trade between Britain and the Continent was mainly in the hands of foreigners. During the Early Iron Age it was almost monopolised by the Veneti, who dwelt on the coasts of Morbihan and southern Finistère, though other tribes, notably the Morini of Belgium whose coins have been picked up on the beach at Selsey, had a small share. The prowess of the Veneti is known to us to-day because they happened to cross the path of Caesar. From his account of the naval victory he found it necessary to gain

A coracle fisherman of the Wye

over them at Quiberon Bay (56 B.C.), as a preliminary to his expedition to Britain, it appears that their ships were stoutly built with prows standing high above the water and that they set leather sails. Not a trace of the Gaulish and Belgic ships which must have traded to our shores has survived, nor, in default of ship burial, a rite for which there is no evidence in Early Iron Age Britain, is it easy to see how they could have done. The same applies to those ships from foreign parts which we know must have visited us in periods even more remote. There is plenty of evidence to suggest that in Neolithic times and at the dawn of the Bronze Age maritime activity reached its zenith in prehistoric Europe; the diffusion of the idea of collective burial in rock-cut and megalithic tombs, the spread of early metal forms like the halberd and the trading of exotic trinkets, such as the faience beads noticed in the last chapter, are only a few examples which might be quoted to illustrate how closely knit together was the whole sea-board of Europe from Iberia to Scandinavia. Beyond the fact that the voyagers were men of higher culture than those among whom they moved, we know disappointingly little about them or the boats they sailed. Yet, if we reflect a moment on the evidence likely to be available to archaeologists of the distant future about the ships of the European traders who opened up the coast of West Africa, we need hardly feel surprised. A few trinkets and some bottle glass might mark the trail, but of the ships themselves no trace would be found.

7

Hill-Forts

Hill-forts are among the most numerous, striking and significant of British field antiquities. They vary widely in size. Of the 1,400 or so south of a line between Scarborough and the Isle of Man nearly 800 were under three acres in extent, hardly more than defences for single homesteads. The great majority of the remainder range in size from three to 15 or 20 acres. Only a few, notably the great oppida of Wessex, exceeded this. Often these large hill-forts started their history in a more modest fashion, so that for instance the 46 acres covered by Maiden Castle in its later phases represented almost a threefold enlargement of the already substantial hill-fort earlier constructed on part of the site. As defensive earh-works hill-forts were of immense social significance, since survival is after all a main preoccupation of any viable society. The range of size doubtless reflects the size of social group to be protected and the degree of political integration prevailing at the time.

Before discussing more fully their history and the role they played in the social life of their times a few remarks may be offered about hill-forts as military works. Their defensive character cannot be stressed too often. In this respect they offer a complete contrast to the outposts of an advancing imperialism. Whereas the typical Roman fort was but a forward post of an organised system, connected by road and sea with a definite base, the prehistoric hill-fort, although not without some relation to its neighbours, stood alone as an entity. Again, whereas the forts were set in valleys or on open ground, easily approached by road, the hill-forts were placed so as to be as difficult of access by enemies as possible. To achieve this, reliance was placed partly on physical obstacles and partly on securing an uninterrupted view of surrounding country and an unbroken range of fire for missiles, conditions which could only be fully realised by defending a more or less isolated eminence. It would be a mistake to imagine that altitude was of itself a determining factor. In the mountainous country of North Wales hill-forts are rarely found above the 1,000-foot contour. Even in the rolling chalk country of Sussex and Wessex hill-forts are by no means restricted to the highest ridges of the downs. More important than height above sea-level were the facts of local topography, which often made an isolated hill or spur of comparatively low altitude more suitable than what might at first have appeared more obvious locations. One has to remember that the range of missiles during the Early Iron Age was restricted to the distance a man could sling a pebble or hurl a spear, and further, that economic as well as purely military considerations may have played some part in the selection of sites.

Early man was no more anxious to indulge in superfluous hard work than his modern heirs. So we find that where natural defences were available he contented himself with these, supplementing them by artificial works only where necessary. In Wessex, where the majority of English hill-forts is found, nature was grudging in this respect, but the few opportunities afforded were eagerly exploited. Hengistbury Head is a case in point. Defined to the north by Christchurch Harbour and to the south by the sea, all that was necessary to convert the headland into a stronghold was to cut off the narrow approach from the west. By throwing up a couple of banks and ditches an area several hundred acres in extent was effectively isolated. Butser Hill, overlooking the London-Portsmouth road near Petersfield, is another example. The hill-top, roughly defined by the 800-foot contour, is surrounded by a drop of several hundred feet on all sides except the south, the approach to which from Hillhampton Down is cut off by a single bank and ditch. Instances are more numerous in stony regions with more pronounced surface relief. Thus at Worlebury, which nobly crowns the seaward end of Worle Hill, a limestone ridge projecting into the Bristol Channel immediately north of Weston-super-Mare, the defenders were able to save the labour of raising ramparts on the northern side because there a steep declivity gave ample protection. At Leckhampton above Cheltenham and at Bredon Hill, Overbury, in the same county, two sides were amply defended by nature, while at Lydney, Gloucestershire, the promontory had only to be fortified artificially on the north and at the north-east corner. Natural strongholds improved to varying degress by the hand of man abound in North Wales; to mention only two well-known sites, steep cliffs defended the east and west both of Dinorben and of the huge Y Corddyn, while only the south of the former and the north of the latter required powerful artificial works. As a general rule, however, it was necessary to defend the whole site by artificial means, though often some sectors required stronger works than others. Thus, at Mount Caburn, magnificently placed to dominate the valley of the Sussex Ouse, but approached relatively easily from the north, the earth-works were doubled on the vulnerable sector. The builders of Hembury, the finest hill-fort in Devon, surrounded the whole of their site by two ramparts, but recognised the superior strength of the eastern and steepest side by omitting to carry round it their third line of defence. In every hill-fort the entrances were the weak points. Consequently we shall find that as the art of fortification developed increasing attention was paid to strengthening this feature.

The very considerable number of hill-forts which have in recent years been tested by excavation—not one single one has been completely investigated—makes it possible to obtain a fairly clear idea of their history and at the same time to study details of their structure invisible on the surface. It is easy to form quite a wrong idea of what these ancient strongholds were like by gazing on their ruins. We must not allow the scree-strewn slopes of Worlebury, Old Oswestry (36), or Tre' Ceiri to obscure the trim stone walls of which the lower courses lie buried beneath the tumbled mass; nor, on the other hand, should we be deceived by the smooth profiles of downland banks and ditches into forgetting that what we see are the eroded and silted vestiges of once formidable defensive works. To correct this impression it is necessary to look below the surface and see something of what the spade reveals.

Perhaps the best way to understand the principles underlying the construction of hill-forts is to try and imagine how their builders set to work. In the case of earth-work defences thrown up by the Iron Age A people we are greatly helped by the survival of an unfinished example on unploughed downland at Ladle Hill, Hampshire (34). It is evident that after choosing a suitable site the first business was to mark out the course of the ditch from which the rampart material was to be obtained, and which itself played an important part in the scheme of defence. An early stage in the work is preserved at Ladle Hill at points to which the main ditch was never extended, in the form of a shallow setting-out trench. How the course of this was originally traced we can only guess, but it was probably defined by a plough furrow. The next stage was to enlarge the ditch and so obtain material for the bank. The discontinuous character of the Ladle Hill ditch suggests that this was done by separate gangs; the later stage, when the intervals between the separate quarries would be removed and the profile of the ditch carefully graded and trimmed, was never reached. One of the main problems facing the builders of chalk ramparts was to prevent them slipping back into the ditch, while at the same time securing as steep a slope as possible. Of the various methods available, the simplest was to arrange the excavated material in such a way that a firm core of relatively large blocks was heaped up near the edge of the ditch. The turf, humus, and loose surface chalk removed from the first few spits would accordingly be dumped well back, ready to be banked against the chalk blocks quarried from the lower levels. At Ladle Hill we see the process arrested half-way; the chalk core forms an irregular bank, behind which can be seen small dumps of loose surface material which for more than 2,000 years have waited to be added for the completion of the rampart. Recent excavations at Quarley Hill showed that there the same method was followed, the only difference being that additional surface material required to heighten the rampart was obtained from scrapings within the defended area. A refinement observed at St Catherine's Hill and elsewhere was the use of turf to stabilise successive tips of material as they were dumped on the rampart. More elaborate was the device of a timber revetment by which the heavy chalk blocks were contained behind a wooden wall. The post-holes of the main timber uprights of such were found during the excavations at Cissbury, while traces of a stronger version with two rows of verticals were recovered at Uffington Castle, the Caburn, and in the original Iron Age rampart at Maiden Castle, Dorset.

134

To an enemy, defences of this kind must have been very unpleasant indeed to tackle, for, having scrambled up the inner slope of the ditch, an attacker would find himself on a narrow berm with a vertical wall ahead on which the defenders stood at a considerable vantage.

Hill-forts erected in a stone country naturally show methods of construction adapted to the different material. The fact that dry-stone walling is a common feature of hill-forts erected by the Iron Age B people of the south-west is due primarily to the nature of the country settled by them. The B people built plenty of hill-forts with earth-work defences, of which Hembury is an outstanding example, and there are instances where A people found themselves on limestone and built a stone-walled hill-fort like Chastleton, Oxfordshire. Owing to the sharper relief the proportion of promontory hill-forts is higher in the south-western B than in the A territory, though contour camps are still the commoner. Outstanding examples of the former are Lydney, Bredon Hill, Leckhampton, and Worlebury, while of the latter Llanmelin in Monmouth-shire and the three Somerset sites, Cadbury Castle, Dole-bury, and Ham Hill are particularly well known. Among the details of dry-stone construction worthy of special comment are the horned and inturned entrance at Leck-hampton, designed to give maximum flanking protection, and the great north wall of Worlebury, consisting of a rubble core battered and faced with built stone, reinforced on either side by one or more stone dykes, with an overall width of up to 38 feet.

In the extreme south-west Cornwall abounds in sites from great hill-forts like Castle-an-Dinas with three and in places four earthen ramparts enclosing an area 850 feet in diameter, to small stone-built forts and defended promontory sites, but few of these can be precisely dated.

The best explored and one of the few closely dated examples is Chûn Castle, which from its high hill dominates much of the Land's End district. The extraordinary strength of the defences, which comprise two dry masonry walls faced with large granite blocks, each with an external ditch, may in part be due to the sea-mist common in the district under cover of which surprise attacks might be made. The arrangement of the entrance exposing an enemy to a deadly flanking attack at close quarters shows that the defenders wished to leave nothing to chance. Since the walls were dry-built their outer surfaces were made with a batter. How tall they were originally, we cannot say, although a hundred years ago they still stood up to 12 feet in height. Within, irregularly built stone huts were arranged against the inner face of the defensive wall, together with a furnace accompanied by iron and tin slag, and a well. Among the pottery were sherds of red Mediterranean ware, some of them parts of wine amphorae, together with incised pottery and sherds stamped with a duck design, of a type known from northern Portugal, north-western Spain, and western Britanny.

The entrances of hill-forts are always liable to be interesting, because as the weakest points in the defences they, more than any other part, challenged the ingenuity of their builders. One result of this is that they were often reconstructed as notions of defence developed, and so afford clues to the stages through which individual hill-forts have passed. Similarly, by correlating the evidence from a number of sites it is possible to arrive at a general sequence. Thus the simplest type of entrance, a mere gap in the bank and ditch, well exemplified at Figsbury, Wiltshire, was employd by the Iron Age A people when they first began to build hill-forts. At Lidbury it was found that a simple entrance of this kind had been modified already at an early stage of the settlement by filling up a stretch of the original ditches and throwing forward locally the line of the earth-work, which at the point of entry was slightly inturned. The object of this was, of course, to expose an enemy trying to break in to attack from both flanks. The device of setting the entrance slightly askew must have extended the ordeal of anyone trying to force a passage by prolonging the distance over which he would have to repel flank attacks. Both methods were combined at St Catherine's Hill, Hampshire, a work dating from the second stage of the Iron Age A settlement. Here excavation showed that the inturned ends of the ramparts had been faced with clay and retained by a timber wall which may well have been carried to a sufficient height to provide a breastwork for the defenders. At the eastern entrance of Maiden Castle, Dorset, we find yet another device in the shape of hornworks, thrown out in front. The Maiden Castle entrance is particularly notable, too, for its double portals, each set askew and flanked by timber works. In the final phase of the site, when the ramparts were multiplied, the hornworks were doubled.

The construction of hill-forts must have involved a tremendous effort on the part of contemporary society. To take but one example, it has been calculated that the earth-works of the 60-acre camp at Cissbury involved the quarrying of 35,000 cubic yards of chalk, which had then to be lifted from the ditch and systematically built into the rampart; in addition the timber required for the retaining wall had to be felled and prepared, the 15-foot main uprights alone numbering from 8,000 to 12,000. These figures become all the more impressive when it is realised that at the height of the Iron Age in southern

England a hill-fort served only quite a restricted area of country, and that the defences were in some cases doubled, trebled, or even quadrupled. In relation to the standard of economic wealth prevailing at the time the efforts of the hill-fort builders can only be compared with those of modern tax-payers in face of space-rocket programmes. Such a comparison indeed is apposite. Hill-forts were able to command so drastic an economic sacrifice precisely because they were primarily defensive works of a military character. Again, like rearmament programmes, phases of hill-fort building were exceptional interludes, the product of exceptional times. It should never be forgotten that the people who built hill-forts were the same ones who dwelt in peasant communities, cultivated their fields, and herded their cattle. From the work already done it appears likely that hill-forts were erected or their defences strengthened in response to troubles interrupting for quite brief periods a long reign of peace. That hill-fort construction was mainly conditioned by such factors as the influx of immigrant peoples, coming at fairly long periods of time, is proved by the indications of long periods of neglect interrupted by spasms of activity—'evidence for war and peace' as it is aptly described by the excavators of St Catherine's Hill—found on most sites investigated by trained observers. The phenomenon of unfinished hill-forts, dramatically exemplified by Ladle Hill, suggests a rearmament programme rendered superfluous by circumstances; its frequency is significant. On the other hand, there is gruesome evidence to show that defences were sometimes repaired in time, though not always sufficiently strongly to withstand the onslaught of the enemy. In the inner entrance of Bredon Hill camp remains of fifty persons, mostly young men, were found as they had fallen in their last struggle, except that some had been barbarously

138

mutilated with hands, legs, and heads removed. When the Romans stormed Maiden Castle they slew many of the defenders, though they allowed them decent, if hurried, burial.

The time has not yet arrived when we can define with confidence the various waves of rearmament which at different times swept over Iron Age Britain; still less is it possible to interpret each in terms of folk-movements or political events.

On the other hand it looks as though the inhabitants of southern Britain were able to get along without true hill-forts for most, if not the whole, of the first phase of the Early Iron Age. One reason for thinking this is that the key sites of this period either lacked defences, like Scarborough, West Harling, All Cannings Cross or Eastbourne, or, as in the case of Castell Odo, made do with mere palisades. Another is the frequency with which pottery and structural features occur on sites subsequently converted into hill-forts.

It was not until around 300 B.C., at a time when immigrants may perhaps have been coming from the Marne region, that we find the first crop of hill-forts. These forts were single-ramparted and were thrown up by the surviving A people during an early part of the second phase of the Early Iron Age, presumably to protect themselves against intruders. Sections cut through their defences show that they were constructed by people in whom the Hallstatt tradition of fortification was still alive, kept in being it may be by the construction during the preceding phase of timber enclosures. The object of the people who planned and built such hill-forts as Maiden Castle I, Hollingbury or Wandlebury I, was evidently the same as that of their distant relatives in south Germany, namely to make the ramparts as much like walls as they

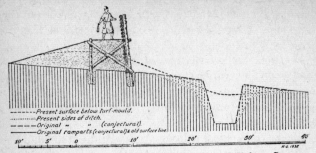

Reconstruction of defences at Hollingbury hill-fort, Sussex

could. This they achieved by building a strong timber face
with stout verticals driven deeply into the subsoil so as
to retain the horizontals against which the soil and rock
from the ditch were retained. To counter the strain caused
by the weight of the rampart material the front timber
face was tied by cross-timbers to an inner row of vertical
posts. So as to give sufficient bearing for the great posts
supporting the wall a platform or berm was commonly
left between the vertical face and the ditch, which was
itself cut steeply to increase its effectiveness as part of the
defensive system.

During the third phase of the Iron Age a new style
of fortification came into use that depended on the
multiplication of banks and ditches, a style which at
Maiden Castle (37) replaced the older type of single
rampart defence. Notable multivallate hill-forts in Wessex,
other than Maiden Castle III, include Ham Hill and
Cadbury Castle, and, further west, Hembury in Devon
(33) provides another outstanding example. The notion
that this increase in depth of fortification was necessarily
linked with the introduction of new people using the
sling as an offensive weapon is no longer so strongly

supported. The new system is one that could easily have grown up in Wessex, and the greater depth of defence would have been valuable against other weapons than the sling. Again, investigation of hill-forts in northern Gaul has failed to reveal any convincing source for the hypothetical invaders. However this may be it, it is obvious that the multiplication of defences must have increased their cost very greatly, testifying at once to the turbulence of the times and to the political authority of petty chieftains at the height of the pre-Roman Iron Age.

The military role of hill-forts is sufficiently evident. What other part, if any, did they play in economic and social life? Were they, as many older writers suggested, essentially refuge places to which people from surrounding districts might repair in times of stress, or were they 'cities', permanently occupied centres, serving as markets and even as political headquarters? As we began by emphasising, hill-forts vary greatly in scale and it would be unreasonable on this ground alone to expect that any single explanation can apply to all of them. In the case of the smaller hill-forts, like the group of multiple-enclosure forts built between c. 200-50 B.C. in the south-west, having inner enclosures set within or tangential to outer ones, excavation has sometimes been sufficient to tell us what they imply in terms of inhabitants. Some of the smaller ones only held three or four huts, such as a substantial family might have occupied, whereas others like Castle Dore held perhaps 15 or 16 huts. The real problem is offered by the larger hill-forts, whose mere size has prevented the examination of more than quite small parts of the interior. Until this has been done—and the use of proton-magnetomers and analogous devices has recently made examination of the interior of hill-forts a much more practical proposition—it is hardly possible to gain a clear picture of the intensity or nature of the occupation of the great hill-forts.

Meanwhile critical investigation of the farmstead at Little Woodbury has enabled us to clear away one fertile source of miscalculation. The more or less circular pits, accepted only a generation ago as pit-dwellings, are now known to have been storage-pits. The effect of this revision on our notions of population will be apparent when it is realised that half a dozen store-pits might go to a single house and that the effective life of each was hardly more than five years. Thus a very large number of pits could mean either a brief occupation by a large population or a prolonged one by a single household. Only the recovery of all the hut plans within an enclosure, together with a precise notion of the duration of settlement, would allow one to draw valid conclusions about the size and nature of the occupation. At the Little Woodbury farmstead approximately 360 pits have to be distributed over a period, which, to judge from the number of reconstructions and from the development of the pottery, probably extended to 300 years. If each pit lasted for five years and the population remained at much the same level throughout, this would give an average of six pits in use at any one time.

It is difficult to work along similar lines in the case of hill-forts, because it is rarely possible to estimate the number of storage-pits. All the same the application of the Woodbury results to those hill-forts for which there is fairly definite information is distinctly suggestive. Thus the eleven pits recovered as the result of extensive trenching at Lidbury might imply one farmstead lasting for ten years, two farmsteads for five years, or possibly a larger number for a shorter time; the 55 pits belonging to the second stage of the Caburn give anything from

142

nine farmsteads for up to five years to one farmstead for 45; or, again, the 100 pits at Worlebury could imply sixteen farmsteads for five years or one farmstead for 82 years. Now it is obvious from the scale of the hill-forts that they cannot have been intended to shelter the inhabitants of a single or even a few farmsteads, so we must conclude that they were meant as refuges for whole communities during times of stress. The large areas enclosed by hill-forts are no doubt explained in part by the fact that they were intended to shelter flocks and herds as well as human beings. In this respect the large camp on Quarley Hill is significant, as it is aligned exactly on an earlier cattle enclosure, itself placed at the junction of a number of separate grazing areas defined by running banks and ditches (9).

The probability is that the larger hill-forts served a variety of purpose. In parts of the chalk areas of Wessex where it has been possible to reconstruct the picture of land-occupation with some approach to accuracy, it has been found that each chunk of countryside had its own hill-fort. If we are right in thinking that the mass of the population lived in scattered farmsteads, it seems to follow that the hill-forts formed natural centres. The very scale of the fortifications, and the fact that the work must often have been undertaken in a hurry to meet some sudden threat, argues that the people of the surrounding country must have contributed their labour. As has often been pointed out, this in itself argues for the exercise of political authority and it is reasonable to suppose that the wielder of this was based on the strongpoint of the territory. Occasionally it would seem that hill-forts were centres of some special economic activity: for instance the inhabitants of Hunsbury seem to have been engaged on mining and working the local iron-stone. Yet their prime

143

function must surely have been to serve as the castle of the local chieftain, the rallying point and also the refuge of the countryside.

The hey-day of the hill-forts passed with the social conditions that gave rise to them. In many parts of the country petty chiefs survived down to the Roman conquest —and for that matter much later—but within the territories ruled by Belgic princes they gave way as a rule to fortified towns set by river fords and screened by linear dykes traversing and enclosing broad stretches of open country. Thus we find the Belgae establishing themselves beside a ford in the Lea Valley at Wheathampstead and then setting up in the neighbouring valley of the Ver the precursor of the Roman *municipium* of Verulamium. Or, again, in the coastal region of Essex we see Cunobelin protecting his headquarters by throwing dykes across the gravel peninsula between the Colne and Roman rivers, enclosing in all an area of some 12 square miles. Here, again, as in the mass production of wheel-made pottery, the importation of luxuries from Italy and Gaul, the inscribing of coinage and the increase of naturalism in art, we can see in the final phases of Belgic occupation the shadow of Rome over Britain.

Burial

ANCIENT graves have always been one of the richest sources of prehistoric antiquities. That this is so is due to early man's belief in a life after death and to the practical way in which he expressed his faith. Ever since Upper Palaeolithic times there is evidence for ceremonial burial and the provision of grave goods for use in the next world. The oldest burial yet found in Britain was uncovered over a century ago in the Upper Palaeolithic deposits of Paviland Cave by Dean Buckland. Although the learned author of *Reliquiae Diluvianae* mistook the sex of the individual concerned and post-dated the 'Red Lady of Paviland' by many thousands of years, his description tallies with numerous finds in the French caves. With the skeleton—in reality that of a young man of twenty-five—were parts of an ivory armlet, a number of rods of the same material, and a couple of handfuls of shells *(Nerita littoralis)*, the whole being enveloped in powdered red ochre, symbolic of blood.

One of the most striking developments of Neolithic times was the diffusion throughout much of western Europe of tombs built of megalithic masonry, resembling in plan the subterranean rock-cut tombs of Mediterranean lands. The British Isles shared in this to the full, lying athwart the sea routes by which megalithic tombs were spread along the Atlantic sea-board. Within the limits of England and Wales, however, megalithic tombs of the form most widely spread in Europe, those having a single burial chamber approached by a well-defined passage, are comparatively rare. Our most elaborate tomb of the basic passage grave form is Bryn Celli Ddu in Anglesey, a round cairn slightly indented at the entrance to the passage (39) and covering two central slabs, one incised with a meandering patten, surrounded by a circle of free-standing stones and a broad trench in which were set two rows of contiguous slabs. Unfortunately nothing was found in the chamber at the time of its recent exploration.

The chamber itself is polygonal in plan, being formed by five megalithic slabs, and was originally roofed by large capstones, only one of which survives. Anglesey can boast another passage-grave of outstanding interest at Barclodiod near Holyhead. This has a markedly cruciform plan, the main chamber having smaller ones at the end and either side, a type at home across the Irish Sea in the Boyne Valley, Co. Meath. Traces of a cremation deposit in one of the side chambers of the Barclodiod monument shows moreover that its builders used the same rite as the makers of the Boyne tombs. Again the schematic figures engraved on stones at both the Anglesey tombs and the spirals found at Barclodiod find analogues both in the Boyne group and significantly far to the south in Iberia.

The other main class of megalithic tomb in southern Britain having well-defined characteristics belongs to a particular variety of large gallery-graves having one or more pairs of side-chambers or transepts. Transepted gallery-graves are concentrated in the Cotswold-Severn area, mainly on the Cotswolds, but important concentrations occur north of the Bristol Channel in the Black Mountains and south on the Mendips, with another to the east on the Wessex downs. Close analogies for these tombs are found in Morbihan and the Loire Inférieure, and there seems little doubt that they represent the result of a movement from the Biscayan area up the Bristol Channel.

146

In building a tomb of this kind the chamber was the first to be set up, thin slabs of stone stood up on edge being used for the purpose; gaps were filled with dry-stone walling, and the whole was roofed by overlapping slabs in the corbelling technique (38). The structure was enclosed for protection in an elongated wedge-shaped mound built around by dry-stone walling, in turn revetted by courses of inclined slabs. Access to the chamber, which was placed at the broad end of the mound, was obtained by way of a funnel-shaped forecourt formed by the inturning of the marginal dry-stone walling. As a rule there is an ante-chamber, defined by transversely set slabs, at the entry. Except when unsealed for burials, the tomb was effectively closed by plugging the forecourt with a stone packing. The number of transepts varies from the single pair of Nympsfield or Wayland's Smithy to the three pairs of Nempnett Thrubwell and Stoney Littleton. Where there are two pairs these may be separated as at Notgrove, or contiguous as at Uley. A feature worthy of special notice is the rotunda at Notgrove and West Kennet, a round dry-stone construction built around a small megalithic cist in line with, but quite distinct from, the main chamber.

Examples with three transepts are an elaboration of the introduced form, but insular development mainly took the line of degeneration. While the wedge-shaped long barrow with its horned forecourt at the broad end persisted, the megalithic structures which it masked underwent great changes. Sometimes, as at Tinkinswood, the grave, while shrinking to a small rectangular chamber, continued to fill the position formerly occupied by the gallery. More often, however, the chambers were inserted into the side of the barrow, the former position of the entrance being marked by a 'dummy portal', a couple of uprights with a lintel and blocking stone, features well illustrated by the

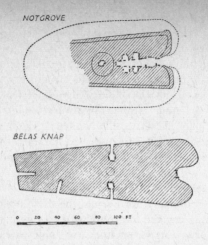

NOTGROVE

BELAS KNAP

0   20   40   60   80   100' FT

northern end of Belas Knap. The survival of the forecourt
and the provision of a false entrance only serve to
emphasise the ritual importance of the broad end of the
barrow in the original monuments. It was of course
through the entrance that successive corpses were borne to
their resting-place in the tomb, and it was in the forecourt
between the horns that the ceremonies antecedent to this
event probably took place. As a rule the side-chambers
were small enough to roof with a single capstone. They
were commonly approached by an ante-chamber between
which and the chamber proper there were sometimes
placed a couple of upright slabs with semi-circular hollows
flaked out of contiguous edges so as to form a more or less
circular hole. A recently discovered example in the
Rodmarton long barrow was found with its original dry-
stone plugging in position, showing that the aperture was
left open only for the actual insertion of a body. Another
detail to be noted in the same tomb is the carefully laid
flight of steps.

148

In regions easily accessible from the Irish Sea there are a few gallery graves of the type commonly represented in northern Ireland and in south-west Scotland, having compartments formed by septal slabs. One of the finest is Cashtal yn Ard in the Isle of Man, the chamber of which has five compartments opening on to a paved forecourt defined by a hollow façade of upright slabs. At one time the tomb was covered by an oval stone cairn which, banked against the façade, projected in the form of horns on either side of the forecourt, but the material of the mound has long since been robbed for field walls. The Bride Stones near Congleton mark the site of a similar horned cairn covering a long chamber. Others, even more ruinous, are known from Holyhead and from Anglesey.

The majority of the megalithic tombs, found mainly in south-west England and Wales, are simpler in form. A localised group is that of the entrance-graves of Scilly and Penwith, the megalithic chambers of which have constricted entries and are incorporated in small round mounds with megalithic kerbs. Commoner and more generalised in form are small squarish or polygonal chambers or 'dolmens', many of them free-standing and often more or less ruined. Most of these 'dolmens' represent more or less highly devolved versions of more elaborate types of chamber-tomb, though a few are remnants of monuments originally more complex. Dolmens include some of the best-loved monuments of the countryside from Kits Coty House in the Medway Valley and the Devil's Den near Marlborough to Trethevy and Zennor down in Cornwall. Although much can be learned on the historical side from a study of the morphology of megalithic tombs, their social interest lies in the idea of which they are the architectural expression. In the final analysis megalithic, like rock-cut tombs, are chambers designed to be opened

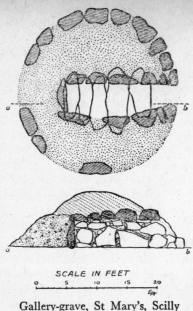

SCALE IN FEET

Gallery-grave, St Mary's, Scilly

and closed easily, such as would be needed for the
reception of burials over a period of time. That they were
in fact used as family vaults is proved by the nature of the
human remains found in them. It has been the common
experience of excavators to find traces of numerous skeletons in varying stages of disarray. In Britain we have many
records of the number of individuals represented in the
material from different tombs—thus, there were at least
17 at Nympsfield, 28 at Uley, 36 at Belas Knap, and so
on, but accurate accounts of the contents of undisturbed
burial chambers are rare. One of the few exceptions is the
side chamber recently discovered in the long barrow at
Lanhill, Wiltshire. Constructed of megalithic slabs with a

150

single capstone, it was of such slight dimensions, only 4 feet 8 inches in length and varying in width between 2 feet 6 inches and 3 feet 8 inches, that the seven more or less complete skeletons found within could hardly have been inserted as corpses at one time. On the other hand, the disposition of the skeletons, the one nearest the entrance being articulated, the others pushed together as though to make room for successors, does not support the theory that they were deposited as bones. It seems much more likely that we have to deal with a series of successive burials. The individuals comprised a man of over 50, one between 30 and 40, and another of 30, an aged woman, a woman of between 30 and 40, and a child of from 12 to 13. Expert examination has shown that they were almost certainly members of the same family. In addition, stray bones were identified from two other individuals, a youth of 20 and a year-old baby, possibly vestiges of a previous sequence of burials all other indication of which had been swept from the chamber.

From this it follows that grave goods found in megalithic tombs are likely to belong to the last stage of their period of use. Moreover, their very nature made them more liable than earth-graves to spoliation by early antiquaries. This often makes it difficult to decide who built a given group of tombs, though we may safely attribute those of the Cotswold-Severn and Irish Sea areas to Western Neolithic communities, even though, as at West Kennet, Peterborough and Beaker pots were inserted in a later phase.

In regions deficient in stone suitable for megalithic construction, and in a few where it was present, long barrows were built of turf and timber heaped over with subsoil quarried from ditches. Most of these monuments occur on the chalk, centring on the downs of Dorset, Wiltshire,

Hampshire, and Sussex; there are isolated examples strung out along the course of the Icknield Way, and outlying groups on the Wolds of Lincolnshire and Yorkshire with outliers in the north-west. Externally they resemble long mounds with megalithic chambers, except where their quarry ditches are visible. In size and proportions they vary considerably, but the Lincolnshire average of 175 feet by 57 feet gives some idea of scale. The original height of the barrows is often difficult to judge, although Giants' Hills, Skendleby, Lincolnshire, must have been at least 12 feet. Their effect was enhanced by the presence on both sides, and sometimes round one or both ends as well, of quarry ditches as much as 12 feet deep. Further, it has to be remembered that when freshly built the chalk covering must have gleamed white against the greensward. The artifical covering of white quartz which originally adorned the great mound of New Grange on the Boyne suggests that the whiteness of chalk barrows had more than an accidental significance. It is not impossible that the surface of such mounds was periodically scoured: the chalk-cut White Horse of Uffington has been kept white for nearly two thousand years.

During recent years several earthen long barrows have been excavated by modern methods and much information has been added to the pioneer discoveries made by General Pitt-Rivers at Wor Barrow in Dorset. Although many traces of timber structures have been found (p. 153 ff.), there is no indication that anything comparable with a megalithic chamber accessible from outside the mound existed. Corresponding with this structural difference there was a profound functional one. In the sense that a number of persons were buried in each, both were collective tombs, but that is where the similarity ends. Whereas megalithic tombs were designed for the reception of successive burials

38 Stoney Littleton, Somerset: inside the burial chamber

39 Bryn Celli Ddu,
Anglesey:
entrance of the
passage to the
burial chamber

40 Winterbourne
Stoke, Wiltshire:
long barrow and
bowl, bell and
disc barrows

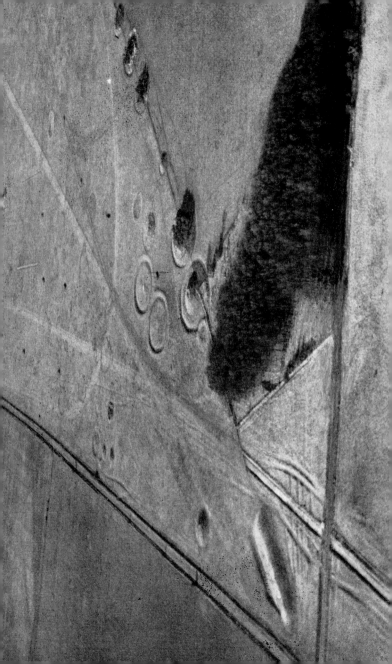

41   Arbor Low, Derbyshire, from the air

42   Woodhenge, Wiltshire: crop-marks, from the air (*cf.* p. 176)

43 Stonehenge, Wiltshire: general view from the air (*cf.* p. 181)

44 Stonehenge: curvature of the lintels

45   Stonehenge: upper part of second trilithon

46   Stonehenge: the second trilithon

47 Avebury Circle, Wiltshire, from the air

48 Avebury: section of the great ditch

49   Overton Hill Sanctuary, Wiltshire, with Silbury Hill in the background: sketch by Stukeley, 1723

50   Silbury Hill, Wiltshire

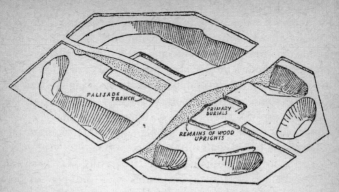

Wor Barrow, Dorset: the rectangular funerary enclosure under long mound with quarry ditches (*c.* 1:1700)

over a period of time, earthen long barrows were themselves thrown up over human remains previously placed in position, sealing them as for all time. Usually the bones from earthen long barrows comprise crouched skeletons which can only have been deposited as corpses, and scattered over them loose bones from bodies previously buried or exposed. If the corpses were fresh at the time of burial, they would seem to imply some form of human sacrifice for service in the next world, either as male retainers or as wives or concubines, but it is by no means improbable that corpses may have been dried and kept against the great occasion when the barrow was to be built. At Wor Barrow and Giants' Hills bones and corpses were laid together on beds of chalk slabs within great timber enclosures, scene of the final rites before all was covered by the piles of turf and loads of chalk which formed the material of the barrow.

There is evidence from several sites that timber enclosures were commonly erected as a preliminary to the building of the barrows themselves. In most instances it is evident that the enclosures were open to the sky, but smaller structures revealed at Nutbane long barrow seem to have had ridge-roofs. It seems likely that they were built to contain bodies until such a time as it was decided to go forward with the formidable task of erecting a barrow. Clearly some such temporary resting place would be needed, especially when it is remembered that it was customary to bury several people under one mound and that all the burials had to take place at one time. Although it seems to have happened fairly frequently that barrows were erected over such enclosures, this did not always happen and morturary enclosures have sometimes been found without any trace of a barrow; for instance a rectangular one some 200 feet by 65 feet was found on the line of the Dorchester Cursus (see p. 167).

There has been much discussion about the relationships between earthen and megalithic long barrows. Against the old view that the former were in some sense devolved forms of megalithic tomb, it has been urged that they may be related in some way to the Kujavian graves of Poland and analogous tombs on the North European Plain. The older view may yet prove nearer the mark, because whereas the Polish tombs were for single burials, the earthen long barrows of Britain were collective in the sense that as a rule they covered a number of individuals, even if unlike the chambered tomb rite the burials must have been inserted at one time. There seems no doubt on the other hand that we must look east to account for the small Medway group of chambered long barrows, geographically so widely separated from the other megalithic groups of Britain. The small chambers and rectangular stone settings, most completely preserved at Coldrum, suggest comparison with the tombs known in Denmark as *dysse,* and which date from the latter part of the Early Neolithic phase in the prehistory of that country.

In certain Yorkshire long barrows there is evidence that after the erection of the mound the bodies and bones were subjected to partial cremation. The arrangement varied in different barrows, but at Westow Canon Greenwell found the cremated remains—three articulated skeletons and bones from four others—resting on a stone pavement along the middle towards the eastern end. Turf and wood had evidently been heaped over the interments, and over this was a ridge-shaped roof formed by inclined slabs of oolitic stone reaching to the top of the mound. The draught was introduced from the eastern end of the mound, for the last 12 feet of which the pavement gave way to an inclined trench reaching a depth of 3 feet below surface level at the edge, where it was joined by a cross trench extending into the open. Reddening of the soil under the pavement and in contact with the roof of the burial area shows that the firing must have been subsequent at least to an advanced stage in the construction of the mound. Although combustion was sometimes assisted by flues it was not always fully effective, as shown by Greenwell's remark that 'in the case of the Scamridge and Rudstone barrows the burning gradually decreased in intensity towards the west end of the deposit of bones, where it was found to have died out, leaving them entirely uncalcined'. None of the pottery from crematorium long barrows has proved to be of the normal Western ware, and it may well be that they represent a regional and rather late development, a view supported by the occurrence of a similar rite in certain round barrows in the same area.

Nothing specific is known about the burial customs of the makers of Clacton-Rinyo ware as such; nor are we much better informed about the makers of Peterborough ware, though here we can point to the burial of disarticulated remains of two adults in a stone cist built against the wall of a rock-shelter in Church Dale, Derbyshire.

With the Beaker people matters are very different, the great bulk of our information about them having been derived from a study of their burials. In some parts of the country they inhumed their dead in flat graves, such as are only likely to be found by the process of gravel-digging and other commercial exavations. Observation of prolific localities has confirmed that the graves were sometimes arranged in cemeteries, examples of which are known from Eynsham and Cassington, Oxfordshire, and Ely, Cambridgeshire. But not the least of the Beaker people's contributions to our prehistory was their introduction of the practice of marking burials by circular mounds or round barrows. The round barrow is, indeed, not only the most typical monument of the Bronze Age, but, although vastly diminished in numbers, is still among the commonest of all our prehistoric field antiquities. On the chalk downs, or on desolate moors beyond the margin of existing cultivation, round barrows preserve their original contours but slightly moulded by the age-long processes of erosion and marred only by burrowing animals or the tell-tale depression left by some antiquarian barrow-digger. In many ways they are most satisfying to the eye, silhoutted against the sky, as their builders set them, on some sinuous fold of down. From the air they assume a somewhat macabre appearance like lunar craters in reverse. Yet when all surface traces have been ploughed away observation from the air may be the only method of finding them; the ditch and sometimes even the central grave will betray themselves through the deeper colour of the infilling soil, or by extra luxuriant crop growth.

Round barrows frequently occur in cemeteries. These

may be set out either in a line extending beyond or on either side of a foundation barrow or else nucleating round it to form a cluster. Striking examples may be quoted from the Stonehenge area of Salisbury Plain, notably the linear cemeteries of Normanton and Winterbourne Stoke (40) and the nucleated one of Lake, but barrows occur in cemeteries in Yorkshire, Derbyshire and other parts of the country. Individual barrows vary in size very greatly: they may be as little as from 4 to 5, or as much as from 50 to 60 yards in diameter, while in height they range from a few inches to 20 feet. Their character was strongly influenced by geology. In the highland zone it was usual to build the mound from surface materials such as boulders and stones. Sometimes, as in a number of cairns in South Wales, Devon, and Somerset, the structure was composite, the core being built of turf or earth, the outer rim of boulders. Turf was also used in the construction of barrows in the lowland zone, but here it was usually supplemented by material quarried from an encircling ditch and laid on as a capping. It is certain, though, that the ditch had significance in virtue of encircling the grave as much as in providing material for the mound.

In the basic and long-persisting bowl form introduced by the beaker people the ditch was immediately contiguous to the mound. It continued to be a feature of the bell and disc barrows that served as burial places for men and women respectively of the better off people of the Wessex Early Bronze Age, even though in the former the mound no longer occupied the whole inner area, leaving a distinct berm or platform, and in the latter had shrunk to a mere lump in the middle. The same basic idea of keeping the dead enclosed in a circle seems to be emphasised by the rings of driven stakes, wooden posts and upright stones found in individual barrows.

At the dawn of the Bronze Age inhumation was the general rule. Inhumed bodies were normally buried individually, in marked contrast with practice in the long barrows, though both men and women were fairly often accompanied by children, and the collective burial of adults did occur in rare instances like Greenwell's barrow XXVIII at Ganton in the East Riding of Yorkshire. In the great majority of cases the dead were buried in the attitude frequently adopted for sleep among modern primitive peoples, the knees drawn up to the stomach in a crouched position. Where the requisite stone slabs were easily obtainable they were commonly protected by boxlike cists. An excellent example was found by Lord Londesborough under a round barrow at Kelleythorpe in the East Riding. Here, in a neatly made cist, was buried a man of some consequence. A Beaker was near his ankles, a bronze dagger with traces of wooden handle and sheath near his hips, and on his right wrist an archer's guard of bone with gold-plated studs, the bronze buckle of which was found in place under his fore-arm. A mass of linen was found under the entire skeleton. The hawk's head found between his elbows and knees was probably magical in intent: had it been a bird used for falconry we might surely have expected more than the head. There are many records of oak coffins having been used, especially in the East Riding, though in no case are the remains as well preserved as in the famous Danish finds. The coffin found by Canon Greenwell under a small clay barrow at Rylston consisted of an oak trunk, 7 feet 3 inches long and 1 foot 11 inches wide, split in two and hollowed out; the exterior was left untouched, but the ends were partially rounded. The Gristhorpe Cliff coffin had a hole in the bottom to drain the liquids of putrefaction. One found recently at Loose Howe, Rosedale, and now in the British Museum, was

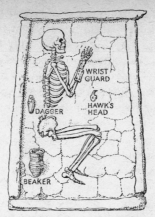

Cist burial under barrow at Kelleythorpe

accompanied by the two halves of a larger trunk carefully
shaped to a boat form, symbolic perhaps of the last voyage.
In addition to several more from Yorkshire, oak coffin
burials have been recorded from Dorset, Wiltshire, and
Sussex. At Dysgwylfa Fawr, Cardiganshire, two oak dug-
outs were found within a ring of standing stones at the
centre of a round barrow: the larger was empty, but the
smaller contained a cremation accompanied by a food-
vessel and a flint knife, a good example of the survival of
an old usage.

From the fragments of cloth in the Rylston coffin and
the few impressions from other burials it is difficult to
determine whether the dead were buried in clothes or
shrouds. The tall, round-headed man from the Gristhorpe
coffin is certainly said to have been wrapped in a shroud
of animal skin fastened by a bone pin at the breast. On the
other hand, the frequent occurrence of buttons of amber,
bone, or jet, sometimes described as having been found

159

'in front of the upper part of the chest', almost certainly belonged to cloaks, which, as in Denmark, seem to have been worn exclusively by men, probably over kirtles with shoulder straps. No buttons have been found with women, who probably wore a skirt and jacket. The fairly frequent discovery of bone pins behind women's skulls suggests that they wore their hair in buns. The string found by Mortimer behind the skull of an aged woman in a barrow at Garton Slack (barrow 82) was probably used, like the complete one from the Danish Egtved find, to tie the hair. Important differences exist between the grave goods associated with men and women. Among the Beaker people pots were common to the two sexes, but men might be supplied, in addition, with a dagger of flint or metal—one of the former was found clasped in the hand of a skeleton on Acklam Wold (barrow 124)—a stone axe-hammer at the shoulder, and a full archer's equipment, flint arrowheads, stone wrist-guard, and, almost certainly, a bow and other perishable items; women, on the other hand, were more meagrely provided with metal awls and flint scrapers, signs that during life they were busily employed at handwork. During the full Early Bronze Age in Wessex certain burials were furnished with extreme richness. An outstanding example is the Bush Barrow, near Stonehenge, which was opened by that famous antiquary, Sir Richard Colt Hoare, in 1808. The inventory of the objects found with the skeleton of the 'stout and tall man' buried therein included a flat bronze axe, two bronze daggers, one of which had a handle inlaid with hundreds of fine gold pins, two quadrangular plates of sheet gold, a gold sheath mount, and a ceremonial mace. Nor was such lavish provision curtailed at first by the passing of inhumation: the individuals buried in many of the most famous barrows of the Wessex Early Bronze Age, including the 'Gold

Barrow' at Upton Lovell, with its gold sheets, beads, and boxes, its gold-plated shale cones and its thousand or more amber beads, were cremated.

By the Middle Bronze Age cremation, established since Neolithic times in Britain and practised alongside exhumation during the Early Bronze Age, had become the dominant rite. Barrows continued to be built, but the tendency was to utilise existing ones. The ashes contained in a bag or a pottery urn would be inserted in small holes cut in the material of the barrow. Sometimes after a number of secondary burials had taken place a second ditch would be cut and the height of the barrow raised. Grave goods were provided, though on a greatly reduced scale. In the Late Bronze Age regular urnfields came into use, the urns sometimes being let into flat ground, sometimes intruded into the material of earlier burial mounds, demonstrating afresh the persistence of sanctity attaching to well-marked places of burial. There is also evidence that, even in regions like Hampshire directly affected by immigration, barrows, low and saucer-shaped and comprising mainly scraped-up material, continued to be built at this time. How far this was due to the persistence of native tradition and how far to absorption of ideas from the South German tumulus culture by our urnfield immigrants prior to leaving the Continent, it is difficult to assess. As a rule the urns are found inverted over the ashes, although sometimes they stand the right way up. Rather meagre grave goods in the form of worked flints, beads, bone needles, and bronze blades continued to be deposited with a fair number of the native hooped and encrusted urns, but as a general rule the cremations of the intensive Deverel-Rimbury urnfield culture were unaccompanied by personal possessions for use in the next world.

Considering how much is known about their domestic sites it is astonishing how meagre is our information about the burial customs of the Iron Age A people. From the scanty, and not always too satisfactory, evidence it appears that the rite was mixed, inhumation and cremation being associated indifferently with flat graves or burial under a round barrow. Children were commonly buried under huts or pushed into disused storage-pits. The frequency with which human bones—sometimes worked into implements or utensils—are met with on Iron Age A sites is consistent with cannibalism or with some form of exposure of corpses. In either case it helps to explain the rarity of burials.

More is known of the burials of the Iron Age B people. The remarkable chariot burials of Yorkshire have already been described in Chapter 5. From the West Country we have flat cemeteries like those at Trelan Bahow, St Keverne, and Harlyn Bay, at the latter of which 130 stone cists were unearthed, each containing a contracted skeleton. The graves of important women were sometimes marked by the provision of a splendid bronze mirror. The beautifully engraved example from Birdlip was found by quarrymen with the extended skeleton of a woman in a stone cist between two others containing men; the woman was further accompanied by two bronze bowls, hammered thin and turned on the lathe, a silver brooch gilded, four bronze rings, a tubular bracelet of the same material, a bronze knife handle modelled into the shape of an animal's head, and a necklace of large ring beads of amber, jet and grey marble.

In those parts of England settled by the Belgae cremation cemeteries were the rule; indeed, it was upon a study of those at Aylesford and Swarling, Kent, and Welwyn, Hertfordshire, that archaeological proof of their invasion was first founded. The poorer graves in such cemeteries consist of round pits 2-3 feet in diameter, sometimes arranged in irregular circles, indicative perhaps of separate families. Generally they were simply furnished with one or two cinerary urns, but the principal grave at Aylesford yielded, in addition to pots, a stave-built wooden bucket containing cremated bones and brooches and bound with bronze bands, the upper of which was embossed with a frieze of stylized horses and motives derived from the classical palmette. Even more elaborately furnished were the two vaults at Welwyn, which produced two bronze jugs, a tankard with bronze handle, a bronze *patella*, a pair of silver cups of Italian make, the silver handle of a footed cup, three bronze masks, a bronze bowl, an iron frame, five large wine amphorae, and three pairs of iron fire-dogs of the type found in similar tombs at Stanford-bury, Mount Bures, Snailwell and Barton, Cambridgeshire. Richest of all was the princely burial under a round bar-row in Lexden Park, Colchester, which comprised the re-mains of a chariot, silver-studded chain mail, enamelled studs and discs, bronze plates, handles and hinges and a tray of the same material, a series of bronze statuettes of classical character, including a griffin, a bull, a boar and a cupid, and finally a silver portrait medallion of Augustus, cut from a denarius of 17 B.C., the prized possession of a Belgic chieftain beglamoured by Rome. From the 'Red Lady of Paviland' to the Lexden burial is a far cry, but the motive remains the same, to honour the dead and ensure the enjoyment in the next world of possessions favoured during life upon earth.

9

Sacred Sites

STANDING stones, whether isolated monoliths or grouped in alignments and circles, have probably attracted more widespread attention through the ages than any other antiquities. The people of the countryside and a whole succession of learned chroniclers from Geoffrey of Monmouth onwards have puzzled on their meaning, but, though the stones stand free for all to contemplate, what they signify no man can say. Let it be confessed that scientific archaeology has brought us little nearer to understanding them. Yet it is evident the erection of stones, sometimes more than 20 feet in height and weighing many tons, can only have been undertaken under the influence of some compelling motive, to commemorate ancestors, encourage fertility, or in some other way to further the vital interests of society. Even if we could visit Bronze Age Britain and study at first hand the rites and practices associated with them, it would be difficult enough to comprehend their underlying meaning: to probe the innermost consciousness of men who lived thousands of years ago by measuring and classifying stones, however meticulously, is manifestly vain. Still, the stones are abundantly worthy of study, even if only as symbols of a religious life which may for ever elude us.

Simplest and most numerous are the single monoliths which abound in highland Britain and in the lowland occur sporadically where suitable stone was available. It may be said as a preliminary that quite a number of stones popularly referred to as monoliths or menhirs are in reality purely natural—glacial erratics or natural 'stacks' left by denudation like the Buck Stone, Staunton, and the Longstone, English Bicknor. In a few instances, also, artificially erected stones, which appear to be isolated to-day, are in reality vestiges of megalithic tombs, alignments or circles. Some monoliths may have been set up to mark boundaries. Others, like the tall one at Tresvennack, at the foot of which two Late Bronze Age urns were found, the larger containing cremated human remains, may have been erected to mark burials, though it is not always easy to decide whether these are contemporary with or subsequent to the erection of the stone. In the vast majority of instances there is no indication of purpose. It seems legitimate to conclude that the veneration of stones as such, a veneration which in Brittany has survived the introduction of Christianity, contributed in some degree to their erection.

Although we have nothing to compare with the magnificent alignments of Carnac, there are on Dartmoor something like sixty analogous monuments. As a rule they comprise one or two rows of stones, but occasionally, as at Challacombe, triple rows are found. In many cases the stones are only a few inches high and they rarely exceed 2 or 3 feet. An unexplained feature is the frequent presence at one end of a transverse 'blocking-stone'. They vary widely in their spacing. The average overall length is about 150 yards, but several examples on Dartmoor are over 400 yards, and one attains some two miles. Mostly they tend to run east and west, but to some extent their direction was modified by the lie of the ground. Quite a number, including the three at Drizzlecombe, approach burial cairns. Outside Dartmoor alignments are rare. There is one at St Columb Major in Cornwall. Wales can show eight, all of them small, the largest, Parc y Meirw, attaining only 130 feet in length. A few isolated examples are recorded from the north of England, including one nearly 300 yards long at Thockrington Quarry House Farm, Northumberland, which approaches a cairn like many of those on Dartmoor. Beyond noting their association with the dead, nothing profitable can be said at this stage about the motives which inspired the building of alignments in early Britain. Among modern primitive peoples similar monuments have been regarded as symbols for ancestors in religious rites; alternatively, as in Assam, they have been imagined as vehicles for the souls of the dead in fertility cults. It is possible that the Devil's Arrows, close to the Great North Road, on the south-west side of Boroughbridge, may once have belonged to a double alignment, though to-day there are only three stones. The distance between the two extremes is about 360 feet. Their heights above ground are $16^1/_2$ feet, 21 and $22^1/_2$ feet, to which, when estimating their total length, one may add 5 feet, the depth below ground established by the antiquary, Dale, early in the eighteenth century. From the nature of the stone it is known that the monoliths cannot have been quarried nearer than Plompton, $7^3/_4$ miles distant. The surface of the stones has been dressed by pecking, but the vertical runnels on their upper portions are the results of weathering.

In the context of stone alignments a word must be said about another from of elongated monument, this time constructed in earthwork. The original Cursus monuments, a Greater and a Lesser, were observed and planned by William Stukeley in the neighhourhood of Stonehenge. Modern field archaeology has revealed many comparable structures scattered widely over the country, from the Dorset downs to the Thames gravels at Dorchester (Oxfordshire), the Maxey district near Stamford and Thornborough near Ripon. In age they seem to date back to Middle Neolithic times. They are formed by more or less parallel banks with external ditches and are squared off at either end. By length they are the largest monuments of their period. The Greater Cursus at Stonehenge, up to 110 yards across and some 3,030 yards long, is by no means the most considerable of its class. For instance the Dorset cursus between Blandford and Dorchester, originally running from Thickthorn to Bottlebush Down and later extended past Pentridge and almost to Bokerly Dyke, attained a total length of nearly $6^1/_4$ miles and a width of about 100 yards. In relation to the population and its productivity the work involved in these structures was stupendous. Since they served no apparent practical end, one must suppose that they were built for some religious purpose. A clear indication that this was connected with ideas about the dead is given by the intimate physical association between Cursus monuments, long barrows and funerary enclosures. Thus the Dorset Cursus begins and ends close to pairs of long barrows and the Pentridge section actually incorporates another in its northern bank; the Greater Cursus at Stonehenge abuts on a long barrow; and the southern side of the Dorchester Cursus traverses an oblong funerary enclosure. Perhaps William Stukeley was not so far out when he interpreted Cursus monuments as courses for races, even if these can hardly have been for chariots as he suggested. It could well be that they were used for foot-races as part of funeral games like those described by Homer as having been held at the burials of warriors in the Trojan War.

The third, and much the most interesting class of standing stone, comprises those arranged in megalithic free-standing circles. Small circles of boulders should be treated warily, as they may once have been covered by burial mounds, since denuded. Sometimes stone settings can be shown to belong to funerary monuments of a different kind, like the 'Druid's Circles' on Birkrigg, Westmorland, where within the inner of two small concentric circles were found four burials by cremation, one accompanied by a Bronze Age urn, sealed beneath the two layers of rough slab paving which occupied the greater part of the interior of the monument. Circles made up of more or less contiguous slabs almost certainly represent the kerbs of vanished cairns, or the last traces of hut-circles. There remains, however, a large number of stone circles which, from their size, can hardly have been covered by vanished mounds, and to which no obvious function can be assigned.

Circles of this kind, which we may fairly describe as sacred, are widespread in the highland zone. Characteristic examples from the northern counties are the Keswick circle, having thirty-nine stones set on a diameter of from 100 to 110 feet, Long Meg with fifty-nine stones and a diameter of from 305 to 360 feet, and one on Summerhouse Hill, Yealand Conyers, Lancashire, the remaining four stones of which give a diameter of 460 feet. The small circle at Shap in Westmorland, partly destroyed by the railway, is of special interest because approached by a double alignment or avenue half a mile in length.

The Welsh circles, though numerous, are disappointing, being composed of smallish stones and mostly ranging in diameter between 60 and 80 feet. Their distribution is markedly upland, two-thirds of them being in Montgomery, Radnor, and Brecknock. Outlying stones are a common feature, Cerrig Duon, Traen-glas, Brecknock, having, in addition, an avenue 130 feet long which, although it does not approach nearer than 40 feet and is not aligned directly on the circle, was obviously designed to form part of the same complex. Central stones also occur occasionally.

The circles of West Cornwall resemble those of Wales both in scale and in details of form. Thus, the Nine Maidens of Boscawen-ûn has a large central stone, while the

Merry Maidens on Rosemodres has two tall outliers. They are particularly rich in legend. The commonest tale is that the rings represent girls turned to stone for dancing on the Sabbath, while outliers are explained as petrified pipers. It need hardly be added that the dance legends attached to megalithic circles are far older than Sabbatarianism and even antedate the spread of Christianity. An alternative story has to do with warriors and conflicts. According to this the Merry Maidens were set up on the spot where the Cornish King Howel was overcome by the English under Aethelstan, the outliers marking the positions of the two leaders. Some of the circles in the eastern part of the county are rather larger, notably the three Hurlers. According to Camden, writing in his *Britannia* in 1587, 'the neighbouring Inhabitants terme them Hurlers as being by devout and godly error perswaded that they had been men sometime transformed into stones, for profaning the Lord's Day, with hurling the ball'.

Of the Dartmoor circles one at Fernworthy has an attendant alignment. At Stanton Drew in Somerset there are three circles, having diameters respectively of 97, 368 and 145 feet, the former two with avenues approaching from the north-east. A third of a mile to the north there is a single stone called Hauteville's Quoit, which has been claimed to be on the line of the axis of the two larger circles, while to the south-west there is a group of three stones known as the Cove, which may be the remains of a chambered tomb. Writing of Stanton Drew some two hundred years ago, William Stukeley recorded that 'this noble monument is vulgarly called the Weddings; and they say 'tis a company at a nuptial solemnity thus petrify'd. In an orchard near the church is a cove consisting of three stones like that of the northern circle in Abury...; this they call the parson, the bride, and bridegroom.'

Even more remarkable is the folk-lore attaching to the Rollright Stones on the Oxford-Worcester border. The story, as recounted by Sir Arthur Evans, is that a certain King set forth at the head of an army to conquer England, but as he advanced up the hill the Witch who owned the ground appeared. Just as he approached the crest of the hill, from which the village of Long Compton would be visible, she halted him with the words 'Seven long strides shall thou take', and

> 'If Long Compton thou canst see,
> King of England thou shalt be.'

Exulting, the King cried out:

> 'Stick, stock, stone,
> As King of England I shall be known',

and strode forward seven paces. But lo! instead of Long Compton there rose up before him a long earthen mound, and the Witch replied:

> 'As Long Compton thou canst not see
> King of England thou shalt not be.
> Rise up, stick, and stand still, stone,
> For King of England thou shalt be none;
> Thou and thy men hoar stones shall be
> And I myself an eldern tree.'

The King became a single stone and his men a circle. The stones of the neighbouring burial chamber, the 'Whispering Knights', are said to be 'traitors, who, when the King with his army hard by was about to engage with the enemy, withdrew themselves privily apart, and were plotting treason together, when they were turned into stone by the Witch'. An alternative version has it that they are at prayer. Among the other lore attaching to the stones is the saying that they cannot be counted. At night the King Stone and the Whispering Knights are supposed to go down at midnight to drink of a spring in Little Rollright spinney. At the same hour the stones of the circle are said to become men again, join hands, and dance in the air. Lastly there is the story that, when it was purposed to use the capstone of the chamber to bridge the brook at Little Rollright, it took a score of horses to drag it downhill, and then only by such a strain as broke their harness. Every night it turned over and lay down in the meadow, until in desperation it was decided to restore it to its rightful place. Only one horse was needed to drag it up the hill again.

By far the grandest sacred site in Britain is Avebury (47). As William Stukeley remarked in his *Abury,* in 1743, it shows 'a notorious grandeur of taste, a justness of plan, an apparent symmetry, and a sufficient niceness in the execution: in compass very extensive, in effect magnificent and agreeable. The boldness of the imagination we cannot sufficiently admire.' Since his day the monument has been sadly mutilated, although later rehabilitated in one sector enough to show how, if the treatment were completed, the whole might regain its former dignity. The great encircling bank remains virtually intact, save where for a stretch in the north-west sector it has been levelled for farm buildings, and it is possible to walk round almost the whole circumference of about 4,440 feet. The effect, looking down into the sacred area within, is enhanced by an inner ditch the original depth of which can only be gauged by imagining it cleared of its 20 feet of silting (48). When freshly made the vertical height between the crest of the bank and the bottom of the ditch must have been fully 50 feet. What this means in terms of human labour and—let it be added—of social organisation can only be adequately imagined in terms of the small population of Beaker times, and the slight technical means at the disposal of the builders. The tools chiefly used were the antler 'pick', the shoulder-blade shovel, and, no doubt, strong wicker-work baskets, and a simple hoisting tackle.

Bank and ditch are breached by four entrances, three of which are known to have been original. The enclosed area which is only approximately circular, covers $28^1/_2$ acres. Round its margin are disposed the uprights of the largest megalithic circle in Europe, over 1,100 feet in diameter. Within this there are visible to-day two smaller circles, which according to Stukeley each had an inner ring. Recent excavations at the northern entrance have shown that another circle, on the same axis as the other two and of approximately the same size, disproved the claim made some years ago that a third circle formerly existed on the same axis as the other two and of approximately the same size.

The completed monument, which according to Stukeley's fantasy was designed in the form of a serpent passing through a circle, extended far beyond the bank which encircles the central portion. The existence of the tail, in the shape of an avenue of megaliths describing a sinuous curve in the direction of Beckhampton, has yet to be proved: the two stones popularly known to-day as Adam and Eve, and by Stukeley dubbed the Longstones Cove, still stand midway on the course of the supposed Beckhampton Avenue, but it is not improbable that they relate to some quite different structure. No such doubt attaches to the Kennet Avenue, which approaches from the southeast, running for some distance with the Marlborough road, and was regarded by Stukeley as the serpent's neck. When he counted the stones in 1722 in company with Lord

Winchelsea, he found 72, a number which had until recently dropped to 19. To-day, thanks to the restorative work already mentioned, a sufficient number of monoliths has been re-erected along the last half mile of the avenue's course to show what it must once have been like. The course of the avenue is sinuous without being tortuous, having been laid out in a series of straight stretches. The stones were set up in pairs averaging 50 feet apart at intervals of 80 feet, though near the entrance the avenue narrowed and the intervals shortened. The stones, like all those at Avebury, were of local origin, being of sarsen, a siliceous sandstone which must in ancient times have occurred quite commonly on the Wiltshire Downs in the form of isolated boulders. Although it has often been said that the stones of Avebury are unworked, they have in fact been roughly dressed by pecking. The monoliths were in the first instance selected for shape with a view to balancing well. No attempt seems to have been made to match the size of pairs or to grade successive pairs. The blocks were presumably hauled into position on wooden rollers, shallow cavities were scooped out of the ground, and the bases of the monoliths levered into position. The final process of adjustment must, in view of the great weight of the stones, have been a show one performed with great deliberation. At some distance from the cavity strong stakes were driven into the chalky sub-soil to take the strains on the ropes used to steady the monolith, while smaller ones were set against the steeper side of the cavity itself to reduce friction. Altogether the handling of the stones must have been even more laborious than the excavation of the ditch and the building of the massive bank. But the Kennet Avenue is not the end of Avebury, for after running for more than a mile it used to climb Overton Hill and terminate in two small concentric circles, variously described by Stukeley as 'The Sanctuary' and 'The Hackpen', and fondly interpreted by him as the serpent's head.

When Stukeley sketched the site in 1723 many of the stones were still standing, and it was possible to make out the Kennet Avenue sweeping downhill and away northwards to the great circle, itself hidden by a fold in the ground (49). The year after the sketch was made the remaining stones of the Sanctuary were removed and the ground cleared for winter ploughing. When, after a lapse of more than two centuries, it was decided to excavate the site, nothing visible remained, but the area of search was limited by Stukeley's remark that it was possible to see the serpent's head from its tail. As at Avebury itself, digging not only confirmed his observations by revealing the socket-holes of stone uprights, but, in the shape of no less than six concentric circles of post-holes, has brought to light remains of the wooden structure which pre-existed the stone version known to Stukeley. The general lay-out of the site has been made plain to visitors by concrete stumps set in the post- and stone-holes.

The disappearance of the Sanctuary emphasises that the monument, of which, in its later stage, it formed a part, is itself a mere torso. Many of the stones have been buried in pits, from which they can to-day be raised. It was in digging out one of the buried stones of the great circle that excavators recently came upon the skeleton of a man accidentally killed by the fall of the stone. From the scissors found with him he was evidently a barber, while the coins in his pouch date him to the first quarter of the fourteenth century. Fortunately the more vicious method, involving the breaking of the stones, did not come into use until late in the seventeenth century, and Stukeley arrived just in time. Besides planning the stones still standing, many of them subsequently destroyed, he left us an instructive sketch of a stone in process of destruction 'The method', he tells us, 'is to dig a pit by the side of the stone, till it falls down, then to burn many loads of straw under it. They draw lines of water along it when heated, and then with smart strokes of a great sledge-hammer, its prodigious bulk is divided into lesser parts.' The natives of French Guinea destroy rocks in the same way at the present day in the course of road-construction. The Avebury stones were mostly incorporated into the little village whose 'wretched ignorance and avarice' Stukeley so bitterly deplored.

Happily the age of the monument in its developed form can be tied down within fairly narrow limits to an early stage in the Beaker settlement of Wessex, on current chronology round about 1800-1900 B.C. Neolithic Peterborough ware has been found under the bank, in the lower silting of the ditch, and on a domestic site overlaid by the Kennet Avenue. On the other hand, Beaker sherds (Type A) have been found in the overlying silt of the ditch, while Type B Beakers accompanied burials at the foot of stones in the avenue. Similar pots were buried with inhumations at the foot of one of the Sanctuary monoliths, and—for what it is worth—at the foot of 'Adam', one of the Beckhampton 'Longstones'.

It would be impossible to take leave of Avebury without mention of Silbury Hill (50), situated close to the Bath Road some 4,750 feet from the centre of the great circle. The largest artificial mound in Western Europe, it covers more than five acres of ground, is 125 feet high, and could carry the stone circles of Stonehenge on its summit. Many people have tried to probe its secrets without avail. It was bored from top to bottom by the Duke of Northumberland in 1777; in 1849 Dean Merewether tunnelled to the centre from one side; and in 1922 trenches were cut from several

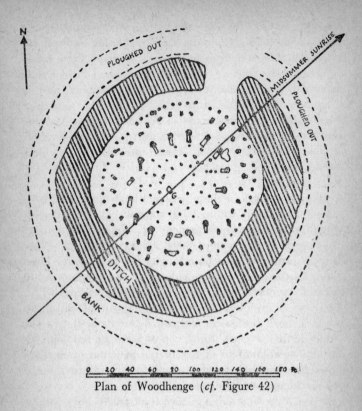

Plan of Woodhenge (*cf.* Figure 42)

points. It remains as much a mystery as ever. All we can be certain of is that whoever put it up must have been impelled by an overmastering impulse.

While there is no other sacred site in southern Britain approaching Avebury in grandeur, modern research has made it plain that it belongs to a numerous category of kindred monuments of Late Neolithic and Chalcolithic age, of which Stonehenge is the most famous. Because of this fame the term 'henge' has become attached to the whole series of embanked and ditched circular monuments with uprights in the interior, even though Stonehenge itself is the only one for which there is evidence for hanging or lintelled stones (or for that matter timbers), the etymological basis for the name. Two classes of henge monument have been distinguished according as they have one or two (in the case of Avebury originally four) entrances; and probably connected in some way with these is a group of mainly smaller monuments, lacking uprights and generally associated with cremation burials.

In some respects the most remarkable of the penannular henges is the original Woodhenge (42) discovered from the air by Wing-Commander Insall, V.C., in December 1925, when flying at a height of 2,000 feet over the parish of Durrington. Only four years later the same observer found a simpler example of the same kind at Arminghall, near Norwich. At Woodhenge there were as many as six concentric oval settings of timber uprights of which the third from outermost was made up of markedly stouter posts. The timbers at Arminghall were only eight in number and formed a horseshoe setting open towards the causewayed entrance to the monument, but they were on a massive scale, a yard thick and sunk between six and seven feet into the subsoil. Like the larger posts at Woodhenge and the sarsens at Stonehenge, the timbers at Arminghall were erected by cutting a slope down to the required depth, hauling them upright and then filling in the ramp. It was noted that the Arminghall timbers had been stripped of their bark; whether they were carved or painted one can only guess. In two cases sites of similar type had stone uprights. The more complete of these, the Stripple Stones, some seven miles north-east of Bodmin, had a circle of 28 monoliths, four of them still erect, disposed around a circular area defined by an inner ditch and outer bank. The other one, Mayborough, situated on a tongue of land between the rivers Eamont and Lowther, near Penrith, differs in lacking a ditch, but in this case plenty of river pebbles were at hand to build the bank; at present only one stone is left standing, but we have it on Stukeley's authority that two concentric circles of monoliths once stood in the central area. Mention should also be made here of penannular ditched and embanked sites of similar scale, but with no indication in their existing state of the presence of uprights. At Gorsey Bigbury on Mendip only the great rock-out ditch remains. Excavations at Maumbury Rings, Dorchester, which yielded pottery of Clacton-Rinyo character and revealed the presence in the ditch of a series of huge holes up to 35 feet in depth, also showed that the surface of the central area had been destroyed when the site was converted into an amphitheatre by the Romans.

To the second class of henge monument may be assigned sites with stone uprights and others of large size which may have carried timber ones. At Arbor Low (41) in Derbyshire we have a circle of monoliths, all now recumbent, disposed around a more or less circular area defined by a rock-cut ditch and bank with two opposite entrances. Remains of a megalithic structure exist near the middle and close by the skeleton of a man was found by excavators. Some indication of date is given by a round barrow of the Early Bronze Age that appears to have been made from material robbed from the bank. Some ten miles to the north-west a similar monument exists in the Bullring, Doveholes, which up till the time of the French Revolution had a single monolith still standing. An impressive group of probable henge monuments is the series of three circles at Thornborough and the single one on Hutton Moor in the Vale of York. The Thornborough rings, the largest of which is nearly a hundred yards across, are formed by banks with external as well as internal ditches, each separated by berms. The large southern circle at Knowlton, Dorset, probably belongs to the same class.

A third category of round sacred site, and one which some would regard as ancestral to the other two, comprises sites, generally about the size of a round barrow, which never had uprights. This group was first recognised in the course of excavations at Dorchester, Oxfordshire. As a rule it has a ditch, either circular or more often penannular, made up of very short sections with causeways, like a setting of almost contiguous pits; in one case the ditch seems to have been cut continuously and then enlarged locally to give the same kind of effect. In addition small pits were either sunk in the floor of the ditch, reminding one of the much larger ones at Maumbury Rings, or arranged in a penannular setting in the central area. No surface traces of banks survived, but silting in the ditches suggested that in most cases these had been external. In one instance there was an inhumation burial, presumably dedicatory, set in line with the entrance. Cremation burials scattered over the central area and ditch are normal. The few finds suggest that these monuments were set up by Late Neolithic people.

The interest of the Dorchester sites is that, though smaller, they closely resemble the initial phase at Stonehenge, the most famous prehistoric monument in Britain (43). To an observer on the ground the most prominent features of Stonehenge are the standing stones, comprising an outer circle of sarsens, lintelled to form a continuous circle, a ring of bluestone monoliths, an U-shaped setting of five trilithons or pairs of lintelled monoliths, a recumbent 'Altar Stone' lying across the axis within the U-setting, and a number of outliers, namely the 'Slaughter Stone' and its companion the other side of the entrance, the Heel Stone on the main axis outside the entrance and the four station stones set more or less on the perimeter of the sacred area in such a way as to describe angles of 45° between diagonal pairs. Closer inspection reveals a low bank and ditch outlining the monument and an avenue of parallel banks and ditches that approaches the entrance and link this with the river Avon nearly two miles distant. Excavation has brought to light a number of features no longer visible on the ground and has made it possible to define the main stages through which the monument passed in the course of something like five hundred years.

Stonehenge I, of Late Neolithic age, consisted of an irregularly quarried ditch, a low inner bank and a circle of pits, which because they were observed by the antiquary John Aubrey, are known as the Aubrey Holes. Careful examination has disposed of the notion that the Aubrey Holes carried uprights. Presumably they served some such ritual purpose as those at some of the Dorchester sites and it is suggestive that cremations, sometimes with a particular kind of bent bone skewer, precisely like those at the Oxfordshire sites, were found both in the pits and on the site of the bank. There is no question that this first phase of Stonehenge was contemporary with and closely associated with the cult represented by the Dorchester monuments. The one vertical feature on the site at this time was probably the Heel Stone, the only undressed sarsen monolith on the site.

Stonehenge II, built by the chalcolithic Beaker people, was marked by the first appearance on the site of the famous bluestones from the Prescelly Mountains of Pembrokeshire. These were erected in a double ring (Q and R holes) having an entrance to the north-east, approximately on the axis of the sunrise at summer solstice. The Avenue

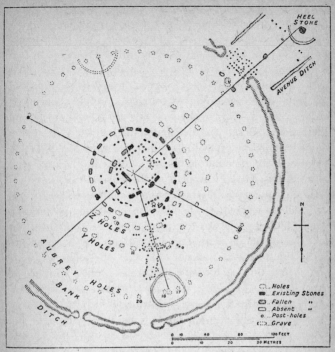

Plan of Stonehenge (*cf.* Figure 43)

linking the site whith the Avon was made at this time, probably to mark the route by which the bluestones were dragged to Stonehenge. Since the Avenue was rather wider than the original entrance causeway, a few feet of the original ditch had to be filled in on one side.

The third stage at Stonehenge, attributed to the activities of Early Bronze Age Wessex chieftains, was more complex and three phases have been distinguished. Phase IIIA was marked by the uprooting of the bluestones and the erection of the sarsen trilithons and lintelled circle, the Slaughter Stone and the four station stones which presumably served as surveyor's markers. Phase IIIB saw the re-utilization of the bluestones, now in dressed form. At first they seem to have been set up in an oval that included at least two trilithons. Later it looks as though it was intended to erect the remaining bluestones in two concentric circles, but the work never seems to have got beyond cutting the sockets in the chalk, the so-called X and Y holes revealed by excavation. The final stage of all (IIIC) witnessed the erection of the bluestones in their existing settings, duplicating the plan of the sarsen ones.

The frequency with which Stonehenge was reconstructed in itself bears witness to the long-sustained veneration with which the site was regarded. The vast effort involved in its construction is another indication. The mere assembly of the stones was a major task. The bluestones, weighing up to four tons each, had to be transported a distance as the crow flies of some 135 miles. Almost certainly they must have come by water, probably lashed to platforms between pairs of dug-out boats. First they had to be got down from the Prescelly Mountains to Milford Haven, then shipped coastwise to the Severn estuary, up the rivers Avon and Frome, overland on sledge and rollers to the Wylye, by which they were floated to Salisbury, and thence by the Avon to the point from which they were finally hauled up the line of the Avenue to their final destination. The 6¼-ton Altar Stone, which came from the Cosheston beds near Milford Haven, presumably followed the same route.

Although the sarsens came from much closer at hand, their transport presented more serious problems, partly because of their much greater weight—up to some 50 tons —and partly because they would have had to come over-

182

land, most probably from the Marlborough Downs, a distance of some 24 miles that involved the traverse of the Vale of Pewsey. Hardly less onerous was the task of preparing the blocks for use. Much of the preliminary shaping was presumably done where the original blocks were selected, but the presence of numerous flakes and of the stone mauls up to 60 lb. in weight used to dress the monoliths, shows that the final work was done on the site of Stonehenge; indeed some of the final adjustments connected with lintelling must have been done after the monoliths had actually been erected. It has been estimated that some three million cubic inches of rock have been laboriously bashed away from the sarsen monoliths alone, and in addition the surfaces of these were further regularised, especially on the inner faces, by being ground smooth. Finally there was the onerous work of erecting the monoliths and still more of getting the lintels in position, a task most probably achieved by means of levers and timber cribs successively built up until the lintel-stone was level with the top of the uprights onto which it was designed to fit.

Although in its general appearance Stonehenge may strike us as barbarous, the monument has been laid out with great precision and the sarsens themselves have been meticulously planned and shaped. The lintels have been most carefully secured to their uprights by tenon and mortice and to their neighbours by tongue and groove joints. In plan they have been perfectly curved to fit the outline of the circle (44) and they have been fitted so that the tops form an even line. Again, and in some ways most notably, the lintels of the trilithons are some 6 inches wider at the top than the bottom (45-6) in order to give the illusion of verticality. When we recall that the sarsen structures at Stonehenge were almost certainly the work

183

of the Wessex chieftains whose graves cluster round the monument, we are left to wonder how far the architecture was inspired from Mycenae, the ultimate source of Wessex wealth. The recent discovery of the engraving of what may be a bronze dagger of Mycenaean type on one of the sarsen uprights at Stonehenge has even prompted the suggestion that a Mycenaean architect may have designed the sarsen lay-out. Yet one must remember that the great mass of engravings on the sarsen surfaces depict axes of robust native form. At most one can admit that certain refinements in the temple architecture, as in Wessex gold-smithery, may derive from Mycenaean inspiration. In any case we have to remember that, before ever the lintelled sarsens were thought of, Stonehenge had had a long history rooted in native Neolithic tradition.

The earliest stories to survive about Stonehenge—those recorded by Geoffrey of Monmouth (1136)— accord so well with two of the main facts established about the monument by archaeology, namely the uprooting of the bluestones and their transport from the far west, as to make one wonder whether oral traditions can have survived from prehistoric times. The story tells how Ambrosius, king of the Britons, consulted Merlin as to how best to commemorate his nobles slain in battle by Hengist the Saxon and how the king was bidden to fetch the Giant's Dance from Mount Killaurus in Ireland, a magic circle the stones of which would stand forever. The king defeated the Irish in battle, but not surprisingly his soldiers tried in vain to shift the stones. Only with the aid of Merlin's magic did they finally succeed in carrying them away across the sea and re-erecting them at Stonehenge. The idea that Stonehenge was a kind of war memorial was long in dying. An alternative theory was that it served as a place of election for kings. All who have studied the monument agree that it was designed and used for some supreme purpose. Probably most people would agree with the opinion of Inigo Jones, who, on returning from his mission of enquiry on behalf of the king, reported to King James I '... concerning the use for which Stone-Heng was first erected, I am clearly of opinion it was originally a temple'.

There are reasons for thinking that ideas connected with death played an important part in the systems of belief of which Stonehenge and the other henge monuments are the architectural expression. As we have already seen, circles were a common feature of burial mounds. We have only to imagine the disappearance of the cairn of New Grange, for example, to obtain a free-standing megalithic circle, in the shape of the surrounding peristaliths. At Callernish on the Isle of Lewis the process is in fact half accomplished, a diminutive cairn being surrounded by a large stone circle, approached by eight alignments of megaliths. With this latter can be correlated the attachment of the Dartmoor alignments to cairns. The conjunction of double alignments, or avenues, with circles can, of course, be matched at Cerrig-duon, Stanton Drew, and Avebury. Again, the stone settings at Stonehenge seem to reproduce important elements of megalithic tombs, the circles equating with peristaliths, the graded U-settings with forecourts, and the lintelled trilithons with portals. In the same direction point the dedicatory burial at Woodhenge and the inhumations set at the foot of several of the sarsens of the Kennet Avenue at Avebury and of one of those of the Sanctuary on Overton Hill. The cremations found in two-thirds of the 'Aubrey holes' at Stonehenge may have been subsequent to the erection of the posts, but in this case they only go to confirm the sanctity of the site. The close connection between sacred sites and burial is well brought out in the unique monument at Bleasdale, Lancashire, where a small round barrow is set almost tangentially within a circular timber stockade. The barrow itself had a causeway across the ditch, defined by sideposts as if to give access to the central grave. This contained Middle Bronze Age funerary pottery and was itself surrounded by a circular setting of timber uprights. Finally, it is pertinent to remark that barrows and cairns tend to cluster round free-standing circles, whether of stone or of wood, simple or defined by ditches. Many of the most famous barrows in the south of England are found within a short radius of Stonehenge.

As already stated, both Stonehenge and Woodhenge are orientated in such a way that the axis of each points to the midsummer sunrise. It would be rash to infer from this anything definite about the religious outlook of their builders, though it does betray some preoccupation with the sun, and, in the case of Woodhenge, the axial line of which divides at right-angles the burial set in the innermost ring, seems deliberately to associate its maximum potency with the grave. It is possible that we have here an expression of the idea that life proceeds from death, one which may easily have been combined with fertility cults. Yet there is no need to read into the fact of orientation any more than that the builders of Woodhenge and Stonehenge shared an interest in the solar calendar common to most people whose livelihood is in any degree bound up with husbandry. In all essentials the great circles retain their mystery.

List of Books for Further Reading

ATKINSON, R. C. J., *Stonehenge,* Hamish Hamilton, 1956

BULLEID, A. and GRAY, H. St. G., *The Glastonbury Lake Village,* Glastonbury, 1914

CLARK, GRAHAME, *Archaeology and Society,* Methuen, 1960; *Excavations at Starr Carr,* Cambridge, 1954; *World Prehistory: an outline,* Cambridge, 1961

CLARKE, R. RAINBIRD, *East Anglia,* Thames & Hudson, 1960

CURWEN, E. C., *The Archaeology of Sussex,* Methuen, 1954

DANIEL, G. E., *The Prehistoric Chamber Tombs of England and Wales,* Cambridge, 1950

FOX, Sir CYRIL, *A Find of the Early Iron Age from Llyn Cerrig Bach,* National Museum, Cardiff, 1945; *Pattern and Purpose: Early Celtic Art in Britain,* National Museum, Cardiff 1958

GRINSELL, L. V., *The Archaeology of Wessex,* Methuen, 1956

FRERE, S. S. (ed.), *Problems of the Iron Age in Southern Britain,* London University Institute of Archaeology, 1961

GRIMES, W. F., *Guide to the Collection illustrating the Prehistory of Wales,* National Museum, Cardiff, 1938

HAWKES, JACQUETTA, *A Guide to the Prehistoric and Roman Antiquities in England and Wales,* Chatto and Windus, 1951

HAWKES, JACQUETTA and CHRISTOPHER, *Prehistoric Britain,* Chatto and Windus, 1942

HENCKEN, H. O'N., *The Archaeology of Cornwall,* Methuen, 1932

OAKLEY, K. P., *Man the Tool-maker,* British Museum (Natural History), 1949

PIGGOTT, STUART, *British Prehistory,* Oxford, 1949; *Neolithic Cultures of the British Isles,* Cambridge, 1954

POWELL, T. G. E., *The Celts,* Thames & Hudson, 1958

POWELL, T. G. E. and DANIEL, G. E., *Barclodiod y Gawres,* University of Liverpool, 1956

THOMAS, NICHOLAS, *A guide to Prehistoric England,* Batsford, 1960

Note: Much of the detailed evidence is published in the periodical publication of learned Societies. References to these may be found in many of the books cited. Most of the newer prehistoric material will be found in the *Proceedings of the Prehistoric Society,* Cambridge. The best review ranging over the whole field of archaeology is *Antiquity,* Cambridge. Important papers will be found in *The Antiquaries Journal* and *Archaeologia,* published by the Society of Antiquaries of London.

General Index

County Index of Prehistoric Sites

(including Ireland, Isle of Man, Jersey, Scotland and Wales)